Single Wish

Single Dads of Dragonfly Lake

Amy Knupp

Chapter One

Magnolia

I could see the neon glowing even before I unlocked the door.

The Moments by Magnolia sign that hung prominently on the inside brick wall of my business had been a gift from my new girlfriends, Presley, Rowan, and Chloe, when I opened my event-planning company a couple of months ago.

It was only three words, but that sign symbolized my future, my hope, my redemption. Maybe that sounded over-dramatic, but I had so much to prove—to this town, to my terrible father who'd disowned me, but most importantly, to myself.

Two years ago, I'd gone from being a member of one of the wealthiest families in Dragonfly Lake to having nothing literally overnight. The rich-girl version of me had never quite managed to form any true, deep friendships. The new version of me, well...let's just say work in progress.

Maybe opening a business in a town where everyone

knew my history was a mistake, but a few weeks in, I had a few customers and more than a few stubborn glimmers of hope. A boatload of doubts too, and we're not talking a little canoe. More like a big, filthy river barge.

On this Monday morning in early October, I'd walked from my studio apartment above The Lily Pad, across the town square, to my month-old storefront. I used my key to enter, then closed my eyes for an extra second to breathe it all in. The undertaking. The potential. The soothing aroma of peppermint, wild orange, and lime essential oils recommended by the girls at Earthly Charm.

The back wall of the main room where I hosted clients and potential clients was brick, with a wet bar for tea, sparkling water, or champagne when they signed a contract. Above the bar was my cherished logo sign—the word *Moments* was on the top line in a simple font, and *by Magnolia* was in a smaller, graceful script below.

I stepped into my personal office and felt the remnants of my nighttime doubts and fears dissipate. This was my refuge. My happy place, with peaceful plum, gray, and white decor and a tall, elegant vase of faux magnolias between two plush, comfortable chairs by the large windows that filled the room with natural light.

Daylight was so much easier to navigate than darkness.

I sat behind my pretty but sturdy white desk and pulled out my laptop to plan my day. It was ten till eight, morning rush time next door at Presley's coffee shop, The Bean Counter, so I'd wait to fuel up with my one daily splurge.

My business hours didn't officially begin until nine, but I'd much rather be here, trying to prove myself, than alone in my dinky apartment.

As I opened my planner, I heard the outer door close. I leaned so I could see who it was.

"Good morning," Presley sang out with an obnoxious amount of cheer.

"Hey, Presley," I said, happy to see her and the two coffees she carried. "Are you starting a new service? Free delivery to souls in need?"

She smiled warmly as she waltzed into my office and set one of the cups in front of me. "One-time deal. I might have an agenda. How was your weekend?" she asked as she sat in the chair across from me.

"Really good. The party Saturday night was a hit, and I gave out several business cards."

"Congrats! Did you do anything besides work?"

"I binged a show and finished a book yesterday while recovering from the late-night job. What about you?"

"Oh..." She shrugged nonchalantly. "I got engaged yesterday."

"What?" I slapped my hand down on my desk, coming alive with excitement. "West proposed?"

She held out her hand to show off the beautiful diamond on her left hand, her face lit with joy and excitement.

With a gasp, I hurried around the desk, took her hand, and checked out the bling close up. "Presley, it's gorgeous. Congratulations."

The princess-cut diamond wasn't obnoxiously huge, but I'd learned the hard way money and bling meant nothing compared to love and affection. I leaned over and hugged her, ignoring the selfish pang in my chest.

"Thank you. He stunned the heck out of me."

"I'm not surprised in the least. Have you seen the way he looks at you?"

Her grin stretched even wider. "I have. I love that look he gets. But we said we were taking it slowly."

3

"Because of the girls," I said.

She nodded. "I think it was more for him to be sure. The girls are beside themselves. You should've heard them when we told them last night."

"I bet they were excited. I'm so happy for you, Presley."

I meant that from my heart, but at the same time, I was sad on my own behalf. Presley and I had grown close over the past two months. I was the one she'd called when West had his head up his butt and broke it off with her. I'd hated that she was hurting, but I'd never before been the girl somebody turned to in their time of need. I'd made it a point to step up and be there for her. Presley's late-night texts back then had resulted in a sleepover and the beginnings of what I considered my first *true* friendship.

It didn't hurt that Presley was new to town and didn't know the old me. I was sure she'd heard plenty of stories; in fact, I'd told her some of the hardest parts of my past myself. But she hadn't been here to experience the past me I was ashamed of now.

When she got married and became stepmom to three daughters, our friendship would inevitably be affected.

Stop being so self-centered, I scolded myself as I forced a bigger smile on my face.

"I'm dying to hear how he proposed," I said, genuinely interested.

"Well..." She scooted to the edge of her chair. "It was right after I gave him his birthday present."

"The painting?"

She nodded. "He loved it."

"I told you he would," I said.

She'd showed me the painting Shawna Jenkins had created from a photo on Presley's phone. Back before she and West were a thing, his girls had insisted on a group

4

photo with Esmerelda the llama at the Honeysuckle Festival. It was of West, Presley, and the three girls, family-photo style—plus the llama. The finished painting was both heartwarming and humorous. There was no way West wouldn't adore it.

"I was so worried it would give off the wrong message—"

"That you were ready to be an official family," I filled in.

"Right. And then after I gave it to him, he pulled a ring box out of his bag, went down on one knee, and asked me to marry him."

"He'd planned it all along?"

"He said he couldn't think of a better birthday present than me saying yes...with the painting a close second."

"Oh," I said, loving that she was so smitten with West and that he felt the same way, maybe even double, from what I'd seen. "Congratulations again. That's the best news."

"Thanks, Mags. I'm hoping you'll be my planner."

"Of course I will. I'd be devastated if you asked anyone else."

"You might want to know the details before you agree," she said hesitantly.

"What details?" There wasn't much that could prevent me from throwing one of my closest friends the wedding of her dreams.

"We're hoping for a Christmas Eve wedding."

My brows shot up as I counted off the dates in my head. Approximately eleven weeks away. "Okay," I said, drawing out the word as my mind spun with the pitfalls of such a short turnaround time. "What are we talking for size and venue?"

"Not too big. We're only having two attendants each. Chloe and Rowan are my bridesmaids. You'd be my next one, but selfishly, I need you for my planner."

"I'm much better at planning than bridesmaiding." I'd never been a bridesmaid before.

"You're the best. West and I both have small families, but we definitely want all our friends on the guest list. I'm thinking maybe a hundred fifty people?"

I nodded. That was manageable. "The biggest challenge will be finding a venue with availability."

"We've already got that," she said. "Or we hope so." She eyed me in such a way that set off an alarm in my head.

"Where do you have in mind?"

She pressed her lips together before answering. "Saturday night at their dads' group, Luke announced he's converting his big barn for events. He's hoping for a new revenue stream that will be steady regardless of Mother Nature, unlike his crops. West wants to support him."

I sat up straighter, taking that in, trying not to think about the Luke part of the equation. "Barns can make beautiful wedding venues."

"West says he'd feel more at home in a barn than a fancy hotel."

"I can see that from your blue-collar guy."

"I'll just come out and ask. Do you think you can work with Luke?"

I tried not to let my true feelings show as I smiled and said, "For you, I can work with the devil himself."

"Are you calling Luke the devil?" she asked, tilting her head.

"Not at all." I laughed to act as if I didn't have a doubt in the world.

"But there's bad blood between you," she said. "Right?"

"I wouldn't call us BFFs, but this is business. *My* business." My business that was everything to me—my means of supporting myself, repairing my reputation, and proving my hateful father wrong. "I've got you, Presley."

She let out a squeal that was so not the norm for the former investment banker, but who could blame her? She was marrying the man she loved in less than three months. I could barely imagine what that must feel like, but the joy pouring out of her gave me a strong indication.

We hugged again, and she bounced with excitement.

"So tell me what you have in mind," I said, leaning my backside on the edge of my desk. "General idea. Colors? Music? Will the ceremony be at the barn too or just the reception?"

Presley flopped back into the chair as if those simple questions wore her out. "I was never the kind of girl who dreamed of a wedding and planned everything out. I never thought I'd get married. So basically I'm overwhelmed. West and I talked about evergreens and silver. That's literally the only thing I know."

"That's a starting point," I said, a kernel of excitement blooming in my gut at the possibilities. The events where I had more freedom, where the people involved had fewer ideas of what they wanted, were my favorite. They allowed me to flex my creativity, which was what I loved most. "You're in the middle of your morning rush at the shop. We can set a time to get serious about planning. But it has to be soon if you want Christmas Eve."

"I want Christmas Eve. I don't want to wait any longer than that to start my life with West. Rumor has it my eggs are rotting."

I laughed at her choice of words but not too hard, because my thirty-five-year-old eggs were in the same rotting boat. While she had a good chance to have babies now, I wasn't sure that would ever be in the cards for me.

I shoved the threatening anxiety down. This was a happy moment, a significant milestone in my friend's life that called for joy and celebration, not to mention a new client for me.

"Is it too early for a champagne toast?" I asked.

Presley glanced at the time on her phone as she sat up straighter. "I need to get back to help Glenda, but here's the deal with the venue. West and I have a meeting with Luke at six tonight to see the barn. He's just starting to remodel it, but he swears he'll have it ready in plenty of time for the holidays."

"He could book other events if he's ready by early December," I said, my party-planning mind taking over and allowing me to ignore that it was Luke Durham we were talking about.

"It sounds like there's a lot of renovation work. West agreed to help him with some of it. Anyway, right now it's bare bones, but I was hoping you could come too?"

I worked to keep my expression blank as I mentally ran through my admittedly loose schedule. "Of course. We have so much to plan. Seeing the barn is important."

"Okay." She studied me, and I smiled again to hide my feelings toward Luke. "It should be pretty fast. Just a look around while he explains what the final space will be like."

I nodded. "It's fine, Presley. It's good. Let's do this."

She stood, hugged me yet again, then picked up her coffee. "You're the best. I know the timetable's a big ask, but I have every bit of confidence that, if anyone can pull it off, it's you."

Her confidence warmed me clear through. I knew I could do it, because I'd put everything I had into it. It wasn't like I had any kind of life outside of building up my business.

The timetable? It would be a challenge, but this was where not having a huge client list yet would be a benefit. Presley and West's wedding could get the majority of my time.

The venue owner? That part would be unpleasant, but I'd just put on my professional, get-out-of-my-way-we-have-an-event-to-pull-off face and ignore him as much as possible.

I wasn't about to let an insignificant thing like a man who hated me get in the way.

Chapter Two

Luke

I loved farming with all my soul. It was in my blood.

I'd lived on this land my entire life, and I planned to work it until I was dead. It was my family's legacy, dating back to my grandparents, and I hoped Addie would love it the way I did and continue the tradition.

There were days though...

Today had been one hell of a Monday so far, and though it was after five o'clock, our work was nowhere near done.

"How close is Gary?" I asked Scotty, my right-hand guy and the manager of the apple orchard, as we stood staring at the truck that apparently needed a new alternator.

"ETA is five forty-five," Scotty said. "He oughta be here any minute."

"I hope he's right that it'll take no more than an hour and a half."

Scotty chuckled. "You doubting Gary's skills now?"

I shook my head and glanced at the sky, reassuring

myself it was still clear, as the weather app promised it would be. The truck was full of crates of apples to be delivered to local stores. They needed to reach their destination as soon as possible since it wasn't refrigerated.

"Your dad know you hired out?"

I shook my head and gave him a look that said, *No need to tell him.*

"When did Cheyenne say she'd be here?" I asked.

"I told her six. That'll give her time to eat and relax a spell."

I nodded, trusting Scotty and Cheyenne to take care of the apple deliveries. They were two of my top people and did what they said they'd do no matter what. Scotty had been with us since I was in grade school, working with my dad back then. He knew all our operations as well as I did. Cheyenne was in her sixth year with us. This was far from her first time distributing apples to the retailers during the season.

"Weren't you fixin' to check on Gage before your meeting?" Scotty asked.

"I'm heading that way. Call me if anything unexpected comes up."

"Will do. Get outta here."

I climbed into my truck and pointed it toward the outbuilding where Gage was checking the shakers and balers to make sure they worked and were ready to go for Christmas-tree season. When I pulled up, he was coming out the door.

"Everything good?" I asked as I got out of the truck.

"The shakers and balers are ready to go, but Matilda needs a battery. I can pick one up tomorrow before I come in."

"Sounds good." Matilda was one of our tractors, and

yes, they all had names, a tradition started by my mother years ago.

"Yeah, that's the good news," Gage said. The look on his face had me bracing for the not-good news he seemed to have.

"And?" I prompted.

"The Heinrich kid took a different job."

"The guy we hired Friday?"

"One and only. He was supposed to show up at four, after school. Texted me at twenty after to let me know."

Dammit. "Better now than two weeks into the season, I guess. How many more interviews do we have set up?"

"Three tomorrow and two on Wednesday. Plus there's the Webber kid we couldn't decide on. We got prospects. We'll get a crew in place."

"Fast, I hope. How's the pricing going?"

"Slow but steady. We'll get there."

Though our cut-your-own-tree operations wouldn't open for six weeks, we had a shit ton to do before then, including going through acres of trees and pricing the ones that were ready to sell. That was a project one of us full-timers had to do, but harvesting the trees that would be shipped out for wholesale demanded lots of hands and was time sensitive. Our seasonal crew would help out with that once they went through training.

"You taking off soon?" I asked him.

Gage nodded. "Got a hot date tonight." He raised his brows till they nearly touched the beanie he usually wore once it wasn't ninety in the shade.

"Go on then. Good luck, man."

"I'll bring the battery in with me tomorrow."

"Thanks. See you then."

As Gage walked to his truck, I noticed my dad and my six-year-old daughter making their way in my direction, holding hands. When I waved, Addie looked up at her grandfather and said something. At his nod, she dropped his hand and ran toward me, lightening my mood like not much could.

"Daddy!"

When she reached me, long before my dad did, I hoisted her forty-eight pounds into my arms.

"Hey, doodlebug, how was school?"

Addie threw her arms around me, her grin big and happy. "It was super awesome. I got Star Speller for the week!"

"What? No way."

"Yes way." She giggled, meeting my gaze with her big brown eyes. They were the one feature she got from her mother, Jessie, who was full-time military but spent any time off she could with our daughter. The arrangement worked for all three of us.

"How'd you do that?" I asked Addie. "I'm not sure a Durham has ever been Star Speller before."

"I practiced and practiced, and you quizzed me, and Pops quizzed me, and I learned all the words."

I hugged her tight, proud of her achievement, then lowered her to the ground as my dad approached.

"What the hell is Gary doing here?" he asked.

I glanced in the direction of the truck in need of repair, even though I couldn't see it from here. "Alternator went out in the delivery truck."

He glared at me as I'd known he would.

"Replacing an alternator is the last thing your back needs, Dad," I said before he could come at me.

"Gary doesn't come cheap, especially after hours."

"He's worth every penny if it means you don't hurt extra for the next week."

"I'd be fine. I don't need to be babied."

"I'm looking out for you since you don't look out for yourself," I said, my jaw tight.

"I look out for myself just fine. Quit trying to shut me out of everything. I'm not dead yet. I can't lift, but I can repair."

Could and *should* were two different things. My dad's doctor had told him no more farm work after his second back surgery hadn't eliminated his pain. He still struggled with his forced retirement, but Addie gave him a new purpose. Having him at home to care for her took a load of worry away. He might grumble, but our arrangement was win-win-win.

"You know Gary's trustworthy. I have a meeting about the barn in—" I checked my watch. "Hell. Five minutes ago. I gotta run. You guys good?"

"Just came out to share her news," my dad said, an unmistakable sparkle of pride in his eyes for his grand-daughter.

Addie did a dance at my side and made up a song about Star Speller. I leaned down and kissed the top of her coffee-brown head.

"Congratulations, bug."

"Thanks, Daddy! Will you be home in time for dinner?"

"I hope so. I'm meeting with someone who wants to have their wedding in our barn. Gotta go," I told them, kissing Addie one more time. "If I'm late for dinner, start without me."

"Okay. Bye, Daddy!"

As she took my dad's hand and the two of them headed toward the house, I jogged to the main barn. It was old, big as hell, and majestic, with red paint we'd updated two years ago and a stone foundation that had weathered decades.

When I came around to the front, there were two vehicles parked there, one I recognized as West's. I'd left the barn door open and figured West and Presley must be inside checking it out.

I went in and found West just inside the door, leaning against the wall.

"Hey, West," I said.

"Luke. What's up?"

We bumped fists in greeting.

"Sorry I'm late," I said. "Crazy day around here." That was true, but every day was chaotic.

"No worries."

"Hi, Luke." Presley appeared from behind one of the piles of junk I hadn't yet cleared out.

"Hey, Presley. How's it going?"

"Good." She half turned as someone else stepped closer. "I brought my wedding planner with me. I hope that's okay."

I switched my glance, and there stood the woman who'd hurt my family irrevocably all those years ago.

Chapter Three

Luke

What a nightmare.

I should've expected this.

When West called this morning to discuss a Christmas Eve wedding in my barn, I should've guessed Presley would hire Magnolia fucking James as her planner.

Back in the spring when I'd first had the idea of renovating our barn for event space, Magnolia hadn't opened her event-planning business. Now here we were. I was opening a venue I had every hope would become one of the hottest wedding spots in town just as she was starting a planning business.

This likely would be the first of many times I had to work with this woman I detested if I wanted the barn to be profitable.

I not only wanted it; I *needed* the barn to be profitable. My doubting Thomas of a father was only one reason.

Our farm wasn't in trouble, but revenue each year

varied widely. The weather could screw us. Pests could screw us. Economics could screw us.

We were lucky in that we had three different crops that could balance each other out, but the event space would be a new revenue stream that wouldn't depend on Mother Nature. I wasn't sure where I'd get the time to manage it, but I damn well would. Apparently I'd have to figure out how to work with Magnolia as part of that.

"Magnolia," I finally said, hoping my opinion of her didn't show on my face.

"Hello, Luke." She didn't smile.

I looked past her and pulled my thoughts to the purpose of this meeting—showing West and Presley what I planned for this admittedly dirty, in-need-of-work space.

"Thanks for coming out to see the place," I said. "I hope you can squint a bit and see the vision I have for it instead of the state it's in now."

"It's bigger than I expected," Presley said.

"The main space will get smaller when we put in restrooms and a catering area." I walked farther into the barn. "I'm planning on that corner for restrooms with the catering area next to it." I pointed.

"How big will the catering area be?" Magnolia asked.

I showed them roughly where we planned to put walls in.

"That's not very big," Magnolia said, and I tried not to bristle. "Once you put commercial refrigerators and ovens in, it will be difficult to fit in a serving staff." She spoke without looking at me, and I fought with myself to disregard the source and consider what she was saying.

It might be a decent point, but I didn't acknowledge it out loud.

"Will there be a separate area for a ceremony?"

Magnolia continued, striding toward the center of the room. "Or cocktails between the ceremony and reception?"

"Are you planning to have the ceremony here as well as the reception?" I asked West and Presley.

"We haven't decided about the ceremony yet," Presley said, glancing at West. "Honestly we haven't decided on much besides the date, the reception venue, and the planner."

Magnolia turned and smiled at her friend. Then her smile dropped, and she pegged me with another question. "What will the capacity be for guests?"

"I don't know yet. I'd like to shoot for up to three hundred, but that'll be determined once the space is finished. We'll be adding two extra exits and keeping the windows intact with that in mind."

"And what's the plan for electricity?" Magnolia asked.

As much research as I'd done, I was beginning to feel like she was on the attack. She might think I didn't know what I was getting into, but I wasn't stupid. I'd studied up. I'd made phone calls to key people. West had agreed to help me with construction.

This was going to be what I hoped was a significant part of my livelihood. I hadn't gone into it lightly.

"We'll be greatly increasing the electrical capacity," I said, coaching myself not to snap.

"You'll want all kinds of lighting options, plus the ability to have a DJ or a band. Speakers, microphones, kitchen appliances..."

"I'm well aware," I said, and I was, for the most part.

If she were anyone else, I'd be appreciative of the information, the expertise. Frankly I just wanted Magnolia off my property, but that wasn't in the cards.

"Like I said, we'll be running a lot more electricity, plus

water lines, a heating system upgrade, air-conditioning, all the necessities." I aimed my answer at Presley, who was, after all, the customer.

"What about a room for the wedding party to get ready in?" Magnolia asked.

Presley nodded, her eyes lighting up. "If we decide to have the ceremony here, that would be really convenient."

That was something I hadn't committed to, but I could. We had the space. When my grandfather had built the barn nearly eighty years ago, he'd gone big.

"We could wall off this side over here," I said, walking to the opposite side from where we planned to add restrooms. "West's going to help me with a plan."

West nodded. "I don't know the first thing about wedding venues, only construction. We could use your input, Magnolia."

"I've got a pretty good handle on it," I told him, hoping to kill the idea of Magnolia helping me with anything. I didn't trust her and sure as hell didn't want to spend any more time with her than I absolutely had to.

"My clients are taking a risk," she said, "going into this blind and hoping you'll build what they need. The problem is, if you don't, they're trapped."

"There will be a contract," I said. "I'm not going to screw over my friends."

"What about the timetable?" Presley asked, her voice friendlier than her planner's.

"Christmas Eve won't be a problem," I reassured her. "Once we get the plan hammered out, we'll start immediately. My goal is to be done with the big stuff by early December."

"That's plenty of time. Do you mind if I wander?" Presley asked, waving toward the other end.

"Not at all." *Take your bulldog with you, please,* I thought to myself.

Presley and Magnolia headed away from us, leaving West and me to talk construction details.

As we discussed who would do electricity and plumbing and how soon I could get them in, we both faced the large, open room, which made it easy for me to keep my eyes on Magnolia like I would a rattler coiled in the corner.

Her change in fortune when her father had kicked her out was evident in her wardrobe these days, I thought as I watched her slender body move away from us. Before, she'd generally dripped in prissy designer labels I didn't know the first thing about, plus flawless makeup on her flawless face. In high school, I'd been intrigued by her, in spite of the superficial layers.

Today she was dressed more simply in a short skirt, a plain short-sleeved shirt, and boots that nearly reached her knees, showing off her legs. Her makeup was minimal, but she didn't need it. I might not be able to stand her, but I couldn't deny she would seem attractive to the casual acquaintance who'd never experienced her cold-hearted ways. I'd been sucked in once by her porcelain skin and gorgeous mane of strawberry-blond hair.

Never again.

"Luke," West said in a low voice, "level with me. You gonna be okay working with her?"

"I'll be just fine," I said, allowing zero doubt to infiltrate my tone. "This is business."

He sized me up from the side, my gaze still on the women, mainly to avoid his. I meant what I said, but it was damn hard to hide my feelings for Magnolia James.

"You're one of my closest friends, but if anything fucks up this wedding for Presley..."

I grinned, even though I didn't feel it. "I know, man. Don't screw over your woman. I won't. Even though I should since you left me the last single dad standing. Lucky for you, I like Presley."

"But not Magnolia."

"I don't have to like her to work with her. My stakes are high here, man. Whether she's part of it or not, I need this to work. I need this to work well, or I'll never hear the end of it from my dad."

"He's still not on board, huh?"

I shook my head. "He won't be, probably not even if I turn this into a six-figure business."

"What's his deal? He doesn't like money?"

"He's all about the land. Tradition. The way we've always done things."

"Times change," West said. "For what it's worth, I'm damn glad you're doing it. Can you imagine me at the fancy-schmancy Marks Hotel? I'd do it if Presley insisted on it, but this place... It's gonna fit us better."

"You definitely belong in a barn," I cracked.

"Asshole," he said, laughing. He sobered. "So I have a question for you."

"Seems to be the theme of the day," I said, frowning at Magnolia as she and Presley walked back toward us.

"You think you can pull off being the venue owner as well as one of my groomsmen?"

I shot my gaze to him to make sure he was serious. "You asking me to stand up for you?"

"Seems like it," he said, his hands in his front pants pockets as if he felt awkward.

"Hell yes, I'll be a groomsman. Even if you did betray our single-guy pact."

"We didn't have a pact," he said as if I was a drama

queen, and maybe I was, but it sucked with a capital S to be the last guy in our group to find a wife.

The painful irony? Out of the six of us in the once-single-dad group—West, Max, Knox, Ben, Chance, and me —I was the only sad sack who actually *wanted* to get married. My involvement with Addie's mom had barely lasted a year and a half. I was ready for a lifelong partner.

The joke was on me, obviously.

West held his hand out for me to shake. I took it, and we did the man-hug, back-smack thing.

"Thanks, Luke. It means the world," he said. "Chance is my other groomsman."

"I'm honored, man."

"When do you want to meet about this?" He nodded toward the rest of the barn.

"You tell me when you're available. The sooner the better."

"We need all the time we can get. Shouldn't be any supply issues with the basics, but you'll want to order appliances and windows ASAP."

"How does Saturday look?"

"I'll check with Presley and let you know tomorrow."

"Good enough," I said as the women approached.

"We came up with more questions," Presley said.

"Will there be a coat room for guests?" Magnolia asked.

I hadn't given that a single thought, but it was a valid concern. "There'll be a place for coats," I said noncommittally.

"What about a room for gifts?" Magnolia pressed. "One with a lock?"

I was starting to wonder if she was just trying to be a pain in my ass or if people expected a lockable room for gifts. Did people really steal from the bride and groom?

"I'll have a full layout once West and I put pencil to paper." Again I addressed Presley with my answer because I found it easier to smile when I didn't have my nemesis in sight.

"That's fair," Presley said. "I can't wait to see what you settle on. I have no doubt it's going to be perfect."

Out of the corner of my eye, I saw Magnolia's brow go up slightly, as if she wasn't sure about that.

Damn her. There'd been a time when I'd thought she actually believed in me, but now she was my biggest doubter.

Was I out of my element with an event venue?

Maybe.

But I damn sure wasn't about to let that get to me—let *her* get to me.

I'd never had the advantages she'd grown up with. I'd spent my life working against the odds—the farm kid, the C student, the dude who wore old jeans and a bargain T-shirt to school every day.

This project was a significant part of my and my daughter's future though. I'd sure as hell figure it all out.

Chapter Four

Magnolia

At the risk of sounding like a mushy greeting card, sometimes a person came into your life and changed everything—including you.

Dotty Jaworski was that person for me.

She'd been my first lesson in gratitude after my father cut me off and kicked me out.

We were the unlikeliest of friends. She was in her sixties, had come from a humble upbringing, been married twice, and was well-known and loved throughout town. I was the opposite in every way. And yet I trusted her like I trusted no one else.

"Whatever you've got cooking, it smells delicious, Maggie May," she said as she entered my apartment bearing a bottle of wine.

I took it from her, and we hugged.

I said, "I hope you like a simple bowl of chili mac and cheese."

"You know me. I'll eat whatever you cook."

"The bravest guinea pig known to mankind."

"I'm still standing, my dear. I even survived buffalo chicken and pasta night."

"Stop," I said, grinning. "I told you that you didn't have to eat it. You're the stubborn woman who insisted on trying in spite of the hot sauce bobble."

"You mean the great hot sauce spillage of the decade?"

"I can't help it if I didn't understand the tiny little hole in the lid was intentional." Frustrated with how slowly the sauce had come out, I'd taken the whole lid off—and managed to spill way too much in the bowl.

"You've never made that mistake again," Dotty said as she sat at the petite round table in my petite kitchen area.

I'd been hosting Dotty for dinner weekly for nearly two years. I'd first extended an invitation for two reasons—one, I wanted to pay her back for rescuing me the morning after my dad had cut ties, and two, I needed to learn to cook, and having a guest was motivation. Now it was our ritual, and it was all about our friendship.

I didn't entertain anyone but Dotty in my tiny studio apartment. It was awkward, what with the bed in one corner and a love seat and two chairs squeezed into a tiny sitting area butting up against the kitchen table.

Dotty, bless her soul, ate everything I made for her without complaint. Except for the buffalo chicken. The dish had ended up so spicy that both of us had eyes and noses running by halfway through the meal as we laughed and laughed.

"Thanks for this," I said, checking out the wine label. "You don't know how much I need it tonight."

"Rough day at the office?"

I opened the wine and poured. "I'm starting to think I made a mistake. I'm not sure about this whole business-owning thing." My eyes filled as I said it, and I kept my back to her an extra few seconds as I reined in control of my emotions.

"What happened?"

I breathed in deeply and blew it out, picked up one of the glasses, closed the three feet to the table, and offered it to her.

"I'm not getting any younger," she quipped.

I sat in the other chair. "I lost a client before they could sign."

"Well, damn. But that's going to happen sometimes."

I swallowed, knowing I was going to spill the whole story but trying to gird my loins beforehand. Not because of any reaction Dotty would have, but because it meant digging up the old Magnolia.

"This was for a large wedding in June," I told her. "You probably know the groom. Joel Hightower. His fiancée, a sweet girl from Birmingham, met with me last week, and it went really well. They have money to spend and wanted me to help. Or *she* did. Then Joel found out, and he basically said over his dead body."

"I'd say we need to off him, but then there wouldn't be a wedding at all."

That made me grin in spite of my angsty mood. "No use killing off the groom."

"What was his reasoning?" Dotty asked carefully.

"He didn't spell it out, but I'm sure it was because he believes I hurt his little sister years ago. Back in high school, she was dating a particular guy. They broke up, and I went out with the guy. Let's just say we got caught kissing after a football game, and everybody found out. She accused us of having a thing before they broke up, which was false unless you counted some low-key flirting that *he* started."

"So you were made to look like the jerk in the situation."

"Yes, ma'am. Honestly, I didn't know how recent their breakup had been, and I'm not sure it would've changed anything if I had, but somehow I was the one who hurt Joel's sister. Not the guy she'd been dating."

When you were the girl who didn't quite fit in, it was easy for others to put the blame on you.

"That's been how many years?" she asked.

I thought back. "I was a senior, so like seventeen?"

She shook her head. "I'm sorry, my dear. The more events you put on, the more people in this town will see who you are today. They'll forget all about their petty ideas from the past."

I shot her a skeptical look. "This small town has a long memory."

"Perhaps, and there will always be those who flake. That's a *them* issue, not a *you* issue."

I nodded, knowing she was right but also finding it hard to let it roll off, particularly in light of...

"I didn't tell you about yesterday." I hopped up, unsettled just thinking about the meeting at Luke's barn and also realizing I needed to check dinner.

"What happened yesterday? Does it have anything to do with Presley and West getting engaged?"

"They're hiring me as their planner," I said.

"Naturally. They'd be stupid not to."

"They've already picked out their venue."

"That was fast."

"Luke Durham is renovating his barn to host events like weddings and parties."

"That big, pretty, red barn?"

"That's the one."

She sat back in her chair, watching me. "You and Luke aren't buddies."

I laughed at that innocent understatement. "Luke hates me with a passion."

"Does Luke even really know you?"

My brows shot up as I pondered the irony of that question. There was a time when I'd thought he knew me better than anyone. That wasn't saying much, really, because to this day, I wouldn't say many really knew me. According to Dotty and Jolene, my therapist, I didn't make it easy for people to know me because I didn't like being vulnerable. I couldn't argue with that. I absolutely had trust issues, but I was trying to learn how to open up so I could make meaningful connections.

I took the pan off the burner, determining the chili mac was done, then added grated cheese as I considered how much of my Luke history to share with Dotty. I'd never told a soul about it, with the exception of Jolene, and she didn't really count. I'd intentionally chosen a therapist in Nashville to ensure she wouldn't be familiar with any of the people involved.

Being in the same room with Luke, talking to him, finding myself in the position where I had to work with him... I was aching to spill it. It felt like a weight I carried around, a part of my past that I couldn't let go of as long as I kept it secret.

It was just like Dotty to sit there quietly, patiently, letting me wade through my thoughts.

I emptied the pan into a serving bowl, grabbed two smaller bowls and forks, and carried them all to the table.

"When I was in high school, Luke's mom cleaned our house every week," I said once I'd sat and we'd both filled our bowls. "Spring of our junior year, Luke started picking her up each week when she was done. One of those nights, I found him in his car in the driveway, waiting for his mom, who wasn't quite finished working. We started talking, just the two of us out in the driveway in the dark."

I shoveled a bite into my mouth, allowing myself to remember in a way I hadn't for years. My curiosity upon seeing him idling there in the partial glow of our security light, watching me with unhidden interest. His slow, handsome, unsure smile as I walked closer. The way my name rolled off his lips when he said, *Hey, Magnolia.*

"I'd known Luke since grade school, but I didn't really *know* him. Just that he was on the football team, he lived on a farm, and his family wasn't well-off. The two-dimensional ideas you have about most of the kids in your grade, you know?"

Dotty nodded, her mouth full of food, her expression telling me she was engrossed in my story.

"Talking to him had felt exciting and a little forbidden that first night. If anyone from school had seen us, they would've thought what an odd pairing. The rich girl and the farm boy. But there was nobody around. We could let our guard down and maybe be ourselves a little more easily. We just...talked. For maybe thirty minutes, until his mom came out."

"Ahhh," Dotty said, as if everything was falling into place in her head. But there was more.

"It sort of became a thing," I continued. "Every Wednesday night, Luke would show up a little earlier. I'd watch for him and sneak outside. There was a part of our driveway that couldn't be seen from the house, not that my parents were looking. They were too wrapped up in their own drama to worry about what I had going on."

Dotty watched me intently as she ate. I took a bite, giving myself time to remember.

"He wasn't like the other guys who just wanted, well, you know what high school boys want," I said. "He seemed to see me as a real person, not a conquest and not just a spoiled rich girl. Anyway, we had a secret thing going for a few months. He was there for me when my mom took off. I listened to him as he debated whether to apply to colleges or dedicate himself to the farm. Our conversations were *real*, you know?"

"Indeed," she said. "But something must have happened to make it end badly?"

"Yeah." I shoved more food in my mouth, stalling. I chewed slowly, swallowed, then went on. "For my sixteenth birthday, my parents gave me this stunning, heart-shaped emerald ring with diamonds in a white gold band. I loved that ring. I wanted my parents' love so badly back then, and the heart shape..." I shook my head, feeling foolish. "I liked to pretend it was a token of their love. When I showed people and told them it was from my parents, the easy conclusion was that they loved me, and that's what I wanted everyone to believe."

Dotty reached over and patted my hand. She and I had discussed my parents many times over, so she knew I was more of a hassle and a pawn for them.

I swallowed and went on. "That summer, I noticed the ring was missing. I looked everywhere for it. I mean *every-where*. One day, my father walked into the living room when I was searching for it in the cracks of the furniture. I admitted I couldn't find the ring. Long story short, he accused Luke's mom of stealing it. He fired her even though she denied it."

"Oh, hell," Dotty said, as if that explained everything.

It did—almost.

"He wouldn't listen when I pointed out we couldn't prove that and that I didn't believe Mrs. Durham took it. The next thing I knew, he'd blacklisted her by calling the other four families she worked for and telling them she'd stolen from us. I don't know what power he held over them, but he has ways of making people do what he wants. Within two days, Mrs. Durham was let go from all her cleaning jobs."

"And Luke blamed you."

I shrugged. He obviously did. "I tried to talk to him several times, but he ignored my texts and calls. When school started that fall"—I shook my head, remembering—"he was so cold to me."

"Did the ring ever turn up?"

I shook my head. "Maybe she did take it. Who knows? I didn't know her well at all. She was very quiet and kept her distance. Professional boundaries and all that, and honestly I didn't try to get too close because I didn't want her to find out about Luke and me. It was our secret."

"Have you ever been able to discuss with him what happened?"

"No. He was a brick wall. I was hurt for a long time, but then I got mad."

Even today, when I thought about it, about how unfair it was of him to never even talk about what happened, my blood boiled. Because obviously everything I thought we'd shared had been nothing in reality. Lesson number two hundred forty-seven that guys were not to be trusted.

"And now you're being thrown together on a project that your livelihood depends on. And his too, presumably."

I couldn't care less about Luke's livelihood, but she was spot on about mine.

"Right. And possibly not just this one. If he builds the venue he claims he's going to, the likelihood of other clients being interested is high."

Assuming I would sign other clients. Some days I had so much doubt I could taste it.

We fell into silence while I caught up on eating my dinner. The chili mac wasn't half bad, if I did say so myself.

Dotty set aside her fork and turned her attention to her wine, picking up the glass, taking a sip, then studying the deep burgundy liquid.

"Tell me something, Maggie May. When you think about your life in five years, your ideal life, what do you imagine?"

I'd spent so much time thinking about this; I didn't hesitate to answer. "My business is killing it. I'll have a personal assistant, at least one, plus a handful of other planners. We'll have enough business to keep us all busy year-round. We'll be the premier, in-demand planners for anything anyone plans in the area. I don't need to make millions. I don't *want* to make millions. I want to be able to live comfortably and make sure anyone who works for me does too."

"And what about your personal life?"

"In theory, I'd love to have a family. In reality, I don't know if that's possible."

"Why wouldn't it be possible?" she asked.

I laughed to lighten the subject, then pointed at my head. "I've got a lot of baggage in here."

"We all do, I imagine, but you might have more than most," Dotty said. "At any rate, I love your business vision, my dear. I believe in you. The next question is, are you going to let a pesky little thing like Luke Durham stand in your way?"

Just the thought of that had my jaw tight. "No, ma'am, I am not."

"Then you need to figure out how to work with him. On Presley's wedding as well as others. So you can either blow everything off and bury the past, or you can confront him and air it all out."

I nodded slowly, imagining both options. They both sucked llama balls.

There was a part of me that wanted to march out to his stupid farm and have it out. Give him a piece of my mind. Rant at him about how immature and unfair he was to go silent all those years ago, and how petty and small-minded he was to hold on to his grudge for *eighteen years*. Half of our lives, for God's sake. Maybe it would bring me closure to force him to hear my side of the story.

Then again, that could backfire. It could cause problems for Presley and West's wedding. I would *not* let anything prevent them from having the wedding of their dreams.

I'd bitten my tongue around Luke for years. I could continue to do that at least until after Christmas Eve. For Presley's sake.

An idea blossomed as I pushed away my empty bowl and picked up my wine with as much enthusiasm as if it was my favorite dessert. Today it was a fitting dessert, and we still had half a bottle to go.

"I'll work with him when I have to," I said eventually, "and ensure Presley's day is memorable and amazing. But I'll also scour the surrounding area to see if there are other barn event venues for my future clients. It never hurts to have options."

"That's my girl," Dotty said, grinning. "See? You have a very good business brain. You just need to believe in it. A smart businesswoman doesn't put all her eggs in one basket.

Someday you'll need more than one barn because three of your planners will have barn weddings on the same date."

"I like the way you think, Dotty," I told her.

Luke Durham had taken too much of my mental energy already. I'd work with him when I had no other choice, but I'd do everything I could to have multiple better options for my clients.

He wanted to get into events? Well, sadly for him, I'd gotten into them first. I'd be a lot of people's first contact. He'd have to fight to get my clients to book with him.

Chapter Five

Luke

Being among acres of Christmas trees, surrounded by cool, crisp air and pine scent, had always soothed me, even when I was working my ass off.

It also tended to make me lose track of time, particularly when I became engrossed in a task like pricing.

I was deep in the Fraser firs when I realized I had exactly two minutes to make it to my meeting with Presley at the barn. I stopped what I was doing and jogged to my truck at the edge of the trees, then jumped in and hauled ass. By the time I drove around the corner of the barn, I was a minute late.

An old BMW was parked near the barn door. Seconds later I realized only one person sat inside, and it was Magnolia. Presley must be meeting her here. The upside was I wasn't the only one who was running behind.

I got out and headed toward the barn door, giving myself a pep talk to be pleasant to the planner. If I was lucky, she'd wait for Presley in her car so we wouldn't be alone and have to make small talk as if there wasn't a cargo train's worth of baggage and history between us.

No such luck. I heard her car door shut behind me.

I opened the barn door, shoving down my bone-deep dislike and steeling myself to be neutral if not pleasant. Then I turned to watch her approach.

Her hair was back in a ponytail, and I couldn't help thinking again that she dressed differently these days. She wore leggings, those same knee-high boots, a long shirt, and a puffer vest. The old Magnolia never would've been caught dead in a puffer vest. As she drew closer, her head down, I noticed a big scuff on one of the boots, which was even more unlike the high-school version of this girl. Guess that's what happened when you didn't have Daddy's millions behind you anymore.

"Presley must be running late," I said, skipping a fake greeting.

"Presley isn't coming. West's stepfather is in the ER with a possible heart attack, so West went to Nashville to wait for news with his mom. Presley has the girls. She asked me to handle this."

"I hope the guy's okay," I said, knowing West thought the world of his mom's husband and their daughters had embraced him as their grandfather. "Come on in."

The truth was, Magnolia was the person whose expertise I needed today, so Presley's absence wouldn't affect this meeting. If West hadn't suggested it, I wouldn't have initiated it. I would've spent however many more hours on the internet, doing more research, spinning my wheels.

But time was money, and when West and I had been faced with reining in the rooms and areas we could fit in the barn plans, he'd suggested very practically that we get Magnolia's input on what to prioritize to make it as appealing as possible for future events, not just his wedding. The logical side of me hadn't been able to argue.

Now that I was alone with this woman who made me feel so damn much—both back in the day and now, though those were polar-opposite sentiments—I was second-guessing myself. Maybe we should've rescheduled. But it was too late to change the meeting without looking like I couldn't handle it.

Once I'd latched the door to keep the brisk air out, I turned to find Magnolia watching me with a slight scowl. Time to get this over with.

"West and I met to hammer out the plans, and we had a hard time fitting in all the features we discussed during our first meeting," I said. "We can't do them all, so what's most important?"

She narrowed her eyes and tilted her head. "So you want me to do you a favor," she stated. "Since this isn't about my clients' wedding."

Hell. It wouldn't look like that if Presley were here and we could narrow down *her* needs for her wedding.

This was not a position I was comfortable in.

"I'll pay you as a consultant," I said.

I didn't expect her to do anything out of the goodness of her heart, because I wasn't convinced she *had* any goodness in her heart. Even if she did, I sure as hell didn't want to owe her anything.

She looked me over, seeming to consider the offer.

"Look," I said, "my immediate goal is the same as yours: to give one of my best friends a memorable wedding. To do that, I need to be able to renovate this barn in such a way that it'll serve as a sought-after venue for years to come. Bill me for your services, and let's get this over with."

"You want me to trust you to send payment," she said with a touch of disbelief in her tone.

"I do what I say I'll do," I bit out. "Do you want the job or not?"

Seconds ticked by as she considered. All the while, I thought through a plan B in case she told me to fuck myself and walked out. If I was going to pay someone, I could contact another planner for input. Or combing the internet was still free, minus the time it would take.

"I'll answer your questions," she finally said. "My rate is two hundred an hour."

That was a racket, but fuck it. I'd have her out of here in one hour, have my plans, and move on.

"Fine." I led her farther into the cavernous room, which I'd cleared of the rest of the junk and debris since her last visit. "We're keeping the arched beam details of the ceiling intact. We'll keep this double door as the main entry"—I pointed to the door we'd come in—"and the far end will serve as an altar for couples who have the ceremony here."

"With the window centered above and some kind of portable arch that could be removed, in addition to decor options like draped fabric, greenery, or string lights, that would make for stunning ceremony photos."

"We intend to wall off both sides from the point where the roof angles out." I walked over to show her what I meant. "So we'd have the main open area stretch the full length. On the far end, we'll keep the full width open so it's a T shape. Besides close-up photos of the wedding party and altar, a photographer could get shots of the entire space from this end and capture the architecture as well as the wedding."

"String lights along the arched beams..." She nodded,

her eyes lighting up as if she'd forgotten who she was helping.

It momentarily took me back to nights in her driveway, in the dark, just the two of us, when something I said would light her up the same way.

I shook my head to rid myself of the memory. That was a lifetime ago with someone I thought was a different person. I was no longer the naive teenager who fell for the act.

"The issue we're up against is a limited number of square feet for the extra spaces," I explained. "Restrooms are a necessity. They'll go here. The service area for caterers, with refrigerators, running water... I'd like to put that next to the restrooms so the plumbing's all in one area."

"What do you think of putting a window from the service area to the main room? Maybe one that could be closed if it's not in use."

"I could do that." I strode farther down. "With winter events, we can't skip the coatroom. And if we need two rooms for getting ready, that doesn't leave much for a gift room, a utility room, storage..."

"You'll want a bigger room for the women, with well-lit mirrors, plenty of space for changing, sitting, photos. Men require less space. Although putting a couple of video games in or a pool table wouldn't be a bad idea."

"We don't have room for that."

"Fine. It was just a thought." She paced away from me, glancing up at the ceiling, then eyeing the area that would be walled off. "The gift room could be a closet within one of the prep rooms. It doesn't have to be large. Most people give money or send gifts to the couple's home these days."

"What about the first look?" I asked.

"During the warmer months, that can be outside. Do you plan to create any outdoor spaces for weddings?"

"Like what?" I was so concerned with the barn itself that I hadn't considered the outside yet.

"Like a paved terrace or covered dining area for spring or fall when it isn't unbearably hot. Some photo-op areas. Sitting areas. The sky's the limit, really. Or rather, how much space you have."

We had the space. Budget, well, I'd have to figure that out later, as my priority right now was for indoor events.

"And have you thought about parking?" she asked.

"Still working on that, but if nothing else, we have a lot of parking for the pick-your-own areas and could shuttle people to the barn. But back to the barn. I'm thinking the larger prep room over here and a smaller one there."

"Have you considered separate entries for those? That helps couples avoid seeing each other before the ceremony or the first look."

I made a note on my phone because, no, I hadn't considered that, but it wasn't a bad idea. "Okay, so what about storage? There's no room left for it."

"Don't you have like a hundred acres of land?" Her tone said I was an idiot.

"A lot of that is accounted for."

"But not all. Why not build a storage shed?"

"Some of us aren't made of money," I snapped.

An expression flashed over her face, just for half a second, enough to tell me my comment got to her. I wasn't sure quite what I'd seen—regret? Shame? Sadness?

I shrugged it off. I didn't have it in me to worry about her feelings.

"You could look into renting a portable storage unit for a

few months until you've booked a few weddings to finance a permanent one," she suggested.

It was a plausible idea.

"Using your venue square footage for storage would be a dumb move," she said, and my scowl returned.

"Kind of like making false accusations that get people fired?"

She whipped around and faced me with fire in her eyes. "I didn't make false accusations," she said with venom.

"My mom didn't steal your precious ring," I bit back.

Magnolia narrowed her eyes. "You can pay me two hundred an hour to bicker about the past, or you can pay me to help you figure out your precious barn."

Damn. I hadn't meant to go there. I didn't need her to know how much her careless actions had devastated me.

"Right. I still need to know what to do about the first-look area. Then you can go."

"Just to clarify, I can go whenever I choose to go. I'm doing you a favor."

I let out a sardonic chuckle. "Damn expensive favor, but fine. Let's do this so we can be done. What would you suggest?"

She paced toward the far end, her arms crossed, fist on her chin. I watched her, taking in her fit body, the curves of her hips, the slight messiness of the long ponytail going down her back. Her body had matured since high school, filled out to be more womanly, alluring. She was admittedly a beautiful woman on the outside, but I was not affected by her looks.

"For couples who want a special first-look location," she said from the other end of the barn, "we could make sort of a backdrop along this wall here."

I couldn't help noticing she used the word *we*, as if she

and I were in this together, which we absolutely were not. Not if I could help it. And that was the quandary, wasn't it? I wasn't aware of other event planners in Dragonfly Lake who weren't affiliated with a specific venue like the Marks. She was it until you got to Nashville. So if I wanted to get wedding business, I might need Magnolia's referrals.

"What kind of a backdrop?" I asked as I walked that way.

"One of the other barns I just started working with has a wall of greenery and floral arrangements that makes a gorgeous background. I was thinking of something with rustic wood in a neutral color with string lights, some flowers, possibly even a sign with the bride and groom's name and the date."

"You work with another barn? For weddings?" When I'd gotten this idea months ago, I'd searched online for similar venues in the area and hadn't found any. If there was a competitor out there, I wanted to know about it.

"Yes," she said nonchalantly. "And I'm meeting with a third one next week. It's smaller than yours but has an upper level too. Anyway, outdoors is really preferred for the first look when the weather's nice. You'll want to consider that once you get the inside done."

Hell. Two competitors I hadn't known about? All my dad's naysaying rattled through my head, chipping away at my confidence. Was I making a mistake? This wasn't a small commitment, financially and otherwise.

If Magnolia was in fact the only planner in Dragonfly Lake and possibly even in Runner and the surrounding area, and she recommended these other two barns before mine—because why would she recommend mine when we couldn't stand each other and didn't like working together? —this endeavor could crash and burn fast.

Fuck.

Insecurity rushed over me like a tidal wave. What the hell did I know about event hosting?

I had vague plans to hire someone to run the event business if it got to be too much work, but if Magnolia avoided recommending my barn, would I even get business?

I peered up at the dramatic rafters I'd been in awe of since I was a kid. This might be an old barn, but the architecture was cool as hell. I believed in my bones it would make a spectacular place for weddings and receptions.

I knew lots of people in town, got along with most of them. I could get a marketing expert to help me promote my barn. I could reach out to wedding planners in Nashville, start making connections in the industry just like Magnolia was.

With a nod, I calmed myself down. I did *not* need Magnolia James for this to work.

I took out my phone and added a reminder to research other planners in the state and start reaching out.

I wasn't going to fail. My stakes were too high.

As I stuck my phone back in my pocket, Magnolia walked back toward this end of the barn, still taking in the space, her mind clearly spinning with ideas. If we were on better terms, I'd have loved to be in on those ideas.

Her phone rang as she came closer, and she took it out of a pocket in her vest and checked the screen. She frowned.

"I need to take this in case it's business," she said.

I nodded and turned my attention to measuring and taking notes based on what we'd discussed. Her idea for separate storage was admittedly a decent one.

Though I had no interest in her life, I couldn't help tuning in to her phone call, particularly when she sucked in her breath a few seconds after saying hello. The look on her face gripped me, though I couldn't quite decipher it. Shock? Confusion? Distress?

"I'm here," she said in between long pauses. Then she turned her back to me and said, "I think it's safe to say you don't know a thing about me." She added a series of mm-hmms, yeses, a no, and then, "Look, I'm working right now and can't talk. Can I call you back at this number?"

After ending the call, Magnolia seemed to wilt, her back still to me. I wasn't sure she remembered I was nearby.

"Everything okay?" I asked.

She straightened, verifying my suspicions that she'd forgotten where she was.

"That was my mother," she said, turning but not looking at me. If I wasn't mistaken, she'd gone pale.

I didn't have anything good to say about Bianca James. Magnolia hadn't talked a lot about her parents back when we were close, but I'd learned enough to think they were both assholes. I couldn't fathom a mother who just up and left her family without explanation.

"She wants to meet," Magnolia said.

"Meet?" I asked, unsure what she meant. Meet me? Meet Magnolia? Had she not seen her daughter lately?

"She wants to talk."

"How long has it been since you've seen her?"

Magnolia finally made eye contact with me. "Eighteen years."

"You never heard from her after she left?"

Magnolia pressed her lips together and shook her head. "I tried to reach out to her twice. She never responded." She inhaled deeply, her chest rising with it, and I scolded myself for noticing.

What the fuck was wrong with that woman? Leaving her teenage daughter was bad, but I'd always figured she'd come back around or at least caught up with Magnolia if it was her husband she was escaping.

An expression flickered over Magnolia's features, and I saw a hint of vulnerability. Just for a second. Just enough to send me back nearly two decades to when we'd been... involved.

My hatred began a slow melt, or at least a softening. I knew from experience how tough losing your mom was. My mom's death had hit me hard, *still* hit hard even though it'd been years. I couldn't begin to imagine what it was like knowing your mother *chose* to disappear from your life.

"Are you going to meet with her?" I asked. I might not like her, but I couldn't help feeling a smidgeon of empathy for her.

"I...don't know." She shook her head, seeming to come back to the here and now. Her tone returned to chilly and businesslike. "It's nothing for you to worry about." She checked the time on her phone. "It hasn't been quite an hour. Don't you want to get every bit of your money's worth from me?"

Annnnd any sympathy I'd felt crumbled at the snark in her tone.

"I got what I need," I said. "Send me a bill for the full hour. Thanks for your help."

With her jaw tight, body stiff, she nodded once, then walked out of the barn without another word.

Chapter Six

Magnolia

F riday morning I awoke with a pit of dread in my gut.

When I'd called my mother back, I'd agreed to meet with her in spite of my misgivings.

Today was the day. My office was the place. I'd intentionally insisted on meeting in my "territory" but away from my apartment. I didn't need her knowing where I lived.

In the days since, I'd waffled between drowning in decades-old anger at her and blocking the entire situation from my mind.

If she had contacted me sooner, like years sooner, I'd hold a lot more hope that we might be able to come to some sort of peace. Instead I harbored about ninety-six percent anger and four percent hope that anything good could come of this.

I had no idea why she wanted to meet or why now. Part of me had wanted to refuse her and tell her where to stick it, but I had enough questions that I'd agreed. I'd find out what she wanted, ask my questions, get her out of here, and go on with my life.

I'd made our appointment time toward the end of the workday in case it was emotionally taxing. I was certain it would be.

Now it was nearly time for her to show up. I wasn't a big drinker, but I eyed the bottles of wine and champagne in my drink cooler. I needed to keep my walls strong though, and even a small amount of alcohol could potentially weaken me. I chose a bottle of water instead.

I was sitting at my desk, trying to focus on the bar mitzvah celebration I'd booked yesterday, when the outside door opened exactly on time. My body tensed as I turned my attention to the outer room.

"Hello?" came the chillingly familiar voice from my past.

My stomach roiled as I stood and went to the open doorway. "Hello, Mother," I said through a tight jaw.

"Magnolia," she gushed, smiling nervously. "Look at you. You've grown up."

"That'll happen over the course of eighteen years." I didn't have it in me to fake pleasantness. The wounds were too deep. "Come in."

Her grin disappeared, and she averted her gaze as she entered my office, giving me the opportunity to really look at her.

She was dressed impeccably as she always had been, in a silky blouse, tailored slacks, and high-dollar medium heels. Her jewelry was minimal but dripped with dollar signs as well. She looked almost the same, her face barely aged in nearly two decades—except for her eyes. Her eyes had a life-weary expression that went deeper than a poor night of sleep. I suspected she'd had work done to stay so youthful, because her eyes didn't match the rest of her.

"Have a seat," I said as if she were a potential client visiting for the first time—but with less warmth.

She sat, shooting me a cross between a nervous smile and a grimace. I merely watched her, not making any move to offer comfort or hospitality.

"Well," she said, "I imagine you're very busy and wondering why I've contacted you, so I'll get straight to the point. I owe you two big, major apologies that I know will never be sufficient, but I hope you'll hear me out."

With a shrug, I said, "Go for it," as indifferently as I could.

She inhaled, her insecurity oozing out of her like a bad stench from a dumpster, wiping her hands on her thighs as if they were sweating. "First..." Shaking her head, she looked off to the side. "I'm so very sorry I left you, Magnolia. I know an apology will never take that away, never fix your childhood, but I am genuinely sorry I had to do that. I won't offer you any excuses other than..." She paused, seemingly searching for words, then shook her head again. "I can't easily describe my state of mind then, other than I was beyond miserable, trapped in a terrible marriage, and desperate to get out of your father's grasp."

I frowned at the question that instantly popped into my mind. "Did he hit you?"

"That man's abuse isn't physical. It's much more twisted and diabolical than that."

I nodded, all too familiar with his manipulations and control games. "He was always like that. You left me with him, Mother. I was seventeen years old, and *you left me with that.*"

So much for keeping a lid on my emotions.

"I know," she said in a rush. "I know you have no reason to believe me, but I've regretted that every second since."

"You're right. I don't believe you. If you felt so bad, I would think you'd reach out sooner."

Her face was pale, her eyes even more hollow than when she'd walked in. "I...couldn't." She blew out a shaky breath. "There are things you don't know, Magnolia...things I'm not proud of. Reasons I've had to keep quiet."

I waited her out, wondering if she was going to spill or if this would end up being just more BS from Bianca Lansford James.

"My marriage was an arranged marriage," she said quietly, "dictated by my father for the sake of his business. Felix would not have been my choice. I know that sounds archaic, but believe me."

My brows shot up my forehead, not because I didn't believe my grandfather would do that but because I'd never figured out that's why my parents had gotten married. It all made so much sense in that instant. I wasn't sure why I hadn't guessed before.

"Because of the bylaws," I said knowingly.

Her head whipped up, and she met my gaze. "Felix told you?"

"He didn't mention that's why he married you, but he tried the same trick with me. The bylaws say the company can only be led by a family member or someone who marries into it. I didn't want anything to do with Lansford Development, not that he ever asked. A few years ago, he handpicked the man he wanted to groom to eventually be his second-in-command and one day take over. Then he manipulated me into an engagement."

"Oh, Magnolia," she said as if she gave half a crap about me. "I had no idea—"

"Of course you didn't," I snapped. "How could you when you disappeared from my life?"

"I didn't realize you were married."

"I'm not." I hadn't anticipated *how* trauma-filled this visit would become so quickly.

She frowned. "When are you getting married?"

"I'm not. Initially I agreed to the engagement. Rick was not a love match, but he was good-looking enough and charming and attentive at first."

"At first," she said as if she'd been through the same thing. "When I first married Felix, I foolishly thought maybe we'd find our way to love."

My mother and I had more in common than I'd ever guessed. "Same. I'll give him credit. Rick went all out in the early months. Charm, gifts, kindness. He wanted to marry quickly, but I insisted I needed at least a year to plan a wedding. Turns out Rick couldn't be sweet for that long. Or to be more accurate, faithful."

"I wish I could say I was surprised. So what happened?"

"I called him on it." I thought back to the night more than two years ago at the bonfire, when I'd caught Rick texting some woman suggestive messages. "He had absolutely no remorse. He knew I was trapped and didn't care one little bit about my feelings."

"No," she said. "They don't. So did something happen to Rick?"

That she would assume something happened to him rather than that I stood up for myself was so telling. "*I* happened. I refused to go through life with a husband who was so inconsiderate of me. Cheating itself would be bad enough, but the fact that when I caught him, he showed no remorse? And we weren't even married yet?" I shook my head with emphasis. "I couldn't live like that. I broke off the engagement. Dad disowned me that night. Kicked me out with nothing but two suitcases of clothes and toiletries and my car. He paid an after-hours locksmith to change the locks."

My mother nodded knowingly. "That's how he is. Controlling and manipulative. I'm so sorry you went through that."

"I'm not," I said with no hesitation. "Being free of him is worth it. Free of both of them. You must understand that since you also broke free."

"Not entirely." She averted her eyes again. "I left, but I'm still married to him. Still under his thumb."

I mentally reared back. They were still married? Why, if she went to the effort of getting away from him, was she still legally tied to him? "Why didn't you divorce him?"

My mother leaned back in the chair and reclined her head, eyes closed. "We made an agreement when I left."

"What? He told me you left without telling him, but if you made an agreement..."

She straightened and opened her eyes. "He knew very well I was leaving and how to get ahold of me. He had to in order to send me monthly stipends."

"What's he paying you for?"

"Keeping his secrets, primarily." She shook her head. "Our relationship was so toxic, Magnolia... It still is."

"You still have a relationship with him?"

"Only financially. I suspect I won't after today."

"What is today?"

"Today is the day I tell you everything. Or at least the relevant points."

She looked scared or as if she might get sick, piquing my curiosity. "Okay." I drew out the word and sat back in my chair, settling in.

"Like you, when my father introduced me to Felix James and told me I was to marry him or lose everything, I looked at the groom-to-be with possibility. Maybe we could make a decent life together. He was nice to look at and had this...charisma, I called it. Obviously Felix was dedicated to making my father happy and providing well for us. I didn't entertain the thought of saying no. My dad was my only family, and I'm not going to lie. I liked the type of life his business provided for me. I was into fashion, and fashion wasn't cheap."

I remembered her gargantuan closet in the Dragonfly Heights house I'd grown up in. It was filled with gowns of every color, everyday clothes in the finest fabrics with the most exclusive labels. Her passion had spilled over to me back then. Not surprising when you consider I wore designer duds as an infant. Now the idea was ridiculous, but high fashion, designers, and the trendiest of outfits were a way of life in the James household.

"I was young," my mother continued. "Naive. Stupidly hopeful. I expected better treatment than Felix could ever give me. After a grand, beautiful wedding, it went downhill fast. He was controlling and selfish. His needs were first, second, and third. But he was a master at saying the right things at the right time, not to mention showering me with extravagant gifts to make up for the bad times. But twenty months in, I found out he'd been unfaithful repeatedly. With multiple partners. Sleeping around was his favorite pastime."

I wasn't surprised in the least, though I'd never had proof. "But you stuck around?"

"Eventually I did one better. I had a fling of my own."

My brows shot up because I hadn't expected that. I'd

never heard or seen any hint of my mother stepping out on my father. "Did he catch you?"

She laughed, but there was no humor in the sound. Instantly she sobered and met my gaze. "He found out when I told him I was pregnant."

I tilted my head in confusion.

"That's when he informed me that he was unable to father any children."

My job dropped open as my thoughts went into a spin cycle.

"Felix James is not your biological father, Magnolia."

Chapter Seven

Magnolia

I stared at her, waiting for the punch line, but my mother had never been a joker. "How... How sure are you?"

"One hundred percent positive. Felix is sterile due to an untreated childhood infection. I didn't know that prior to my pregnancy."

"Who...?" I leaned forward, elbows on my desk, head propped in my hands, as if holding myself up could counteract the immense blowing up of my reality, my entire identity.

I wasn't Felix James's daughter?

"Who is my father?" I asked.

"His name was Jimmy. He was in town for a long weekend. Felix was out of town on business, and I confess my objective was revenge for all the times he'd been unfaithful. Jimmy and I spent an unexpectedly magical, unforgettable thirty-six hours together." Her voice had gone slightly dreamy, and a ghost of a smile tugged at her lips. "He knew my situation. We both knew it was a one-time thing. We never exchanged last names."

I sat there frozen, my mouth hanging open as I tried to process everything. My brain moved in slow motion. "So that makes me...a bastard?"

"I'm sorry, Magnolia."

I laughed. For real laughed. "That's... That's actually the best news ever."

I shared no blood with the manipulative, controlling snake, Felix James. None of his toxic DNA. For the past two years plus, I hadn't even had any of his money, with the exception of my eleven-year-old car. I was finally free of the man, save for the psychological damage I was still working through.

My laughter quieted, but my grin didn't fade. I considered taking out the champagne from the drink fridge and popping the cork. My mother, however, still had a grave, heavy expression on her face. This wasn't the right time or person to celebrate with.

I took a swallow of my water instead, my mind reeling. "That explains why he's always seemed to hate me. Because he does," I said almost gleefully.

"Felix James doesn't hold affection for anyone but himself," my mother said. "With you, I believe he resented you from the day you were born, and I'm sorry for that too, Magnolia. You never deserved that."

No, I didn't deserve that. No child did. Only through weekly therapy appointments had I figured out how deep the damage from my father went. From both of my parents actually.

I'd believed I wasn't lovable. I was still undoing that damage, still working on my self-worth. It took a lot of time and effort to undo thirty-plus years of programming. I'd been working with my therapist, Jolene, on loving myself for more than a year, with affirmations, meditations, journaling, and more. She was helping me learn to be kind to myself, to take care of myself in ways I never had, like eating better, treating my body better, and catching negative self-talk and flipping it around. I was a work-in-progress.

And now, in the course of a twenty-minute conversation, my life, my messed-up psyche, made sense like it never had before.

"It helps to know that," I said, less jubilant and more reflective. Another thought occurred to me. "If he knew you were carrying someone else's child, why did you stay in your miserable marriage?"

What could possibly convince Felix James, with his double standards, to keep his unfaithful wife around? Then it hit me before she could say more. He didn't want to lose his big business deal with her father.

My mother stood, stepped to the window, and peered outside. "He and I made an agreement. We both needed to remain married, him for business reasons and me for money. Add to that, he's the type of man who feels deeply ashamed of his inability to produce an heir."

That phrase *produce an heir* was so cold but entirely fitting. For a man with the emotional capacity of a dead possum, fatherhood could only be about carrying on the family name.

"He swore me to secrecy regarding your paternity," she continued, "and with foolish optimism, back then I thought a child ought to have a father figure. I hoped Felix could be one. Maybe not a great one, but I never realized how awful he would be." She turned to face me. "I now understand that having no father can be better than having a bad father. But I was in a tricky position. If I left the marriage, not only would I lose the financial benefits of a wealthy husband, but my father would write me off as well. I had no job history or skills, and I'm not proud to admit I really didn't want to work a nine-to-five job anyway. I liked having money. Felix knew that and agreed, if I kept his dirty little sterility secret, to let me spend generously."

Knowing this woman the way I did, that rang true. I didn't know her from Eve now, but back then, that had to be a dream deal for her—except for having to stay married to a controlling jerk.

"So eighteen years ago, what changed to make you leave?" I asked.

"Two things. One, I hated him so much. It grew with every day I stayed. He flaunted his control over me like a damn peacock. He's driven by power, and while he still reported to my father at work, in our home, he saw himself as a king."

I wrinkled my nose, knowing that was true.

"Two, I was in love with another man."

Ah. That was probably the only thing that would compel her to leave. She'd gone from one man to the next, incapable of being on her own. "Did my fath—Felix know about the other man?"

She shook her head vehemently. "He never found out about Franklin. He wouldn't have agreed to anything if he had. Franklin and I had thirteen wonderful years before he passed away." Pausing, she seemed to reel her emotions in.

"Why didn't you take me with you?" I asked. It was a toss-up whether I would've been better off with her, but I'd always wondered how a mother could desert her only child.

"Felix wouldn't allow it. I believe he thought I wouldn't go without you."

Without the Franklin element, I didn't think she'd have

the courage to leave either. I didn't see her as the type who could forge her own path, even with a healthy bank account.

"Let me guess," I said, my brain spinning, figuring so many things out, questioning just as many others. "He made you swear not to tell me the truth about my paternity."

"You guessed it. That would've taken away his power over you. Our agreement stipulated that I wasn't allowed to be in contact with you at all."

I nodded, pressing my lips together. What a pathetic man he was. Pathetic *human*. Insecure, selfish, weak. "So why now?"

My mother returned to her chair, looking even paler if that was possible. "Could I bother you for some water?"

I got up and grabbed a bottle from the fridge, absorbed in my thoughts. Handing it to her, I sat back down and waited for her to unscrew the lid, which she struggled with, and take a drink.

Finally she said, "Two weeks ago I was diagnosed with breast cancer."

Sympathy tugged at me even though our history was an ugly mess. I might not like her, but I didn't want her to suffer.

"Magnolia, you may or may not believe me, but all these years, I've felt terrible for leaving you with that man, for bending to his demands in every way, allowing you to think he was your father. That's not fair to you, and it's eaten away at me."

I eyed her skeptically, biting down on questions.

"Getting a cancer diagnosis..." She closed her eyes and shook her head, looking downright ashen. "It changes your perspective in a heartbeat."

"I imagine it does. What is your prognosis?"

"I have procedures and appointments next week where I'll find out more," she said, "but regardless of what happens with my health, I decided I couldn't continue to hide the truth from you. What you do with it is up to you. If you choose to go public with it or confront Felix, you have my blessing. It's your truth to do what you need to with it."

"What happens if you break your agreement?"

"I'm prepared to take the stand I should've taken years ago."

"He'll cut off your money."

"Yes. I'm expecting that. Franklin left me everything he had, which wasn't insignificant, so I'll be okay." She took a long drink, then continued, "I'm ready to go on the offensive. I'm going to file for divorce and tell my father everything. The paternity in particular. He could choose to pressure the board of directors to change the bylaws, or Felix could lose his position as next in line for the CEO position."

"Is Grandfather still active in the business?"

"He is to an extent, though at seventy-nine years old, he only works two or three days a week."

"Does he know you've been separated?"

My mother nodded. "As long as we didn't divorce, he could still have Felix as his next in command."

"Do you think the paternity issue and a divorce will make him change his mind about Felix?"

She shrugged. "I don't know, and I don't care. My motivation is freeing myself. I'm nearly forty years late, but as they say, better late than never. I regret so much, Magnolia..."

I didn't know what to say, so I didn't say anything.

Did I feel sorry for her? Yes. She was a weak person who'd needed a health scare to find her spine.

Did I forgive her? I wasn't sure. I needed time to sort through everything she'd dropped on me.

Did I hope Felix's world fell out from under him?

Yes. Yes, I did.

Call me petty and vengeful, but I hoped he suffered the way he'd made others suffer all these years.

My mother picked up her purse from the floor—a Hermes that probably cost more than a new car. She rustled through it, took out a business envelope, and handed it over to me. A small, bulky object made it bulge.

I frowned at it. There was no writing on it, but it was sealed. "What is this?"

"Open it."

Puzzled, I used my letter opener to slice it open, reached in, and pulled out a ring. I gasped.

Between my thumb and index finger, I held the heart-shaped emerald ring that had gone missing eighteen years ago. Right around the time my mother left, I realized for the first time.

"*You* took it?"

The weak woman across from me wouldn't make eye contact.

"I know it was awful of me," she said quietly.

"Yes," I said, astonished and beyond disgusted. "Why would you *do* that?"

She ran her hands over her face, taking her sweet time to say anything. I stared at her, waiting, my mind spinning through the consequences of that single self-centered act of hers.

Who stole from their own daughter?

The same woman who deserted said daughter, leaving her with a controlling asshole.

This woman was something else. I hadn't thought she could drop any lower in my opinion. I'd been wrong.

"Nothing will excuse it, but I'll tell you the story behind it. Felix purchased the ring before you were born. It's a somewhat-famous stone that I can't remember the name of or the history, just that it had some kind of Russian origin. Felix originally bought it to appease me after I confronted him about his extramarital activities."

That sounded like a classic Felix James move.

"He made a big deal of it," she continued, "saying his wife would have the best, which was really about his ego more than me. Anyway, it took several weeks to arrive. While I couldn't wait to see that ring on my finger, his purchase didn't erase my resentment as he'd intended. In the meantime, I met Jimmy and became pregnant with you. In retaliation, Felix informed me I would not be gifted the ring. I never saw it again until he gave it to you, allegedly from both of us, for your sixteenth birthday."

Just when I thought I couldn't be shocked by anything either of my parents did...

Unable to come up with anything to say, I stared at the spectacular green stone surrounded by brilliant white diamonds. How could such a thing of beauty be used for so much hate, control, and revenge?

Then a thought occurred to me.

"Did Felix know you took it?" I asked.

A hint of a sickening grin pulled the corners of her lips upward, making me feel nauseated.

"If you told him it was missing, I'm certain he figured it out."

And he'd ignored that information and instead accused Luke's mother of stealing it. I had no idea why he'd do that. If he'd known about Luke and me, I'd bet he did it to hurt me, but as far as I knew, neither of my parents knew about the time we'd spent together in secret.

"So you stole from your daughter to get revenge on the husband you were leaving," I stated unnecessarily.

"After the agreement he forced on me, I was too mad to think straight. So yes, revenge was part of it. It was also insurance. In case he stopped paying me."

I didn't have a clue what the ring's value was, but with a Russian history and the size, not to mention the quality of the diamonds, selling it would likely be enough for a normal person to live for months. Maybe years. But Bianca Lansford James was not a normal person. The life she was accustomed to consisted of ridiculous spending and waste.

"Did you ever consider just getting a job and earning your living like the rest of the world?"

"Oh, lord, what would I *do*, Magnolia?"

"Whatever you needed to," I said, sitting up straighter. "When you suddenly lose everything, you figure it out. You use the brain God gave you, hope for the assistance of a good-hearted person or two, and do what you need to do."

"I'm not as strong as you."

"It's not about strength," I said angrily. "It's about determination."

Were there moments I'd felt desperate? Yes. A lot of them.

Was I incredibly lucky Dotty had had compassion when she'd found me sleeping in my car? Absolutely.

But was I determined to change my life and make it my own? Something I could be proud of? More than anything.

If I could do it coming from my overdramatic, hate-filled, manipulative background, she could too. The difference was, she hadn't been forced to.

Would I have been able to start over if Felix hadn't

disowned me? I wasn't sure, but I tended to think everything had happened as it needed to in order to get me here, and I was thankful to be where I was: *not* dependent on that hateful man anymore. Not dependent on *any* man.

The fact was, I didn't have any right or reason to feel superior to her. I'd been kicked out and done what I had to do. She hadn't been forced in the same way.

So instead of hatred and anger—because honestly, I knew from experience how those sucked so much energy out of a person—I felt sorry for her.

The woman across from me had never seemed happy in the seventeen years I'd lived with her, and she obviously wasn't a happy person now. She was sad, remorseful, and toxic. The only emotion I could muster for her at this moment was pity.

We had one thing in common, and that was that we were both told who we would marry for the sake of business. The difference was, she'd gone along with it. I'd eventually ultimately refused.

Thank all the stars above.

Sitting across from me was a glimpse of how I could've ended up had I made a different decision and been cowed into marrying Rick two years ago.

In spite of all the baggage and awfulness of the past half hour, a lightness flitted through me. I'd chosen right. I was so much better off than my mother. Chances were, she didn't recognize that. Not while she was still dependent on the money she'd received from Felix and Franklin. She didn't know what it was like to be hungry and scared about where you were going to live and how you were going to eat. I'd gone through some horrible times, but looking at her, it became clear to me just how lucky I was.

"I was forced to find my own way," I said finally. "At the

time, I thought it was the worst thing ever. But now my future is in *my* hands. No one else's. Especially not some misogynistic, pathetic, weak man. I hope coming clean to me somehow frees you, Mother."

"It likely will after I go to my father."

As she'd said, better late than never, but that was her problem.

"Thank you for returning the ring to me," I said, my tone businesslike. I was ready for her to leave.

I tilted the ring from side to side, watching how the light hit it. As gorgeous as it was, I couldn't look at it without seeing the twisted hate and manipulation of my childhood.

I didn't want this ring. I would never wear it. But I put it back into its envelope and stuck it in my desk drawer for now. I'd figure out what to do with it later.

The larger task would be unwinding the ramifications of everything my mother had confessed to me.

Chapter Eight

Luke

Once I'd finished my errands in town Friday afternoon, I glanced at the clock in my truck. Almost five. I didn't know what time Magnolia's business closed, but I needed to catch her before she left.

I had a point to make.

I parked in the lot behind the hardware store and headed to her location by The Bean Counter. The sky was dark for the hour, thanks to heavy clouds that promised one hell of a storm. As I approached the building, I could see a cozy, inviting light was on in her space. Then I shook my head, reminding myself it was like a poisonous spider luring prey into its web.

Raindrops were just starting to fall as I headed down the walkway to the door. It was unlocked, and I stepped inside, noticing her logo in neon on a brick wall. I didn't know what I'd expected, but this was comfortable and classy at once, decorated tastefully without feeling over-the-top snooty.

On the left side was an open door, and I could sense someone was in there, though no one greeted me. I walked to the doorway and looked in just as Magnolia appeared in my face, apparently on her way to see who'd entered. We nearly collided.

"Oh!" she said, stepping back, one hand on her heart, the other holding a half-full champagne flute out of the way. "What are *you* doing here?"

"Why are you drinking champagne by yourself?"

"I asked you first," she said.

I took out my wallet, removed the check I'd filled out at home, and handed it over to her. "Your payment."

She looked at the check as if she'd never seen one before.

"For your consultation services," I said.

She frowned. "You didn't have to deliver it in person."

"I was going to mail it, but I didn't want any chance of it getting lost and you accusing me of not paying you."

"You could've sent it electronically. My username is on the invoice."

"Do you want to argue about how I pay you, or do you want to thank me?"

She wrinkled her nose as if both options sucked, then muttered, "Thanks."

"Your turn," I said.

"My turn for what?"

"To answer my question."

As if remembering she had champagne in her hand, she took a sip, then went to the chair behind her desk and sat. "I'm celebrating." To emphasize, she took another drink.

"New client?" I asked, wondering how often she sat alone drinking champagne.

"Even better." She drained the glass like a beer, then

sized me up, as if judging whether I was worthy of hearing her news. She shrugged. "I don't care if it gets out. I want it to get out."

"Want *what* to get out?" I needed to get home to take care of a couple of pressing items on my to-do list before dinner so I'd have plenty of time for a movie with Addie as I'd promised.

She took a deep breath, her chest rising, catching my attention, triggering my memories. I'd had so many damn fantasies about touching her breasts back in the day but hadn't gotten the opportunity before we crashed and burned. Now they seemed fuller, even more tempting. *If* there wasn't a shit ton of bad history between us.

"I just found out that Felix James is *not* my biological father," she said, sounding gleeful.

I puzzled through that. Felix James was known around town as one of the wealthiest residents. His company owned a bunch of properties, both here and in Nashville. Its reputation as a property manager was mixed. The company mostly maintained their properties well, but he was thought of as arrogant and greedy.

Back during the short time Magnolia and I'd gotten close, I'd gained only a little personal insight from her. Though she hadn't talked about him often, there'd been no question she didn't have a good relationship with him, even back then.

"So that's good news?" I asked.

She narrowed her eyes, morphing from happiness to contempt. "It's great news to learn I'm not related to the most manipulative asshole on the planet."

I wasn't sure I'd ever heard Magnolia swear, which told me even more than the rest of her statement.

"How'd you find out? Did you meet with your mom?"

I'd tried not to wonder about that ever since I'd over-heard her phone call. Tried not to give any mental energy to Magnolia's life and what it must be like to have a mother who'd deserted her and a father who'd disowned her over a broken engagement. But for a few moments last Sunday in the barn, I'd been taken back to those weeks during junior year when Wednesday evenings marked time for me because I got to hang out with her.

Damn, I'd been crazy about her then.

"I did. She left about twenty minutes ago. I'm still absorbing all the bombs she dropped." Her expression snapped to a frown. "You and I need to talk."

"What do I have to do with anything?"

"I've been thinking we need to hash out the past if for no other reason than Presley and West's wedding. But now...some of what I learned concerns you."

What the hell? "What did your mother tell you?" I couldn't imagine the woman I'd never even met knew a thing about me.

"Sit down, and I'll explain."

"Do I need a drink for this?" I asked.

"Likely," she said dryly.

"Got any whiskey?"

Shaking her head, she said, "How about some bubbly?"

"Am I going to want to celebrate?"

"No, but this and white wine are all I have."

"You really think dragging out the past will do any good?"

Her eyes flashed with anger. "You *never* heard my side of the story, Luke. I texted you and called you and tried to talk to you at school, but you shut me out in every way. There were things back then you didn't know, and I just learned even more. So whether it will 'do any good' or not, you're going to hear me out."

I didn't take kindly to being told what to do by anyone, but particularly by this specific person. I debated saying fuck it and walking out.

"Please," she said in a less bossy, more emotional tone that shot me back to our nights outside her house.

Dammit.

I studied her, weighing my decision. I didn't owe her a damn thing, but I did care about West's wedding. I knew he was worried about the friction between Magnolia and me becoming a problem. And I could admit I was curious.

"Fine." I sat, crossed one leg over the other, and waited for her to speak.

Magnolia shot up, went to the other room, and came back with the open champagne bottle. It wasn't Dom or some other high-dollar, snooty brand but a more middle-of-the-road label. She filled her glass as close to the top as humanly possible without overflowing it.

"Want some?" she asked.

I was not a champagne guy. Didn't even own champagne flutes. I had shit to get home to and didn't want to be here more than the five or ten minutes it might take to hash things out. I shook my head. "Just say what you want to say."

She brushed her hair behind her ear and met my gaze directly. "I never accused your mother of stealing my ring. I never believed she would do that."

I scoffed. "Then how the hell did she get fired for it and blacklisted all over town?"

"Felix," she answered simply. "He caught me turning the house upside down looking for it and demanded to know what I was doing. I told him my ring was missing. He asked a few questions, like when I'd last seen it, whether anyone had been in my room. I didn't often have friends inside the house when my parents were in town, only to use the pool in the backyard, so that was an easy no. He asked if Mrs. Durham had cleaned my room that week. She had, but Luke, even if I'd thought your mom was guilty—and I didn't —I wouldn't have told him that. Not when I was getting to know you, learning what kind of person you were, the kind of loving, hardworking family you came from... I didn't know your mom well, but I knew you enough to understand you weren't raised by someone who would steal from her employer. She was always pleasant to me."

"Where're the glasses?" I pointed to her delicate flute, thinking whiskey straight from the bottle would be way more appropriate. I didn't want memories of my mom dredged up here with Magnolia. I'd welcome anything to dull my senses and hopefully the grief that never went away.

"Out there at the beverage station."

She started to stand, but I gestured for her not to get up and went to the other room myself. I picked up a glass and paused for a moment before heading back in.

Magnolia's assessment of my mother was spot-on. She was the last person who would steal anything. She was honest and, like Magnolia had said, loving and hardworking.

Fuck. My eyes burned just thinking about her.

Remembering my mom was enough to choke me up, but add on top of it, Magnolia's revelation that she wasn't the accuser? I couldn't even process that right now.

Painfully aware that Magnolia was on the other side of that wall, waiting for me, I sucked it up, took my glass, and rejoined her. I slid the flute across the desk to her, unable to stop my racing thoughts.

If Magnolia hadn't accused my mom...

A knot formed in my gut.

If she hadn't accused my mom, that would make me the biggest dickhead alive for convicting her without even hearing her side of the story.

Magnolia slid me a full glass of light, sparkling alcohol that was completely inappropriate and insufficient for this occasion. I left it sitting on the edge of the desk.

"How do I know you didn't accuse her?" I asked, unwilling to handle the shift in my reality that would create if it was true.

"Why would I, Luke?" she asked with outrage. She laughed, but there was no humor in it. "What would I have to gain by hurting the family of the boy I had feelings for?"

I leaned forward, planting my elbows on my knees, running my hands over my face. "When I found out my mom was fired and accused of stealing, I thought you'd been playing games with me all along," I admitted.

"How could you think that?"

The pain that flashed in her eyes struck me like a lightning bolt. I knew what I'd believed with every bone in my body back then, but seeing her reaction now had doubts seeping in like water in a doomed ship.

I swallowed, bowing my head. "Back then..." Hell. I hated admitting any of this because I could suddenly see how it was going to come across. "I'd had a crush on you for as long as I could remember, so that first night when you came over to my car and talked to me, with no airs, just what seemed like real talk between us, I rode the high from that for days. At the same time, there was this part of me that couldn't quite believe someone like you would be interested in a farm kid like me. My mom was the help. You were the rich girl whose family employed her."

"But that happened week after week. We were getting to know each other. I thought we were being real with each other."

"I thought we were too. Most of the time. But doubts sometimes crept in."

"So you thought I was faking it? So I could...what? What would be my motivation for that, Luke?"

"I don't know. I was seventeen. Seventeen-year-old boys don't make sense. They're all hormones and insecurity. But you had a reputation for being a mean girl."

Magnolia downed several gulps of champagne. "I wasn't that girl when I was with you," she said quietly.

I straightened so I could look at her. Her eyes were averted, and she was fiddling with her beaded bracelet, so unlike the gold and diamonds she'd worn back then, pulling it around and around her wrist. She looked vulnerable, uncertain, maybe even embarrassed.

A lock of her reddish-blond hair fell over her face. I fixed my gaze on it as I was shot back in time again, recalling when I'd run my fingers through her hair while I kissed her in the front seat of my family's old, beat-up car. I remember thinking how silky and luxurious it was and how surreal that I knew what Magnolia James's hair felt like between my fingers, what her lips tasted like under mine, how sweet her voice was when it was just us. Her wardrobe might've changed since then, but her mane of long, gorgeous hair hadn't. I wondered if it still felt as smooth.

"I was genuine with you, Luke. You treated me like I was special. You made me feel safe enough to be myself. You're the only person who ever saw that side of me."

"You had boyfriends all the time," I pointed out.

"I had guys who took me out and wanted to get in my pants. Not real relationships with any of them. You were different—or at least I thought you were back then, in part because you didn't try to get in my pants, but also because you *listened*. You opened up to me too. But then you cut me out of your life in every way without hearing my side of what happened."

Closing my eyes, I pressed my thumb and finger against the pressure points on my forehead as everything I'd held true all these years unraveled.

I couldn't deny that what she said rang true. I'd thought our fledgling relationship was special too. Real. We'd connected. Until I'd come in from working in the strawberry fields one Wednesday afternoon and found my mom home when she was supposed to be at work.

When my mom had told me what happened, I'd taken it personally. Maybe I'd jumped to conclusions. Maybe I'd let my teenage-boy insecurities take the reins. For sure, I'd been pissed as hell that anyone had treated my mom like shit.

And the aftermath my mother suffered...

I locked down on that memory, unwilling to be bowled over by the emotional tsunami it was capable of stirring.

"You mean what you said about my mom?" I asked in a raw, gravelly voice.

"That she was pleasant and kind? Of course. I grew up with a front-and-center view of what cold, manipulative, and vengeful look like. That wasn't your mom. She was quiet but sweet to me. Respectful. Sometimes I wondered if she knew about you and me."

"If she did, she never said anything, but you know how moms are. They have a sixth sense."

She shook her head. "I don't know how moms are. Not normal moms. Not good moms."

"My mom was good. Kindhearted. Honest. But also depressed. Getting fired and then blacklisted..." I shook my head, pressing my hands together in front of my mouth. "It sent her spiraling. She sank further into depression. She became sickly, staying in bed most days, plagued by chronic pain that the doctors couldn't diagnose." I swallowed hard around the lump in my throat. "She never recovered. Was never herself again."

"I'm sorry about your mom, Luke. Truly. She sounds like a special person."

"She was a good one." My throat swelled with the loss of her.

Silence grew between us. Magnolia emptied her glass again and set it on the desk, but she didn't refill it.

"For the record, I told my fa—*Felix* I didn't believe your mom stole my ring. He didn't care what I believed. And now I know why."

I glanced up at her, curious what she meant.

"He made it all up. After my mom's visit today, I'm ninety-nine percent certain he knew your mom didn't take the ring."

I narrowed my eyes, trying to follow.

Magnolia opened a desk drawer, took out an envelope, and emptied it. A single ring with a large green, heart-shaped stone surrounded by diamonds rolled onto the desk.

"It turned up?" I asked.

"About an hour ago. My mother took it with her when she left."

I listened with my mouth hanging open as Magnolia told me about her parents' history, particularly the parts her mother had revealed to her today, about the battles between her parents and their twisted agreement. It sounded like a damn soap opera, not someone's real life. *That* was the environment she'd grown up in?

Jesus.

"She took the ring because she knew he'd figure it out. In her mind, she won in the end because she got the ring that was supposed to be hers."

I couldn't come up with a response. Her family life was something I couldn't even imagine. No kid should have to be exposed to immature, hateful games like that.

Magnolia skipped the glass and swigged directly from the champagne bottle as I attempted to process her story. I believed it. You couldn't make up shit like that.

"Why would Felix accuse my mother of taking a ring he knew his wife had stolen?"

"I haven't figured that out yet. Your mom was an innocent bystander. A scapegoat. I don't understand what would make him do it."

The bastard clearly had a black soul.

Another question popped into my head. "If you didn't think my mom stole it, what did you think happened to your ring all these years?"

She shrugged. "I thought maybe it fell off when I wore it or went down a drain or into a heating duct without my noticing. It's bothered me ever since. I can't tell you how many times I turned the house upside down searching for it."

"And now you have it back."

"I don't want it. But it's worth a lot. Felix James has always used money for evil. I want to figure out something good to do with it. I don't know what yet."

"Whatever it's worth, you could put that into your business," I suggested, knowing firsthand how there were never enough funds for a fledgling venture.

"I don't want anything from that monster touching my business. It's mine and mine alone. I'll succeed without him."

Studying her, I took my first gulp of champagne. The lightness and bubbles made me shudder, and I set the glass back on the desk.

Outside, the rain intensified, hitting the large windows behind me, pulling my brain out of the morass of history and back to the here and now. My watch said I'd been here for nearly an hour.

"Hell, I need to get home," I said, standing abruptly. "My little girl's waiting for me." I needed to address the shitstorm of everything she'd revealed, but I didn't know what to say, as I was still absorbing it. "Uh, thanks for telling me all of this. I...I need to let it all sink in."

Thunder clapped loudly, suddenly, and Magnolia visibly startled, reminding me she used to be scared of storms.

"Are you okay?" I found myself asking.

"I'm fine," she said stiffly. "Go, get home to your daughter. I'll be fine."

She didn't sound fine, but she wasn't my responsibility. Addie was. The farm was.

Still...

"You're not going to drive anywhere, are you?" I eyed the champagne bottle. I couldn't see how much was left, but she'd gone through at least half of it while I'd been sitting here.

With a dismissive laugh, she said, "I live above The Lily Pad."

The stationery store was a block away, on the other side of the square.

"I'd offer you a lift, but my truck is nearly that far away," I said.

She waved me off. "I'll just ride it out here. Go."

I nodded once and went into the outer room. When I

Single Wish

glanced back at her, her gaze was averted. Instead of the light, celebratory mood I'd walked in on, Magnolia looked sad, uneasy. As if she was all alone to face the ghosts her mother's visit had awakened.

For the first time in eighteen years, I felt more than an ounce of empathy for Magnolia James.

My phone buzzed with a silent text message. I knew without looking it was my dad wondering where the hell I was, so I walked out the door into the storm.

Chapter Nine

Magnolia

By the time Luke walked out, I no longer felt like celebrating.

Once he'd gone, I locked the door to the world so I wouldn't be interrupted as I replayed both the conversation with him and the one with my mother.

Luke might've looked shaken by what I'd told him, but he hadn't bothered to apologize for shutting me out in the past.

But I'd told him. Finally, after all these years, I'd gotten my side of the story out. I felt a little bit lighter, unburdened, even if disappointed.

What had I expected though?

His reaction was on him. I couldn't control whether he was a jerk. Obviously I *had* been wrong about him in high school.

The rain continued to pound outside. I went to the closed blinds to peek out, feeling trapped. Alone. Overwhelmed by all the airing out of the past in the last two hours.

My mother... I'd thought not much could surprise me where she was concerned. I'd been wrong. Though I'd grown up in that cold household with no doubt that neither of my parents loved me, the hateful games between them still stunned me.

I could well imagine the explosion that would occur when Felix found out my mother had broken their agreement, but that was their problem. He'd lost any control over me the day he'd forced me out on my own.

That hadn't seemed like a blessing when it happened, but now I could see how lucky I was to have him out of my life.

And my mother's confessions? I'd felt sympathy for her regarding the forced marriage and the scumbag husband. I knew all too well how it felt to be in that position. I couldn't judge her for that. She'd been nineteen or twenty when my grandfather had basically bribed her into marrying the bottom dweller. I'd gone along with my forced engagement at first too.

For a few moments today, I'd felt a bond with her, a shared experience. But stealing my ring? I wasn't sure if I could forgive or forget that one.

That one decision of hers had affected me and my life more than it ever could've hurt Felix James. Sure, his weak little ego had probably been wounded when he'd figured out she'd gotten the ring in the end, but he'd turned it around, used it to hurt Luke's mother, Luke, the rest of his family, and me, whether he'd known that or not.

What might have become of Luke and me if that hadn't happened?

"Probably nothing," I said out loud as I paced my cozy office. "Because obviously Luke is a jerk."

The one thing I couldn't make sense of was why Felix would lie about Luke's mom. That underhanded man had a reason for everything he did, an underlying, destructive objective.

Thunder crashed out of nowhere again, this time so loud it had to be really close. I jumped, then pressed my hand to my chest as my heart raced. I hurried into my private bathroom, tucked behind my office, seeking the safety of a windowless room, and sat on the closed toilet lid, waiting for the next boom. At least when I closed the door, I couldn't see the lightning.

I took out my phone to check the weather app, wanting a heads-up if I was going to die in my dinky bathroom from a tornado.

The app told me there was a thunderstorm warning and that rain was expected for the next several hours with several storms coming and going. The radar didn't show the rain letting up even a little for me to get home. I was stuck by myself to ride it out yet again.

With the next clap of thunder, the room went dark, and my stress level skyrocketed. Within seconds, the electricity came back on, but not before I was thrown back in time to my childhood. How many times had a storm freaked me out and had me running to my parents' room, only for them to send me back to my room at the other end of the house all alone? They'd offered me nothing but an empty reassurance that the storm would be over soon and insist we were fine.

I hadn't felt fine. I'd ridden out so many storms terrified and alone, whether I was four years old or fourteen. Or thirty-five, it turned out.

My self-centered parents were still affecting me today, biological or not.

At that thought, I stood and whipped the bathroom door open with enough force it bounced back at me. I was *not* Felix James's daughter. I was no longer under his thumb. I didn't have to huddle up by myself and cower from thunderstorms. I didn't have to be afraid. That was the old me, the one he'd conditioned me into, but I didn't have to remain the same for the rest of my life.

I went to the outer room and, through the glass door, watched the rain come down. It wasn't as intense now, but the lightning show was nonstop, and thunder rumbled almost constantly. At least it was less loud for the most part.

I could sit there in my lonely office, huddled in the bathroom, and continue to be that traumatized little girl whose parents didn't see fit to comfort her during a storm, or I could face up to this fear and hurry over to the Fly to be among people, probably lots of them. Maybe I could even find a matchup for a game of pool.

After the day I'd had, I needed people and noise and a distraction—from the storm, my mother, and Luke.

With my heart pounding in my chest, I went back in the bathroom to grab my rain jacket.

Back at the outside door, I watched the light show, my eyes wide. There weren't many people out and about, but there were some. They weren't afraid of being struck by lightning or having a branch fall on them. Which, come to think of it, there weren't any big trees between here and the Fly.

Screw it. I took in a deep, shaky breath, heart still racing, and with a mental eff off to Felix James, I went out into the wild weather, locked my door behind me, and ran toward the bar.

Chapter Ten

Luke

By the time I got back to the farm and replaced the belt on the riding mower so it was ready for tomorrow's final orchard mow of the season, I was nearly an hour late for dinner.

This was the one night I hadn't wanted to be late, as Addie was calling it daddy-daughter date night.

I jogged through the rain from the large-equipment outbuilding toward the house, beyond exhausted. The day had been extra busy as we transitioned from putting the orchard to bed for the winter and gearing up for the holiday onslaught Christmas-tree season would bring. The morning was spent removing any diseased pine trees before the infestation could spread. I'd split the afternoon between helping Scotty repair some of the deer fencing, teaching Gage to maintain the roads the public would use to access the tree farm this year—and now possibly weddings—and squeezing in one more interview to round out our seasonal crew.

The trip to town for errands was supposed to be short

and sweet, but then I'd made the mistake of delivering that check to Magnolia in person. Had I known the bombshells she would drop, I would've figured out how to pay her electronically.

I hadn't had the opportunity to think through anything she'd told me, as I'd rushed home and immediately immersed myself in the mower repair, but the weight of what she'd explained pressed down on me.

Later. I'd allow those thoughts in much later, when the day was over and my little girl was tucked in for the night.

I opened the back door to the house and was instantly hit by two things—the mouthwatering aroma of tacos and my daughter coming at me full speed.

"Daddy!" She hugged me around the waist before I could take my wet flannel shirt off.

"Hey, doodlebug, you're going to get drenched."

I bent down and hugged her tightly anyway, laughing at her giggles because she was indeed not staying dry.

"We waited for you. Pops said the taco meat is gonna be dried out, but I don't care."

"You haven't eaten yet?" I asked as I peeled the wet outer layer off and hung it on a hook. Layer number two, a thick Henley, was also damp.

"It's daddy-daughter date night, silly," she said. "And Pops too, but just for dinner because he doesn't like *The Little Mermaid.*"

"It was fine the first four or five times," my dad said from the kitchen.

Addie had seen it probably twenty times and knew all the songs by heart plus half the dialogue. I was just in it for her and would need to work to stay awake during our date. I'd also need to work not to let my mind go to Magnolia and all that business.

"Thanks for holding dinner," I told my dad as Addie and I walked into the kitchen.

"We waited until you got home to start cooking," my dad said. "At your daughter's insistence."

I knew that was true. Though my dad had spent his life being the one who was late to dinner due to chores that made for extra-long days, now he was devoted to his role as Addie's main caretaker. He sometimes forgot what it was like out there hustling to get everything done, because he was caught up in here, practicing spelling words and addition problems, monitoring screen time, and keeping Addie busy in between it all.

As irritating as my dad could be about the barn, he was a godsend when it came to my daughter.

"I need three minutes to shower," I said to my dad. "And Addie, how about you change into a dry shirt. Or better yet, pj's and we can make it a pajama party."

My daughter skipped off singing one of the *Mermaid* songs, and I headed for my bathroom.

Five minutes later, I returned to the kitchen.

"What can I do?" I asked my dad.

He turned around with a large bowl of taco meat, and I carried it to the table. Bowls of chopped onions, tomatoes, avocados, cheese, and salsa were already set out, and plates were waiting.

"Did you set the table for Pops?" I asked Addie as we all sat down.

"Mm-hmm, it's my job."

"She also helped with the salsa and the cheese," my dad said as he passed me the tortillas.

"You're a great dinner assistant," I told my daughter. "How was school today?"

I listened to Addie's tales of her school day, from one of

the kids getting in trouble for purposely saying words wrong during read-aloud to a Halloween-themed scavenger hunt and the substitute bus driver who brought her home.

"Why were you so late today, Daddy?"

"My errands in town ran longer than I thought they would," I told her.

"What errands did you do?" she asked as I refilled my plate.

"Well, I went to my bank appointment to finalize financing for the barn, stopped by the farm store, picked up a few items at the Country Market, then dropped off a check for the wedding planner."

"Are you getting married?" she asked, her eyes wide as she held her taco up, ready for her next bite.

I laughed. "No. Who would I be getting married to?"

Addie shrugged as my dad shook his head. I was sure that was directed at me somehow, and then he confirmed it.

"If you'd drop this barn nonsense, you could've been here on time," he said.

"That barn nonsense is going to make a difference to the bottom line," I told him, keeping my voice as even as I could.

"What barn nonsense?" Addie asked.

"Remember I told you we're turning the barn into a place where people can have their weddings?" I said.

"Oh, yeah."

My dad shook his head again, and I did my best to ignore him.

"Mr. West and Miss Presley are getting married in our barn on Christmas Eve," I told Addie. "Mr. West is helping me build walls next week, so I'll probably miss dinner every night."

"Can I help?" she asked.

"It's pretty heavy work. Are you ready to learn how to use a hammer?"

"Yes!"

"One day we'll show you how we build walls, and then maybe when it's time to decorate the barn, you can help with that too."

"For the wedding?"

"You never know. That's a long way off, and I've got a lot of work before it."

"During our biggest season of the year, no less," my dad mumbled.

"Pops, why are you being so grouchy?" Addie asked.

I eyed my dad, waiting for him to answer his grand-daughter. He finished a bite of food first.

"This is a working farm, sweets," he said as he helped himself to more tacos. "A busy one with three harvest seasons."

"Strawberries, apples, and Christmas trees," Addie said, her voice going gleeful when she got to her favorite, the trees.

"That's right. It's a lot of work," my dad continued. "Adding weddings in the barn will be even more work. There's nothing wrong with hard work. That's what we do on a farm. But your daddy should be focusing on his crops, not chasing some modern trend that'll die out in a year or two."

"Barn weddings aren't going to die out," I said. "People will always get married, and they'll always need venues. Besides, we hope to host other events too, like family reunions, corporate parties, private parties, whatever people need room for."

"Weddings will be my favorite," my daughter declared. "Just like in *The Little Mermaid*. I can't wait!"

Though it worried me to find out from Magnolia about at least two competitors in the area, it also told me this was a viable endeavor.

"That old barn is a piece of history," I told my dad, even though I knew everything I said would likely fall on deaf ears again. "And it's a stunning piece of architecture inside. We can use it to store random crap in, or we can make it a revenue stream. To me it's a no-brainer."

No-brainer was an exaggeration; I'd overthought the hell out of it, weighed the pros and cons for months. But now that I'd committed, I was all in. His gritching about it was a waste of time.

"That 'revenue stream' could well go in the negative and turn into nothing but an expense. There's no guarantees."

"There aren't, but at least for this one we're not depending on the weather for our livelihood," I pointed out. "I'm already taking steps to get the word out. Telling everyone I know, meeting with a marketing person, making connections with event planners."

"I thought you didn't like the James girl."

"That's neither here nor there now," I said, conscious of my daughter's listening. "I'm working with her."

I took a drink of water, sorting through what Magnolia had told me today. I couldn't say I liked her, but I certainly had more empathy for her at the very least. I debated whether I could say more while respecting Magnolia's privacy.

I set my glass down harder than intended at that thought. Since when had I respected anything to do with Magnolia James? Not since I was a teenage boy with a crush. But considering what I'd learned today about her horrible home life growing up, I realized I was beginning to see her in a different light.

I elected to keep it to myself and changed the subject. Once dinner was over and Addie and I had cleaned the kitchen, she zipped off to get the movie, her plushies, and her blanket ready.

My dad slowly stood. "Going to my room for a show. Night, son."

No matter how hard I tried, I couldn't stay awake for round one hundred seventy-two of *The Little Mermaid*. I did my best to hide it though, rousing enough to respond to Addie's comments when they called for it. Mostly she snuggled up beside me and recited the movie.

This was comfortably familiar. Sitting with her in our cozy family room in the otherwise quiet house was soothing. I was content to listen to her sweet voice and used it to avoid deeper thoughts that weren't at all soothing.

When the movie was over, I cleaned up our popcorn mess while she got ready for bed. I went into her room to tuck her in and found her in bed but dressing her Barbie doll in her wedding gown.

"It's time for lights out, bug," I told her.

"I'm almost done. Barbie's having a wedding tomorrow."

"Shouldn't she wait until tomorrow to put on her wedding dress?"

Addie shook her head, focused on her task. "She doesn't want to miss the wedding."

I summoned my patience while she finished. I held out my hand for the doll.

"I need to put her in her bed. Tomorrow's a big day for her," Addie said, scampering over to her Barbie condo.

I bit down on any comments about how the dress would

get ruined in bed, unwilling to contribute to my daughter's bedtime stalls.

She crawled back under her blankets, and I bent over to kiss her. She wrapped her arms around my neck.

"Love you, Daddy."

"Love you, Addie." We both grinned at our nightly rhyme.

As I was straightening, I spotted an eyelash on her cheek. I gently brushed it onto my finger.

"An eyelash," I said quietly. "Make a wish and blow it away."

She closed her eyes for two seconds as if silently wishing, then opened them and blew the lash off my fingers with all the gusto of a six-year-old.

As I turned off the lamp on her nightstand, she said, "Know what I wished for, Daddy?"

"Aren't you supposed to keep your wish to yourself?"

She shrugged. "I wished for you to get married."

My brows shot up my forehead, likely to my hairline. "Why's that, bug? We do okay with you, me, and Pops, don't we? Plus your mom."

Jessie was deployed overseas, so she wasn't around much, but she faithfully called Addie as often as she could and spent most of her leave each year with her daughter.

"We do okay," she said authoritatively. "But you should get a wedding and a happy ever after."

My heart swelled with love for this little girl who'd used her wish for me. "You're a sweet girl, but I don't see that happening any time soon."

"Mommy wasn't the right one for you."

"She was the right one to give us you."

"Don't you want another wife?"

"I wouldn't mind having one if she's the right one."

She scrunched her face in thought. "How can you find the right one?"

I laughed quietly. "I wish I knew, bug."

The truth was, I longed for a partner to share my life with, to build a future with. While each of the other guys in my dads' group had been staunchly against relationships, love had fallen into their laps. I was over here wishing for someone, and here I was, the last single guy standing.

Irony was a bitch.

"You should go on some dates," she said, starting to sound sleepy.

I chuckled. "Who would I go on a date with?"

Her shoulders went up in a shrug. "Whoever you like."

"I'll take that under consideration," I whispered as I stood.

Her lids were heavy. She'd be out in less than sixty seconds.

"Night, bug." I kissed her forehead, walked out, and closed her door.

To be six years old again, when everything was so much simpler. Black-and-white. Wishes could come true.

In a way, I wished I could keep her from growing up, protect her from the complexities of adulting. Instead I'd do my best to prepare her to handle the easy times and the hard ones.

I headed off to my room for the night, where I knew complexities were lying in wait for me, ready to invade my mind.

Chapter Eleven

Magnolia

I was grateful for my tiny apartment, but some nights—okay, a lot of nights—it was so quiet and lonely I could barely stand it.

This Saturday evening was one of those nights.

A glance at the clock on my stove told me it was just after eleven. Still early for a girl who never seemed able to sleep until two or three a.m. if I was lucky.

Often on nights like this, I took a walk, not so much for exercise but to get out of my head. This evening I was too exhausted to walk after pulling off an eightieth birthday party for Harriet Limberger, but I put on a worn, oversized sweatshirt over my leggings, stuffed my feet into my fuzzy slippers, and picked up my favorite throw blanket, then headed outside.

The late October air was chilly but refreshing. I went down the exterior stairs to the cushioned bench swing Dotty had hung in the cozy alcove beneath the stairs. A string of fairy lights wound around the railing, and more twinkling lights were draped in the evergreen trees that lined both sides of the compact yard-like space behind her store.

She'd created a cute, private conversation area out here where we sometimes sat with her friends for tea or a glass of wine. Besides the swing, there was a bistro table and chairs, plus some additional patio chairs and end tables. Pots of mums in burgundy, pumpkin, and gold livened up every corner.

I sat sideways on the swing, with my back facing The Lily Pad's rear door, an outdoor pillow behind my back and my feet stretching toward the alley. As I tucked my blanket around me, the swing rocked gently, soothingly.

The party had been a success, with Harriet suitably stunned by her daughter's ability to pull off a surprise bash for her. I'd gotten several compliments on the way I'd transformed the new community center's beige-walled rental room into a fall-themed haven. I might've even gotten a new client out of it, as one of Harriet's neighbors had gone out of her way to get my business card for a possible family reunion next summer.

I'd had a busy week, between preparations for Harriet's party, two new bookings, and meeting with Presley to get serious about her wedding. Regardless of being occupied with work, I'd spent plenty of time thinking about the sordid past my mother had revealed to me last week.

My emotions were all over the board, between relief at not being Felix James's daughter, sadness and resentment that I'd been a pawn between him and my mother since before I was born, and a very mixed bag when it came to my mother herself.

I might dislike her, but I felt a commonality with her due to the environment she'd grown up in, because I'd grown up much the same, with a father figure who valued his business and career far above his daughter. I knew how much my own situation had screwed up my psyche, my self-esteem, my self-worth. I'd done a lot of hard, painful work over the past year and a half, and I still had a long way to go. I suspected my mother had never done anything for her mental health. There was a small part of me that sympathized deeply.

As much as it irritated me that she'd gone from depending on one man to another, I hoped she'd found genuine love with Franklin. Maybe love could begin healing someone, but something my therapist had taught me was that you had to love yourself first, before you could truly love and be loved by another. I wasn't sure Bianca Lansford James could claim that.

I'd been pissed that she'd taken my ring, but now that I'd had time to think, I could admit that the disappearance of the ring had actually done me a favor. If something like that could drive an eighteen-year wedge between Luke and me, we'd never stood a chance anyway.

I hadn't heard from my mom since she'd left my office last week, and I hadn't heard talk around town of any blowup with Felix. I still hadn't figured out what to do about him. I could just let it go and move on with my life. That would probably be the best option. But thirty-some years of resentment was a lot to bottle up.

Though I'd only told Luke and Presley the truth about my paternity, I wasn't concerned about maintaining Felix's privacy. He could suck an egg. I wanted the world to know I was not related to that sad excuse for a man, but I also didn't plan to cause a scene about it. Presley had suggested changing my last name, and while I liked that idea, I had no clue what I would change it to. I wasn't a James, thank God, but I sure didn't want to be a Lansford either.

Picking a random surname seemed generic and meaningless.

Movement in the darkness of the alley, maybe ten feet away, caught my attention, and my pulse raced. My eyes widened as I realized...it was the llama. Esmerelda. The frequent runaway.

I froze where I was, thinking she'd meander on past. She was coming from the direction of the bakery, which was less than a block down the street and had been closed for hours, so I wasn't sure what her goal was if she'd walked away from her temple of cookies. Did llamas have goals?

For the first time, I regretted that there wasn't a fence or a wall around this little backyard, only bushy evergreens on two sides that normally offered plenty of privacy. Just...not when there was a stray llama bearing down on you.

She angled in toward the bistro table, pausing to sniff a pot of mums. Apparently they didn't do anything for her, because she walked on by them.

Straight for me.

I tensed, watching every step she took and trying to figure out what to do. I hadn't heard of a llama attacking a human before. Rumor was Esmerelda was spoiled and soft and only wanted cookies, but if that was true, why was she closing in on me? I sadly had no cookies.

She was between me and the foot of the stairs. The back door of The Lily Pad was locked. You couldn't pass from the back to the front without going *through* the shop. Those big, dark eyes were locked on me.

"Hey, Esmerelda," I said in the gentlest voice I could muster as my heart pounded in fear. "What are you doing here?"

She was four feet away.

Llamas don't eat people, I repeated in my mind.

I knew now I should've dashed to the stairs and up to my apartment the second I'd spotted her.

As she closed the distance, I felt for my phone even as I knew I'd left it upstairs on purpose. One of the things Jolene wanted me to work on was simply *being* with myself, no device, no way to block out my thoughts, so that's what I'd intended.

I hadn't planned on a llama assault.

Did llamas eat people? She looked hungry.

I curled into myself as she came right up to the swing. When she slowly eased her head toward mine, I buried my face in my arms like a little kid pulling the blankets over their head when they were scared. If you couldn't see it, you'd be okay, right?

Except that didn't hold true when you caught the faint animal smell and heard her snuffing and breathing. Up close.

Would a llama bite hurt?

Not as badly as a snake bite, I would bet, trying to find comfort in...*anything* as I felt her snout right next to my head.

Then at my neck.

I let out a whimpery sound without opening my mouth as she nuzzled me. Gently.

Was she luring me in for the kill, or was she in fact a mild-mannered beast with no evil intentions?

I wasn't willing to show my face and find out.

And then she let out a creepy low hum that made me wonder if she was offering up a llama prayer before she sacrificed me for her people.

"Help!" I called weakly, still not lifting my head.

"There she is!" A hushed male voice reached me from the alley, shooting my alarm level up for different reasons.

Since some men were known to be even more dangerous than llamas, I forced my head up so I could see what new danger was heading my way.

"Magnolia?" a second male voice said in a loud whisper.

A familiar voice.

"Luke? What are you—"

Before I could say more, Ben Holloway was on the other side of the llama and had a harness on her. Luke wasn't far behind.

Esmerelda let out an irritated grunt.

"Got you, girl," Ben said to the animal.

I expelled a shaky breath.

"Come here, Esmerelda," Ben said. "Give Magnolia room to breathe."

"Are you okay?" Luke asked me, stepping up next to Ben.

I was still trying to breathe regularly as I took inventory and tried not to be affected by Luke's concerned expression. "She didn't bite me."

"I don't think llamas bite people," Luke said, grinning, probably loving that I looked like a big idiot.

"I'm not sure what she was doing," Ben said. "Did you give her a cookie or something?"

Sitting up and turning so my feet hit the ground, I shook my head. "I don't have any cookies. I was just sitting here minding my business when she appeared out of nowhere. I sat super still, hoping she'd keep on going, but she came straight for me. It was freaky."

"Both times I've helped you wrangle her before, she ran away and made us chase her," Luke said to Ben.

"This rebel always runs," Ben confirmed, patting the beast's neck. "Except for tonight."

Luke held out his hand as if to help me up.

I was shaken enough I took it without thought. As his big palm closed around mine, his rough, calloused skin shot me back in time. His hands had been working hands even in high school, though he was bigger, stronger now. I remembered how I'd been so fascinated by the contrast of our hands—mine so much smaller and softer, and his tanned, coarse, and powerful, even then.

Our eyes met for a weighted moment, as if he was remembering too. Then he released me.

I caught my throw blanket before it fell to the ground.

Holding Esmerelda's lead with one hand, Ben pulled me into his side for a half hug with the other. "You're really okay?" he asked. "I've never known her to be aggressive before."

I leaned into Ben but kept all my parts on this side of him, not wanting to tangle with Esmerelda on accident. "She just...nuzzled me, I think. I had my eyes closed. She was aggressive in a...an *interested* way, but I guess not a threatening way." I could see that now that I'd lived through her ambush.

"What were you after, girl?" Ben asked his funny-looking, giraffe-necked pet.

Esmerelda swiveled her head to look up at Ben, who stood mere inches taller than her, then those big, intent eyes found me again.

I straightened and stepped away from the vet before his llama craned her neck any closer. "I'm good. Just...it's not every day I'm accosted by a llama in my own yard."

Ben frowned and shook his head. "I'd say we need to have a talk, Esmerelda, but I know very well you don't listen."

I avoided looking at Luke, whose gaze I could feel on me.

"I'm sorry that happened to you, Magnolia," Ben said. "She's harmless, but I'm sure that was disconcerting."

Disconcerting. Yeah.

I forced a carefree smile and waved him off. "I'm okay. No harm done."

I'd definitely be checking up and down the alley before I relaxed on the swing again.

"Let's get you loaded up and locked in the barn, miss," Ben said to the llama.

"Hand me your keys," Luke said. "I'll go pull the van closer."

As soon as Ben handed him the keys, Luke jogged off without saying goodbye. Which shouldn't have surprised me. He hadn't apologized for shutting me down years ago either.

Obviously that moment when he'd grasped my hand had *not* made an impact on him after all. I must have imagined we'd shared even a split second of memories or connection. He still wanted nothing to do with me.

I said good night to Ben, my eyes locked on his pet, who stared back at me, and went up the stairs, reminding myself the past was the past. That spark of "connection" was my mind playing tricks on me. I did *not* want anything to do with Luke Durham either.

Chapter Twelve

Luke

"You sure you don't want me to follow you home and help get her to the barn?" I asked Ben.

I'd pulled the llamamobile to the end of the alley, where we'd loaded the animal up easily with a single cookie.

"Nah. She knows she'll get another cookie when she gets to her stall," Ben said. "Thanks for your help finding her. I still can't figure out what she wanted from Magnolia."

"The secrets of llamas," I said.

Esmerelda chuffed as if she didn't approve of my comment.

"Good luck getting her home." I stepped back from the driver's window of the van.

"Have a good night," Ben said as he put the old vehicle into gear.

He raised his window and pulled away. I watched him go, waiting till he was out of sight before moving. Because I wasn't heading straight for my truck.

I walked back toward Magnolia's apartment to take care of what I should've taken care of days ago.

I'd been stunned to find Ben's llama with Magnolia, of all people. My dads' group had been at Max's to eat and play pool while watching game two of the World Series. As we'd been getting ready to leave, Ben got a call from Emerson that Esmerelda was MIA. As the guy without a wife to get home to, I'd been the obvious choice to help round up the beast. What were the chances we'd find Esmerelda was snuggled up with *her*?

Magnolia had looked pale and more than a little freaked out when we'd shown up. Understandably. She'd had a llama in her face, literally.

As I ascended the stairs to the apartment above The Lily Pad, I told myself I mainly wanted to be sure she was okay. More importantly, I owed her a follow-up from everything she'd confessed to me in her office last week.

Only when I got to the top of the steps did I question whether midnight was an appropriate time to be knocking on her door.

She'd been awake just twenty minutes ago. Surely she wasn't already asleep. With a shrug, I decided to go for it. I wasn't sure when I'd be able to take time out during the day to pay her a visit, not with tree season about to start. She could tell me to leave if it wasn't a good time.

I knocked and heard movement inside, then a heavy pause on the other side of the windowless door, which I guessed was her looking through the peephole.

The door creaked open just enough for her head to appear.

Magnolia narrowed her eyes and tilted her head, obviously puzzled.

"Either you didn't bother to look who it was, or you did and you opened the door anyway," I said lightly.

"What are you doing here, Luke?"

"I wanted to make sure you're okay."

"It was a llama, not a street gang," she answered flippantly.

"Llamas are creepy," I said, then shrugged. "Don't tell Ben I said that."

A quiet laugh escaped from her, and she opened the door wider. "They really are. Why are their heads so small?"

"And their eyes so big," I added.

"And googly."

Her hair was wet and hung down her back. Instead of the leggings and baggy sweatshirt from earlier, she wore light-weight pants that reminded me of a genie and a thin-strapped tank. I couldn't help noticing her nipples through the fabric.

"You showered off the llama?" I asked.

"As soon as I got in the door, in case there was drool. Anyway, I'm fine and you can go," she said. Her tone wasn't unfriendly, just matter-of-fact.

"Can we talk?"

"Right now?"

"Are you going to bed?"

She grimaced. "What's the point? I won't sleep for hours."

"Can I come in then?"

She studied me, as if trying to discern why I was here.

"I need to apologize," I said, hoping that would get me in the door.

Her brows shot up. Then she opened the door all the way, turned, and walked farther into her apartment. I stepped across the threshold, taking that to be as much of an invitation as I was going to get, and followed her deeper, past closed doors on either side.

Once past the doors, we went through another door as Magnolia explained the others were Dotty's storage for the shop below. This door led to her studio apartment.

There was a bathroom immediately on the left. Once you got past it, the main room contained a kitchen area with a dining table for two, a double bed, a sitting area with a love seat and two easy chairs flanking a faux fireplace, and a compact desk. The furniture looked old, but she'd deco-rated the whole place with a colorful floral theme, from a blanket on the back of the sofa and her bedding, to a rug in the desk area and gauzy curtain panels on the two windows.

When I returned my attention to her, she'd pulled a Lily Pad sweatshirt over her tank.

"I know what you're thinking," she said as she leaned against the kitchen counter.

"What am I thinking?"

"My apartment could fit in the laundry room of the house I grew up in."

I shook my head. "I've never been in the house you grew up in, but I was thinking this is cozy and you have good taste. Girly but good."

She grinned. "Flowers don't have to be girly."

"Addie would love it," I said.

"Your daughter, right?"

Nodding, I said, "The more colors something has, the more she likes it."

She straightened and her grin disappeared. "What did you want to talk about, Luke?"

"Could we sit?"

She gestured to the sitting area, so I sat on one end of the love seat. Magnolia took the chair across from me.

I leaned forward and fumbled around for what I wanted to say. "Last week in your office... I'm sorry I hurried out. That was a lot to process."

"Tell me about it," she muttered.

"I can't even imagine what you went through after your mom's visit."

"An entire shift in identity basically."

I tried to fathom what it would be like to find out, in your mid-thirties, that one of your parents wasn't actually your biological parent. "Did your mother tell you who your father is?" I'd been so caught up in other parts of what she'd told me that I hadn't wondered before now.

"Jimmy," she said flippantly. "Magical, unforgettable Jimmy, whose last name she didn't get."

I straightened. "Just...Jimmy? She doesn't know more than that?"

"I imagine she knows a few very *personal* details about Jimmy, but nothing to help me track down the man whose DNA I share."

"I'm sorry," I said. "Do you plan to search for him?" I didn't know if that was possible with genealogy sites or some other means.

Magnolia shook her head. "I don't believe I will. It's such a long shot. I'm sure any search service would be pricey anyway. I'm just overjoyed to know it's not Felix. That's enough for me."

My thoughts got caught up in her situation for a bit before I remembered why I was there. I stood, paced a few steps until it registered that I was standing at the edge of her bed. I pivoted and went to the empty chair next to her and sat again.

"Magnolia," I said, "I owe you an apology for the past. For my actions after my mom was fired."

She pulled her legs up onto her chair and hugged them, her eyes locked on me.

"I'm sorry for jumping to conclusions," I continued. "For thinking you were the one accusing her. For shutting you out." I swallowed hard, ashamed of how stupid my reaction had been. "I'm sorry I didn't trust that the Magnolia I was getting to know was the real you." I shook my head, regret flooding me, making it hard to keep talking.

"I've been pissed at you all week because I told you everything—more than my friends know, even—and then you just left. This doesn't change the past, but it helps."

I squeezed my eyes shut. "I fucked up big-time. In high school, I mean. Maybe last week too, but I was bowled over by everything you told me. It took some time for everything to sink in."

"I do understand that."

"I was an idiot back then," I admitted. "I'd like to kick my seventeen-year-old self's ass."

"I'd like to *help* you kick your seventeen-year-old self's ass." She didn't smile when she said it.

"Regret is a bitch." My voice came out thick with emotion.

"Yes, well, you can't change the past," she said. "But I do appreciate the apology."

Her tone seemed dismissive, but I wasn't ready to walk away just yet. Was it just the regret talking? Making me want to try to smooth things over? I knew that wasn't possible, but I couldn't make myself get up and leave.

"Have you heard from your mom since she told you everything?"

She shook her head. "She's...going through some things.

She was just diagnosed with cancer. That's what provoked her to tell me everything. And no, I'm not making excuses for her. I'm not waiting around for her to call. I don't know what she'll do. I might never hear from her again."

"Would you be okay with that?"

"I haven't decided yet." She grasped her legs tighter and shrugged. "It's not like we could ever have a good relationship. Not after everything that's happened. I do have her number, so I could call her if I want to, but I don't know. I'm still processing everything too, even though I've spun it all through my head a thousand times."

"It sounds like it was a lot. I mean, *a lot* doesn't begin to touch it. Just what you told me about the battle between her and her husband..." I shook my head. "Sorry to say it's like an over-the-top TV drama."

"I had the same thought." Magnolia shifted her legs to one side and ran her hands up her arms, like she was hugging herself again. She gazed off at nothing, her expression deeply troubled, tinged with sadness.

I wouldn't have thought it was possible, but I had a strong urge to pull her into my arms and comfort her. That would likely get me shoved away. She didn't want solace from me. I understood why, but my brain seemed to be confusing the past with the present, mixing the reality of now with how it'd been between us before her ring had gone missing. The good times, when our connection was crackling with potential and hope.

I clenched my hands together to try to ground myself fully in the here and now.

"Part of me is stunned by the hateful games she admitted to," she said. "Part of me is thinking, yes, that sounds about right. That's exactly the house I grew up in."

"No child should be subjected to that kind of home life."

"Lots of people have it so much worse than I did, honestly."

"That doesn't make it less awful."

She nodded. "Nobody else knows how it really was. I tried to hide it from everyone. It wasn't like they were beating me or locking me in the basement, you know?"

"Just playing devious head games, using you to hurt each other. That's fucked up, Mags."

Her gaze shot to mine. Only then did I realize what I'd called her. Mags. That was what I used to call her. It spoke of a better, closer relationship than what we currently shared.

Instead of apologizing, I carried on. "What are you going to do? Have you talked to your—to Felix? Called him out? Asked him why the hell he accused my mother of something he knew damn well she didn't do?"

She laughed, but it was hollow. "He wouldn't let me in the door if I tried. I'm dead to him."

I narrowed my eyes, hoping karma would come along and clock that fucker.

"I thought about doing a tell-all on the Tattler," she said, a hint of a real grin curving her lips. "Apparently he's mortified by his inability to have children."

I grinned with her, imagining that would hit him where it hurt.

"I'm not going to though. That's so much negative energy. I've had enough of that for a lifetime."

"That's smart."

"Careful, Luke Durham. You nearly gave me a compliment."

"My bad," I joked.

"I just want to move forward. Keep healing. Build my life as Magnolia *Not*-James. Maybe I could be one of those one-name people. Just Magnolia." Her smile was fuller. More peaceful. Pretty.

"You've already started it with your business name," I said, trying to shake off a spark of attraction.

That ship had sailed long ago and crashed into a giant iceberg. It was too late to send a rescue boat out.

Wasn't it?

I stood. Time to take my leave.

"I'll let you get to bed. Thanks for letting me in so late." I laughed to myself. "Weird night."

"*That's* an understatement." She rose and led me toward the door.

I specifically did not let my gaze drop to her ass. Instead I watched the way the damp waves down her back shifted as she moved. An image flashed in my mind of her in the shower, water dripping down her long locks as I joined her...

Forcing my attention elsewhere, I looked at my watch without really seeing the time, then made a point of noticing the flowered ceramic bowl with her keys in it on a small table near the door.

Magnolia opened the first door, led me to the outer one, and stood with her hand on the knob, facing me. When she looked up at me, her long lashes caught my attention as her lids lifted. Her blue-gray eyes met mine, unguarded for the first time in nearly two decades.

Without thinking it through, I stepped toward her, palmed the back of her head, and lowered my mouth toward hers. Inches away, I paused, checked those captivating eyes for a sign of hesitation. Her pupils enlarged as she peered back at me, seeming open, curious.

I kissed her. I intended to make it a brief touch of our lips, but as soon as we made contact, I was compelled to linger, to press my body against hers as I drew the kiss out for several seconds. I ended it before she could, staggering from the impact of that short contact.

"Good night, Magnolia," I said in a rough voice and hurried out the door.

* * *

Magnolia

I shut the outer door, my heart still racing from the shot of ecstasy that was Luke's kiss.

I went into my apartment, locked up, then leaned my back against the door, trying to gather my thoughts. That kiss was short but intense. It swirled the past into the present, leaving me...confused.

I felt lightheaded and bubbly on the one hand, because I'd never been kissed quite like that, with so much history and regret and apology and tenderness and...lust. I hadn't missed his hardness as he pressed up against me.

On the other hand, how dare he just lean in and kiss me after everything we'd been through?

Worse? The thing that made me clench my jaw at the very thought?

I'd let him.

I'd practically welcomed him.

I could've stopped him at any time, but I hadn't. I hadn't wanted to. And that irritated me more than anything else. Because while I appreciated his apology and everything he'd said, I couldn't just forget years of anger and be fine at the drop of a hat—or an apology. The emotions I'd gone through for eighteen years because of his actions... Even if I wanted to, I couldn't just make all that baggage disappear.

But apparently I also couldn't resist his kiss. I touched my lips, remembering how sure he'd been, confident, almost demanding. He was familiar and brand-new at the same time. Teenage Luke hadn't been half as confident as mid-thirties Luke.

His self-confidence was a turn-on.

"Damn that man."

I shoved away from the door, feeling so very drained.

On a normal night, I had about a fifty-fifty chance of sleeping more than three or four hours.

Tonight, I was pretty sure, was not a normal night.

Chapter Thirteen

Magnolia

When I was younger and had unlimited money, shopping was something I did because I could. It was strangely not that satisfying, but I could never figure out why it left me feeling empty. Maybe in part because I'd had to shop either alone or with my mother. I hadn't had true friends to spend a Saturday with in the finest stores in Nashville. Also I'd erred on the side of overdoing it and hadn't cared. Unsure which color of ten-thousand-dollar purse to buy? No need to choose; just throw them both in.

To clarify, I wasn't proud of past me.

Now that I had very little extra money, shopping ironically brought me joy. Every purchase mattered more, required careful consideration. As a small business owner, I valued local stores and supported them whenever I could. Shopping was often a social event for me now, either because I had friends to go with or because I knew the shop owners or both.

Presley and I decided to kick off November by decorating for the season—our businesses and her home. My apartment was too small to add much without it feeling cluttered. Besides, the only person who ever saw it was Dotty.

Well, except for Luke's midnight visit, which I was still trying to figure out. All I could conclude was that the kiss had been a mistake. A slip-up. Not something to still be thinking about more than a week later.

During the lunch hour, Presley and I hit Oopsie Daisies, where she bought one of Piper's beautiful hand-made centerpieces for her dining-room table. She also chose several signs hand-painted with sayings like "Fall is my favorite F word" and "Thankful, blessed, and pumpkin spice obsessed." I selected a simple fall floral arrangement in a mason jar with tiny fairy lights inside to add to my beverage counter at my business.

We said goodbye to Piper and Tansy, then walked past our own businesses and halfway down the block to Earthly Charm.

"Hey, ladies," Harper called out when we came in the door. "Come on in. Treat yourselves to our hot cider bar."

"You don't have to tell me twice," Presley said as we headed toward the festive table set up near the checkout counter.

"Wow, I love this," I said as I ladled cider into my cup and eyed the toppings.

"Clever girls," Presley said. "Look at all these choices."

There were ramekins filled with cinnamon sticks, caramel sauce, caramel bits, nutmeg, and cloves. A can of whipped cream stood at the ready, and there was a beautiful plate of cranberries, orange slices, and apple slices.

"I highly recommend the caramel bits," a shopper I didn't know told us.

I followed her recommendation, threw in a cinnamon stick, and squirted whipped cream on top.

"Cheers," I said, holding up my cup toward Presley. We tapped our paper cups together and sipped.

"This is the best cider I've ever had," Presley said.

"Cambria's creation," Harper said. "If we were at a private party, we'd have bourbon, whiskey, and rum for add-ins as well. For everyone *except* me."

"Let's see that bump." Presley's attention was on Harper's belly, which was officially showing her pregnancy. "How far along now?"

"Twenty-six weeks. I've been pregnant for half a year." She laughed, her eyes lighting up, showing exactly how she felt to be newly wed to Max Dawson and mom to Danny and soon to be a second child.

"You're well past the halfway mark with that little one," I said. I held my cup up as if to toast again.

"Time flies. The baby's going to be here before you know it," Presley said. "Does Danny understand what's going on yet?"

"He's so excited." Harper's smile was wide, and her eyes lit up. "He doesn't get how long nine months is, so he's more than ready to be a big brother and can't understand what's taking so long."

"That's cute," I said, then sipped more cider. I pointed to the topping bar. "I'm stealing this idea. I don't know where I'll use it yet, but I'm going to."

"Feel free," Harper said.

Two women approached the checkout counter, so Presley and I stepped back and let Harper tend to her business. We made our way around the store, touching crystals, sniffing essential oil blends, and admiring Cambria's hand-made candles.

"I'm getting this for the store," Presley said as she picked out a candle shaped like a pile of acorns. "Oh, and this guy has to go next to it." She selected an adorable, bushy-tailed squirrel candle. "I'm going to need a basket."

"Oooh." I grasped Presley's arm as inspiration struck. I pointed to another table with a fall display. "Center-piece idea. Similar to that, but instead of pumpkins and apples, we use pine branches and pine cones. Silver ribbons."

"And one of Cambria's candles," Presley added as she picked up one of the thin slices of tree trunk currently serving as a pedestal for a turtle candle. "Not a turtle. A pillar."

"Yes. Maybe with a tiny string of fairy lights in the pine."

Twenty minutes later, we'd picked out an assortment of tree discs, an elegant silver pillar candle, and string lights to take home and create a prototype with. We'd spread the pieces out on the counter, and Harper had made good suggestions as well.

"We might not have decided where we're having the ceremony yet, but we've got our centerpieces," Presley said victoriously, making Harper and me laugh.

"Hey, girls." Dakota, Cambria and Harper's third business partner, came up to the counter from the back room.

"Welcome, sleepyhead," Harper said affectionately.

"Sorry I'm late." Dakota looked half remorseful. "I did oversleep."

"Mm-hmm," Harper said, a teasing accusation in her tone. "Must be that handsome roommate. Is Ian keeping you up too late?"

"Stop," Dakota said with a playful flick on Harper's upper arm. "You know it's not like that."

"I know no such thing," Harper said.

"Wait, you're living with a boy?" Presley asked the question in my mind.

"Ian Finley owns the farmhouse I moved to when this girl got hitched," Dakota said, pointing to Harper.

"You probably didn't know Naomi, Ian's sister," Harper said. "She was our dear friend who opened the art studio outside of town."

"I knew of Naomi," I said, "but not Ian."

"They grew up in Runner and inherited a farmhouse between Runner and Dragonfly Lake," Harper explained. "I lived there with Naomi for three years."

"She passed away from sepsis a couple years ago," Dakota said to Presley since she hadn't lived here then. "She was like mid-thirties."

"That's awful," Presley said.

Dakota nodded. "She and her brother, Ian, fought about the farmhouse. He wanted to sell it. She saw its potential, or rather the potential for one of the large outbuildings to serve as an art studio."

"So they were estranged when she died," Harper said, watching Dakota. "Ian's this bajillionaire who worked on Wall Street. Complete opposite of his art-loving, creative-souled sister whose mission was to make art accessible for everyone."

"And now you're living with him?" Presley asked.

"We're *roommates*. He's going through a life thing," Dakota explained. "He walked away from his Wall Street job and moved here to get away from the rat race."

"Wow. You two have something in common, huh?" I said to Presley.

Presley nodded sympathetically. "A big something. Is he not dealing well with the changes he's made?"

"I think it depends on the day," Dakota said. "He's not used to having so much free time."

"Yep, I was the same way. I'd advise opening a business," Presley said flippantly.

"He's got a bunch of real estate investments on the East Coast, but he's definitely interested in investing in something in this part of the country," Dakota explained. "I don't know. Getting him to talk is like pulling teeth from an alligator."

"Dakota to the rescue," Harper said, grinning.

Dakota shook her head. "I don't think I'm up for that task. Anyway, Ian is my grumpy roommate, at least for now."

"And he's handsome?" I asked.

"Are you interested?" Dakota asked. I couldn't read whether she was hesitant because he was grumpy and in a bad place...or because she was interested herself.

"Not at all," I said quickly. "I have more than I can handle with my fledgling business."

Plus processing big life issues like my paternity and my mother and...Luke.

Presley was the only one who knew any of that, and I hadn't even told her about Luke kissing me. I wasn't ready to admit to it. I was determined to make it a one-time thing, and if she knew what had happened, she'd watch us closely the next time we had to meet, looking for signs of who knows what.

"Speaking of your fledgling business..." Dakota glanced questioningly at Harper and asked her, "Did you mention it yet?"

Harper shook her head.

"We want to do a holiday open house here at the shop," Dakota said. "We have tons of ideas but no time to organize anything. Is that something you could take over for us, Magnolia?"

"Absolutely," I gushed. "I'd love to."

"We don't have a budget anywhere close to something like a Presley Holiday wedding," Harper said, grinning apologetically.

"Hey, I'm being reasonable," Presley said. "So far."

"We'll work with whatever budget you have," I said.

I jumped into business mode, asking questions about what they had in mind, then setting a time when Cambria would be there too and the three of us could talk without interruptions. Before we checked out, I added their open-house date to my calendar, which was slowly starting to fill up with a holiday party here and there, just as I'd hoped.

Once we paid for our treasures, Presley and I finished our cider, told Harper and Dakota goodbye, and walked back toward our building.

"Congratulations on the booking," Presley said with restrained enthusiasm.

"Thank you. We'll see what they have in mind, but I love their ideas."

"And so many people will show up for that. More exposure for your business."

"Bring it on," I said.

Presley's phone sounded an alert. She took it out of her pocket, swiped, and read. "West and Luke got the basic walls up in the barn last night. Luke wants us to come out tomorrow evening to see it so we can decide whether to have the ceremony there as well as the reception. Are you available?"

Tomorrow was Friday. I didn't have to check my calendar. I didn't have an event, and I didn't have much of a social life. "I am."

That meant I'd see Luke. We hadn't seen each other since that short but unforgettable kiss.

"So you'll go?"

I glanced over at her. "Of course I'll go. Why wouldn't I?"

"I don't know," she said, shrugging. "There was just something weird in your voice for a second. Like hesitation."

"No hesitation," I said quickly.

I suspected what she'd heard in my voice was the *oh, crap* about Luke.

Taking a deep breath of brisk November air, I tried to push him out of my mind and fully focus on shopping with Presley.

In the end, I was maybe eighteen percent successful at that.

Chapter Fourteen

L uke

Thirteen days.

That's how long it'd been since I'd kissed Magnolia.

I'd like to say I kissed her, went home, and put it out of my mind, but that would be a lie.

In reality, I'd thought about that kiss every day since. Relived it. Picked apart Magnolia's reaction. Questioned whether I'd imagined her kissing me back, *not* pushing me away, seeming *into* it.

Less than sixty seconds nearly two weeks ago shouldn't still be top of mind. It was illogical for her to be popping up in my dreams ever since. But it was, and she did.

With Christmas tree season underway, the commercial harvest in full swing, plus the barn renovation, I'd never been busier. Never worked longer days, and on a farm, that was saying something.

I'd been starting before six a.m., juggling the farm work for a good eleven or twelve hours, grabbing a quick dinner with Addie and my dad, then throwing myself into remodeling for as long as my body would let me—usually until ten or eleven.

Some evenings Gage or Scotty stayed extra and helped. Sometimes West made it out to assist for a few hours. Some nights I worked alone, a lot slower but still determined.

Most nights I questioned my sanity to take this on now, during tree season. My dad's objections got in my head and made me doubt my decision. But I was a stubborn dude if nothing else, so I kept going.

After West and I finished hanging another piece of drywall in what would be the kitchen, I checked my watch and pulled off my work gloves.

"Girls oughta be here any minute," West said.

I was well aware. Every nerve was taut with the anticipation of seeing Magnolia again. Of trying to read what that kiss meant to her, if anything.

West strode past me, toward the far end of the barn, where we'd kept it open the full width, from one outside wall to the other, to create a wider space that could be used for a wedding ceremony or a dance floor or both. To one side was the area Magnolia had suggested could be a first-look setting or a photo op for guests.

I blew out my breath as I remembered the day she'd showed up without Presley and agreed—reluctantly—to consult. We'd both been tense and resentful then. It hadn't even been a month, but it was almost as if history had been rewritten since then. At least in *my* mind.

"There's a lotta room here," West said, surveying the ceremony space now that the drywall was up on this end. "I'm all for having our ceremony here."

"Guess we'll see what the boss says," I said, referring to his fiancée.

"Got that right." West chuckled.

Behind us, one of the double doors opened at the other end.

"We're here," Presley called out.

My pulse picked up, but I took my time turning around to face Magnolia, anticipating laying eyes on her pretty face, her blue-gray eyes, her enticing lips.

West went toward Presley, and I followed more slowly. He kissed his fiancée, but I barely noticed because my eyes were on Magnolia.

I swallowed hard as I took in the gorgeous sight of her. She wore an army-green sweater dress that stopped at her mid-thighs and the brown boots she seemed to favor. The dress was shapeless, hiding her figure. My palms itched with the urge to run them under it, up her sides, over the contours of her curves.

Raising my gaze, I met hers and felt a spark of connection as I tried to read her thoughts.

"Hi, West," she said, then her tone turned businesslike. "Hello, Luke."

"Hey," I said, searching for any sign that she was half as happy to see me as I was her.

She kept her attention everywhere but on me as Presley assured West that Allie, their babysitter, had the girls engrossed in a movie and was happy to give the two of them time to look at the barn and go on a late dinner date.

"You guys have gotten a lot done," Magnolia said as she walked past me and looked through the open doorways of each room.

So we were going to pretend nothing had happened.

I wasn't okay with that, but we had a business meeting

to get through. West and Presley were here to finalize an important decision for their big day.

I could fake it till I got Magnolia alone.

"We've got a lot left to tackle," I countered, ever aware of each day that passed.

The first week of November was gone already. I wanted the big projects finished by the first of December to ensure we'd have plenty of time to handle decor and create an arch, photo op areas, and whatever else cropped up. The barn might be rustic and rough around the edges, but the details needed to be refined and crafted with care.

I took the lead and walked toward the wide end of the barn again. Presley joined Magnolia in checking out the individual rooms, the two of them discussing how they would use each space.

At the corner where the room opened up, I stopped and leaned against the wall, summoning my patience. West joined the women, acting as tour guide, allowing me to stand back and watch Magnolia from afar every time they emerged from one of the rooms.

Her wavy hair hung down her back, glistening under the overhead lights, looking more blond than strawberry tonight. Her cheeks were slightly flushed, and I wondered if that was from the cold outside or something else. She'd switched into planner mode with Presley, pointing out how tables could be scattered the length of the center part of the barn, where the head table could go, and a dozen other things I hadn't yet given a thought to.

Now that my years-old anger had melted away, I was fascinated by this talented, competent adult version of the girl I'd fallen for. No question, she was in her element. She thought in details someone like me never considered, like stands of electric candles here and there along the walls, adding a romantic flair to the dinner segment. She might be going through a crazy bunch of personal stuff, but her confidence professionally didn't waver. I found that surprisingly hot.

Though I'd barely had time to pee for two weeks, I'd spent considerable time thinking as I worked—about her, about us, about the past as well as the present.

My attraction to her since we'd cleared the air with her truth and my apology was alive and well, and surprising as hell. I'd fought admitting it to myself for the first few days, but I'd have to be a dense man not to acknowledge that kissing her had turned my world on end. One kiss. Less than sixty seconds.

If she could do that to me in such a short, serendipitous moment, what would happen if we willingly spent time together, getting to know each other as adults?

I wanted to find out.

She was sending signals that she might not want to find out. I'd definitely be addressing that and doing everything to change her mind, but now was not the time.

I needed to get her alone.

Chapter Fifteen

Magnolia

L uke had been eyeing me since I'd walked in the door, watching me when he thought I didn't notice, studying me whenever I spoke.

It was disconcerting. I couldn't read his mood.

I tried to act is if he was merely a business contact. Never mind that I'd sneaked multiple looks at him and couldn't help liking what I saw. He wore an old white tee and faded, dusty jeans with brown work boots. I'd spotted a thick flannel shirt draped over the back of a folding chair and guessed he'd gotten hot and shed it. I secretly appreciated the view of his biceps.

I still hadn't breathed a word to Presley about the llama night, when he'd come back to my apartment. I trusted her and considered her one of my closest friends, but I couldn't bring myself to talk out loud about Luke kissing me. I was afraid that would give it too much significance. I didn't want it to have any significance.

Since I'd kept mum, I'd been on my own to figure out

how to handle this meeting. I'd decided to act like nothing had happened between us. Wasn't that what he'd been doing for the past two weeks?

So maybe I'd had him on my mind this morning when I'd dressed for work, all too aware I'd be seeing him at the end of the workday. I wouldn't admit it out loud.

The truth? I'd had him on my mind every single day since he'd planted that kiss on my lips and hurried away before I knew what hit me.

I hated that I hadn't already let it go. I didn't want any man to have any kind of power over me ever again, whether it was financially or emotionally.

A kiss didn't have to be emotional.

I'd told myself that a hundred times, but Luke wasn't some random guy. He wasn't a stranger. We didn't have a blank slate between us. There was no way to erase the past, no matter how much I wanted to.

"I'm excited," Presley said once they'd committed to exchanging their vows here. "It'll be a beautiful setting for the ceremony. I'm sure we can fit all our guests in the end area."

"While they're dining, we'll remove the rows of cere-mony chairs and open it up for dancing later," Luke said.

"Do you have a staff to handle the transition?" I asked, knowing Luke was one of the groomsmen.

"I figure I can take care of it," he said.

I shook my head. "As a groomsman, you'll be at the head table. You can't miss the toasts or the meal or fold up chairs in your tux."

Presley looked at West as if this was a problem for the two of them to figure out, but it absolutely wasn't. This was why they'd hired me.

"We've got this," I told her. "Luke and I will discuss

how to staff it. You two aren't allowed to worry about any of it."

"Yes, ma'am," Presley said.

"I can get a couple of my crew to work some overtime that night. Some of them are asking for extra hours." Luke shot me a half grin, and I tried to decipher the message in his eyes.

Was it conspiratorial or smug?

Stop overthinking it.

"That might work," I said. "We can discuss it later. We've achieved our goal for tonight. The ceremony site is decided. I know you two want to get to your date."

"You got that right." West put his arm around Presley and pressed a kiss to her temple. "I've worked up an appetite."

With the look they exchanged, I was pretty sure I knew what he had an appetite for, and it wasn't food.

"Any chance you can stay a few minutes, Magnolia, so we can discuss options for some of the barn details?"

I nearly told him I needed to drive Presley home, but then I remembered West had his vehicle, and they planned to ride together.

So much for an easy out.

Just another business meeting, I reminded myself. Surely I could keep up the act that his kiss hadn't messed with me for another half hour.

I checked the time on my phone as if I had plans for later. "I can do that," I said, hiding my nervousness. I turned to Presley and West. "You two enjoy your date."

"Oh, we will." Presley shared another heated look with West.

"Night, Magnolia," West said.

"Thanks for the help tonight," Luke told West.

"You bet. You kids be good." West grinned.

As the men discussed when West could help again, I gave Presley a quick side hug, then headed to the other end of the barn to think about decorations for Christmas Eve now that we had an actual enclosed space to envision.

I was staring at one of the corners, imagining a multitree display with white lights, silver stars, and thick, gauzy silver ribbon for garland.

"You're staring at the wall," Luke said as he came up beside me.

"I'm seeing more than the wall," I replied. "I'm thinking of a cluster of fresh-cut pine trees in this corner and that one. Maybe five per corner? Would that be feasible?"

His attention was on me instead of the stark, drywalled corner. He chuckled. "We have trees if that's what you're asking."

"What do you think of the idea?"

"I think you're avoiding looking at me."

I pointedly pivoted enough to look him in the eye. "What do you think of my idea?"

"It doesn't matter what I think. I'm not the bride."

"You'd make such a pretty one though."

"Are we going to talk about the elephant in the room?"

So much for keeping up my business front. My gaze wandered to his again and found his intent brown eyes locked on me.

"What elephant is that?" I asked, as if I didn't know.

He grinned, looking so handsome I felt it in my chest. "That kiss," was all he said.

"I thought we were discussing barn details."

Several seconds ticked by as he studied me. I held his gaze for as long as I could, but it was as if he could see into my mind, read my thoughts, which admittedly included something like, *God, he's good-looking.*

I looked away first.

"We can talk barn details once we clear up the personal stuff," he said.

I wish I could say I wasn't affected by him, but I was. After all these years, after all the bad blood and the anger and resentment, I wasn't sure how I could feel any kind of attraction to him, but I did. All he had to do was look at me with that intensity, and I felt more drawn to him than I'd felt to anyone else ever.

"We can pretend it never happened," I said.

Luke shook his head. "It happened, and it set me off-kilter for the past two weeks, Magnolia." He shook his head like he couldn't believe it. "It seemed like you felt something too."

I swallowed, feeling something even now, but it was a physical something. Off-kilter? For two weeks? Was he telling the truth? Why would he lie about that?

He wouldn't, I knew. His admission was a step into vulnerability. Even when we'd been enemies, I hadn't thought he was manipulative. Just stupid.

"Whether I felt something or not, chemistry isn't enough for us to disregard the past and pick up where we left off as if almost twenty years didn't happen."

He brushed a lock of hair off my cheek, peering into my eyes, making me feel squirmy. "What if it is?" His voice was a low, sensual rumble that *did* things to me.

I mentally shook myself. "We can't just ignore that we spent half our lives hating each other. Those feelings don't just drop away because you kissed me."

"I agree. Those feelings dropped away because we talked. Because you told me what really happened. Because

I figured out I was an idiot. I apologized for screwing up. It seemed like you'd forgiven me, but maybe I read that wrong."

I thought that over. Had I forgiven him for being an immature blockhead?

He'd admitted to his teenage insecurities, admitted our families' very different tax brackets had gotten into his head. I'd known the two of us as a couple would cause people to talk if word had ever gotten out that we were together, mainly because my family was wealthy and his was not. But when it was just Luke and me, those differences had meant nothing, at least not in my mind. Apparently they had in Luke's.

Though I couldn't exactly understand it, maybe because I'd admittedly grown up privileged in many ways, I could respect his admission.

So he'd been a normal teenage boy with lots of insecurities. I didn't believe he'd set out to hurt me. He'd genuinely believed I'd hurt him first and had reacted. Could I hold it against him now that he'd misunderstood the situation and misjudged me?

No.

"I have forgiven you," I said quietly. "I'm just not sure if I can forget."

"We're adults now, Mags. Adults who are attracted to each other." He nudged my chin up gently with his finger, forcing eye contact. "Are you going to deny that?"

As I peered up into his earnest chocolate-brown eyes, my pulse quickened. My body responded. I couldn't deny it. I merely shook my head, entranced by the connection crackling between us.

"I'm not asking for forever, Magnolia. I just want to kiss you," he said. "Is it okay if I kiss you?"

The spell he'd cast over me had me nodding even as the wise section of my brain screamed, *Bad idea!*

Luke cradled my jaw with his large palm. He moved his face toward mine, slowly, ramping up my anticipation with every inch he advanced. Finally his lips touched mine, solidly, confidently, sensually. There was nothing of the insecure teenager anymore. This man knew how to turn me inside out with a kiss.

His hand found its way to my waist. He gripped it gently and guided me backward the few feet to the wall, then pressed his body flush with mine so we were touching nearly head to toe. Once again I could feel how aroused he was. My body softened and ached in return.

I slid my hands up to his neck, then higher, to the back of his head, pulling him to me, wanting an even deeper connection. I dipped my tongue between his lips, and he opened to me. Our tongues collided, shooting an intense shudder through me, eliciting an audible whimper from me. I didn't care.

The kiss went on, the most tantalizing, sensual, thorough make-out session of my life.

I'd never had an honest-to-God boyfriend, only hookups and a terrible fiancé who didn't put a lot of effort into his kisses. Luke kissed like it was an art form, and he was an international award winner.

Our kisses went on for minutes, just kisses, even though they were hot, sensual. I pulsed with need for more even as I was thankful Luke was reining himself in and going slow. As much as my body craved his touch and more, I wasn't ready for it. He seemed to understand that.

I didn't know how much time had passed when he broke the contact of our mouths and leaned his forehead to mine, his breathing heavy as his lips curved into a smile.

"We're good at that," he said barely above a whisper.

"We are," I admitted on an exhale.

"If we don't stop now"—he brushed a stray strand of my hair away—"we might not stop. I want you so much, Mags, but not standing up in a barn. Not for our first time."

My mouth went dry thinking about that as I stuck my hand in his back pocket and pulled him tighter into me. Tempted. And also terrified. Not of Luke. Just like I knew he wasn't manipulative, I knew he wouldn't physically hurt me or anything like that. I was scared to trust him. He'd shattered me once. He could shatter me again.

"Who said there would be a first time?" I finally managed, my own breathing jagged.

A low, sexy growl rolled out of him. "I hope there will be."

As he straightened, putting a few inches between our faces, looking into my eyes, there was a part of me that hoped so too. Even if it would be a dumb move.

I brushed my fingers over his jaw, noticing the coarseness of his facial hair. "We're supposed to be talking barn details."

"Right. Barn details." He put more space between us, grinning like a kid who'd stolen a cookie from a cookie jar.

"A question for you," I said. "Have you ordered furniture for the getting-ready rooms?"

He frowned. "I haven't even thought about furniture. I've been focused on electricity and plumbing and big-picture things."

"You should order furniture in advance to ensure it arrives before Christmas Eve."

"How long does it take?" He looked slightly panicked as he paced away from me, turned, came back.

"It depends. But you'll want several sofas for relaxing, large mirrors, ottomans, chairs, tables."

"Right. I accounted for that stuff in the business loan but hadn't thought about ordering early."

"My office furniture took several weeks."

"Shit. We're only, like, six weeks out, aren't we?"

"And there's a major holiday in there."

He ran his hand over his mouth and beard.

I counted to ten silently, thinking before I spoke. "I can help you if you want."

He chuckled. "And charge me two hundred an hour?"

"I'd shop with your credit card for free," I said, grinning, but he didn't smile back.

"Yeah," he said, expelling a breath. "I'd appreciate some help."

"Hey, one thing I'm good at is shopping. We'll get it taken care of."

"Thanks."

"So what other details did you keep me after class for?" I asked lightly.

"Right." Luke stepped to the external wall, to the space between two windows where we'd discussed creating a first-look or photo op area. "I was wondering if there's some kind of wall treatment we could use here and on the opposite side that would be permanent and serve as sort of a blank slate for decor. You mentioned a wood slab panel. Does it have to be removable? Or could we build features into the wall? I'm not sure what, but I'm open to ideas."

I turned and considered the space. It was about twelve to fourteen feet between the windows, a blank canvas. "It could use something there permanently, couldn't it?"

Luke came up next to me again. "The walls will be neutral all around, but I was thinking a backdrop on each side would give the place an extra dimension, an unobtrusive point of interest."

"I know what would work perfectly," I said as an idea came to me. "Imagine wood planks, like two by two in a natural finish, and you cut them at varying lengths. You mount them horizontally on the wall equally spaced, maybe two inches between them vertically."

"I'm with you. So just horizontal boards?"

"That's the base, but then you can have all kinds of modular options for decor. You could have removable shelves that slide between any two planks that could be used for plants or flowers or framed photos. Or whatever decor fits the event. You could also create a modular plaque or chalkboard. The sky's the limit once you have the planks on the wall, and they look classy and add warmth even without any additions. People could add twinkle lights, ribbons, whatever suits them."

"What is it with women and twinkle lights anyway?" he asked.

"They're a vibe. They soften anything. Make it more inviting."

"So I need to stock up on twinkle lights."

I nodded. "I think you should hang them along some of the ceiling beams."

He glanced up to the super-high ceiling, looked doubtful, then said, "Let's tackle the wall thing first. It sounds simple enough."

"There's a similar one in the bar at the Marks Hotel," I said. "I could take you to see it."

"You want to take me to a bar?" he said in an amused voice, knowing full well he was twisting my words.

"This is business, Luke. Do you want to see what I'm talking about?"

"Yeah. I do. When can you go?"

"You're about to start Christmas tree season. You tell me when you can make it."

He seemed to think through his schedule. "I could take some time off tomorrow evening, after dinner with my daughter."

"That works for me."

"Okay then." He sent me a slow, sexy smile. "It's a date."

I wanted to contradict him. It wasn't a date, but I could tell by the spark in his eyes he was trying to get a reaction from me.

"It's a business meeting," I said confidently. "We'll get a drink, discuss furniture, and take pictures of the wall feature."

He approached me again, closed in on me, then kissed me soundly on the lips. "I'll pick you up at eight tomorrow night."

Chapter Sixteen

Magnolia

For nearly twenty-four hours, I'd tried to brainwash myself that this was a business meeting with Luke, not a date.

The memory of that kiss last night was louder in my head though.

That and I could admit he cleaned up well. I mean, I found him appealing in his work clothes and a day's worth of dirt and dust, but showered? Wearing black jeans, black boots, and a black, plum, and white buffalo plaid flannel open over a tee? I'd spent the evening so far waffling between reminding myself my goal was Presley's wedding and getting wrapped up in our nonbusiness conversation.

The bar at the Marks Hotel, The Harbor, was calm and classy, with country music playing quietly. I was surprised to find Josh Mulligan, a guy we'd gone to school with, behind the bar, and Sarah Valdez, who was a few years younger, waiting tables.

Luke was fascinated by the feature wall we'd come here

to see. He'd taken several photos of it, and we'd discussed ideas for options. The plank design was simple but versatile. Even though it would be a permanent fixture, it could easily look different for every single event, thanks to the modular elements.

Once we'd checked it out, Luke had convinced me to stay for a drink and a snack. Truth? It hadn't been tough to persuade me. It was just a drink and some mozzarella sticks.

We sat at a high-top table close to the wood-slab wall. Several other tables were occupied, keeping Josh and Sarah, the only server, busy.

The weeks when Luke and I had gotten close back in high school had been in the late spring, when Luke's family's farm was in the midst of strawberry season. Back then I'd made him tell me all about that operation, loving the stories about all the facets of a working berry farm. Tonight I questioned him about the Christmas tree business. He'd explained how they first harvested several acres of trees to be sold in retail outlets around the region. On Thanksgiving, their focus switched to the cut-your-own segment.

"Then things really get chaotic," he said.

"And this year you're opening a new event-venue business at the same time. Your dad might have a point, you know," I teased him. "You've bitten off a lot."

"I'll sleep in January." He smiled as I fought off an image of him sleeping all alone in a big bed...naked. "But not too much because that's when we get serious about pruning the apple trees."

"I don't know how you juggle it all," I told him.

"We have a good crew, some who've been with us for years, so they know the drill almost as well as I do."

"And your dad is retired?"

"Not by choice. His back forced the issue a few years ago."

"Do you ever consider cutting back to just two crops?" I asked.

Luke shook his head. "The three work out well, labor-wise. There was a period a few years ago when we had two terrible strawberry seasons in a row. I considered throwing in the towel on them, but I decided to keep them for two reasons. One, everything cycles in farming. You go through bad seasons, but they always swing around to good ones. Two, strawberries were my mom's pet project."

"That's sweet."

"It started out as a personal garden when she was a little girl. She loved strawberries and wanted to grow her own, so my grandfather helped her plant a small strawberry garden. Each year she took care of it, expanded it a little bit, until my grandfather recognized it would be a good expansion businesswise and made it official. We have a family tradition now that she's gone. The first strawberries of the season, we eat with homemade whipped cream in remembrance of her."

Emotion flashed over his features. Something deep, sadness tinged. I remembered his affection for his mom from the days when he drove her home from work. I instinctively reached out and touched his hand before realizing what I was doing. I kept the touch brief and pulled my hand back to where it belonged.

"I love that you do that," I said. His family closeness was almost unfathomable to me, and yet when he talked about it, I could imagine. It opened up a longing in me for those kinds of close family ties. There was no chance for that with my parents. My only hope was to someday create that with a husband and kids.

I realized someone was approaching our table from the lobby instead of the bar kitchen, so I sat back on my stool, looked up, and nearly messed my pants at the sight of Felix James.

"Magnolia," he said in a falsely magnanimous baritone.

My only response was to raise my brows. I refused to fake politeness with the jackass who'd kept me under his thumb until I finally rebelled, years later than I should have.

"Isn't this cozy," he continued.

Luke turned to see who it was. He must have recognized him, because then he stiffened and focused back on me. I met his gaze, and he seemed to be gauging whether I was okay. I gave a subtle nod.

"What do you want?" I asked my *not*-father quietly but succinctly. I glanced out to the lobby and noticed a woman waiting for him, watching us. She was quite possibly younger than me and dressed for a date. Gross.

Felix shook his head slowly. "After everything I did to steer you toward suitable men, away from this particular person, and here you are."

"Maybe your first mistake was trying to steer me at all," I said. "I can make up my own mind."

Then his words sank in.

"What do you mean you steered me away from Luke?" I asked.

The smarmy asshole grinned, glanced at Luke with an air of superiority, and said, "I fired his mother from her housekeeping job to stop you two from sneaking around together."

As much as I wish I would've controlled my reaction, my mouth fell open. "Why would you *do* that?" Other than because he was a complete, tyrannical piece of crap.

Felix chuckled diabolically. "I was doing my best to

prevent you from ending up with a farm boy." He said *farm boy* as if it was the worst insult. "And yet here you are, slumming anyway."

I pressed my lips together and glanced at Luke. His hands were on the table as if he was about to stand and possibly take a swing. I'd love to see someone knock Felix out, but...

"He's not worth the trouble," I told Luke quietly.

"Isn't that sweet? You trying to save your lowly lover boy."

That did it.

I sat up straighter and bit out, "Luke is one hundred times a better human being than you could ever hope to be. Back then and now. He's honorable, hardworking, and honest. You're evil, selfish, and the most pathetic excuse for a man I've ever had the misfortune to know."

His chuckle was like fingernails on a chalkboard. I clenched my fists under the table. Maybe *I'd* be the one to punch him.

"Now, now," he said with a patronizing calmness to his voice, "is that any way to speak to your father?"

And that was all it took for me to cause the first scene of my life.

"Isn't it lucky that you're not actually my biological father?" I said, my voice strong and sure. I didn't care who heard me. I hoped someone got video and put it on the Tattler.

There was the quickest flicker of something on his face, something like alarm. That was enough to make me keep going.

"It must make a tough guy like you feel completely emasculated to know you're sterile. Completely incapable of producing that all-important heir. And then it must have killed you to find out your wife's baby with another man was a girl."

I sensed that I was drawing the attention of the others in the bar. I didn't care. In fact, it motivated me.

"You know what that tells me?" I continued. "It tells me God knows what he's doing to cut off the James name with you. The end of a despicable, worthless bloodline. When you die, there'll be no one left in your family because you're a worthless, weak, small-minded man."

Anger slanted his brows as he stepped toward me. Luke stood and crowded him on that side.

"Not worth it," I reminded Luke.

Felix pretended not to notice. "I'd advise you to watch it, young lady."

"I'd advise you to fuck yourself, old man. You're not my father. You have no say in my life. The day you disowned me was the best day of my life. You better run back to your little girlfriend. Is she even legal?"

Felix looked down his nose at me, his lips in an ugly snarl as if he was a badass instead of just an ass. I hadn't missed that he'd gone pale, telling me I'd hit him where it hurt, just as I'd hoped.

"A word of advice to you both," Felix spit out acidly. "Watch yourselves."

"Is that a threat?" Luke asked.

"If it is, I have it on video for law enforcement to have a look-see," Josh said as he came up to our table. "Security's on the way to escort you out, Mr. James. You okay, Magnolia?"

I slowly nodded, feeling...exhilarated. Free like I'd never felt before. I wasn't scared of Felix's threats. He didn't have thugs under hire, nor did he have the balls to do physical harm. With him it was all blowing smoke and throwing his power around, but he had none over me anymore. Not a drop.

Trying to act as if he wasn't humiliated—and failing, as the little tic in his cheek told me—Felix raised his chin, pivoted, and stalked out of the bar area to his unfortunate date.

I exhaled heavily and made eye contact with Luke.

"That...was fucking incredible, Magnolia," he said quietly.

"Brilliant in my opinion," Josh said. "That heartless bastard evicted my ex-girlfriend for being two days late with her rent—when she had the flu so badly that she couldn't sit up. He deserves to rot in hell."

"Thanks for getting video," I told him. "His threats are empty, but could you send it to me just in case?"

"You bet," Josh said. "And don't worry. I won't share it."

"You know what?" I paused and took a sip of my martini, thinking before I said more. "I would actually love it if word got out. You know, if that 'leaked' somehow or someone spread the word on the Tattler." I shrugged. "I mean...I'm not going to post it myself, but if someone else were to accidentally put it out there... Oops."

Josh grinned and shook his head. "It'd serve him right. I'm only going to send it to you though. You can do what you want with it."

"Thanks, Josh." We exchanged numbers so he could forward it.

After he walked back behind the bar, Luke reached across the table and put his big, work-roughened hand over mine. "Are you really doing okay, Mags? That was intense."

"It was. But I'm relieved." I sat back, breathed deeply again, and confirmed that was true. "It felt good to unleash."

Still holding my hand, Luke chuckled. "I bet it did. It

would've felt good to punch him too, but you're right. He's not worth the legal trouble."

Sarah, the server, walked by our table, leaned in, and said, "He so had that coming. Well done, girl."

"Did he evict you too?" I asked her.

She shook her head. "He comes in here plenty. He thinks anyone who serves him a drink is beneath him."

That sounded about right. "He's the lowest of the low," I said before she hurried off to the kitchen.

"Sadly for her he'll probably be back," Luke muttered. "Like a cockroach."

"Like a cockroach," I agreed. "But I doubt he'll be back in my life."

Luke held up his pilsner. "Cheers."

I picked up my glass and clinked it to his. Then we both finished our drinks.

"Do you want another, or are you ready to get out of here?" he asked quietly.

"Do you mind if we go? Everyone keeps looking at us." I was fine with the attention while I aired Felix's shame, but now I just wanted to be alone...with Luke.

"Let me go take care of the tab. Then I'll take you home."

With my eye on the lobby in case Felix came back, I nodded. Once alone, I played over the scene with him, for once not wishing I'd had a better comeback. I'd said the things I wanted to say. My words wouldn't do anything to change that hateful, pathetic man, but he was no longer part of my life.

Luke returned and held out his hand. I took it as I slid off the stool. When he slipped his arm around me as we exited the bar and walked through the lobby toward the hotel door, I didn't object. I liked it. I liked *him*. I wasn't ready to say good night yet.

As we made our way toward his truck, I belatedly said, "I owe you for half the bar bill."

"No, you don't."

"Yes, I do," I said, grinning. "That was a business meeting."

"Ah, Mags. That"—he squeezed me closer to his side—"was a date."

I laughed. "That? A run-in with Felix that nearly turned into a brawl? Luke, we need to work on your dating game."

He laughed too. "The night's not over. I'm still angling for a good-night kiss."

With my emotions all over the board from the evening, chances were decent I was going to give him that good-night kiss.

When he helped me up into his truck, his hands trailed over my body, drawing a reaction from deep in my core, and I thought, *Maybe even more.*

Chapter Seventeen

Luke

Magnolia had been through a lot tonight.

I was so damn proud of her for giving Felix James a piece of her mind. Her words had hit him like well-aimed bullets. That piece of shit deserved every bad thing that came to him.

I was still reeling at the discovery that he'd known Magnolia and I were involved back then. We'd always been careful, staying in the shadows on their property, away from the line of sight of any windows, which made me wonder if he had secret cameras.

None of it mattered much now. His attempt to keep us apart was in the past. I didn't know where we'd end up, but that son of a bitch would not be what came between us again.

The drive from the Marks to her apartment wasn't long, and she let me hold her hand the whole way. I was counting that as a victory.

In the alley behind the shops on Main, I pulled up to

the back of The Lily Pad. Magnolia's car was in the single parking spot, but I angled in as close to her vehicle as I could get.

"I'm walking you up," I said, intent on that kiss.

She sent me a nervous smile. I hopped out and jogged around to her side before she could slide out, my heart pounding with anticipation. I couldn't wait to put my lips on those rebellious ones of hers again.

I extended my hand to help her down, then didn't let go once we were walking toward the stairs. The staircase was old and wooden and not wide enough for us to climb side by side, so I slipped behind her, keeping hold of her hand as we ascended in silence.

At the door, Magnolia faced me, pulling me into her until our lips met. She kissed me hungrily, pressing her body into mine, her hands sliding down to my ass, drawing me against her softness. All my blood pounded into my erection as I kissed her back.

"I feel like celebrating," she said breathlessly when she came up for air.

"Yeah? Got any champagne?"

She shook her head. "Not that kind of celebrating."

Thoughts weren't connecting in my brain. I was too busy kissing her some more, not ready to head back to my lonely truck. I barely registered that her hands had disappeared from my backside until she broke off the kiss again, turning her attention to the little wallet thing she wore across her body.

I forced my attention to what she was doing, mourning the loss of contact with her luscious mouth. She took out her keys and turned to unlock the door.

Once it was open, she looked back at me, wove our fingers together, and tugged me inside.

I didn't argue.

Magnolia relocked the outer door, then led me through the hall, past the storage rooms, and to her private door, which she also unlocked.

Her apartment was dark, so I held on and followed her blindly, not caring where she led me as long as she didn't drop my hand. I heard rather than saw her scoot a kitchen chair out of the way. If I wasn't mistaken, she was heading straight for her bed.

She stopped and let my hand go, then took her phone out, setting it on her nightstand and illuminating the area. She picked something up from the nightstand, and I realized she was turning on a trio of LED candles and setting them back down. Then she got rid of the phone light, leaving us in the warm glow of candlelight.

I raised my brows in question, afraid to believe, but before she could see my face, she took both my hands, stood on her toes, and stretched up to kiss me again.

Her kiss started sweet, not quite tentative, unhurried. Thorough. Before long, she deepened it as she ducked her hands beneath my T-shirt and ran them slowly up my abs, over my chest, as if memorizing the shape of me with her magical fingers. I shrugged off my flannel shirt and tossed it to the side, then burrowed my hands beneath her thick sweater, resting them at her waist, thrilling at the feel of her warm, soft skin.

In high school, I'd dreamed of touching her flawless, milky flesh from head to toe, but I'd never had the balls to do more than kiss her. I'd been taking it slow, biding my time, working up the courage, and then we'd been over.

Magnolia lifted my tee over my head. I took over the task and rid myself of it in a heartbeat, throwing it in the general direction of my flannel shirt, not caring where it landed. I pulled her closer, poised to remove her sweater, but before I could, her hands were at my belt, undoing the buckle, then unsnapping my jeans.

Not going to lie. Her aggressiveness was doing it for me.

My boots were loose enough I could kick them off without my hands, and I did that as Mags unzipped my pants, kissing me at the same time. I ran my palms up her sides to the edge of her bra. I was on the verge of sliding my hand beneath the thin, silky fabric when she derailed every thought in my head by dipping her fingers inside my boxer briefs and skimming them over my dick.

I gasped at the sensation and focused for a few seconds on gathering my self-control. I'd waited nearly twenty years for this. I was not going to ruin it by losing it in my pants at the first intimate touch. A growl rumbled from my throat with the effort.

Her fingers moved to my back, dipping down to my ass as she shoved both layers of clothing down, freeing my throbbing dick. She followed my pants down to the floor, removing them one leg at a time, then my socks, my hands on her fully clothed shoulders as she got me naked as the day I was born.

I was about to comment on her overdressed state when she rose slowly, pausing as her lips were even with my crotch. I stopped breathing altogether as I waited to see what she'd do. She kissed my tip, just a gentle flutter of a touch that made me grunt, aching for more contact.

I was getting ahead of myself though. I was buck naked, and she was still fully dressed. That wasn't how I normally operated, but she had me all off-center and bothered as fuck.

"Mags." I helped her stand, groaning as I pulled her

sweet, soft body against my hard-as-steel one. "You're killing me."

An adorable giggle escaped her as she pulled me to her mouth for another kiss. She'd made her intentions clear, and a switch flipped in me. She'd had her fun stripping me down. It was my turn.

I took control of the kiss, intensifying it as I tracked down the clasp on her bra and undid it beneath her sweater. The lingerie loosened, and I wasted no time seeking out her nipple with my thumb, then palming her perfect breast. Both of her perfect breasts. After all these years, it was surreal as hell to have my hands on Magnolia. I reveled at the feel of her pebbled tips, her soft skin, her purr of pleasure, the way she arched into my hand.

I needed my mouth on her, so I hurriedly lifted her sweater over her head, and she slid her bra off. I bent to tease her nipple with the tip of my tongue, determined to drive her higher, but the joke was on me because I couldn't resist closing my mouth over her, sucking, feasting as I teased the other side with my fingers.

As eager as I was to devour her other nipple too, I couldn't wait to have her completely bared. I lowered a hand to the waistband of her skirt, pushing it down over one hip, then reluctantly releasing her breast from my mouth so I could focus on getting every stitch of clothing off her.

She stepped out of her skirt, leaving her in string bikini panties and ankle boots. I dropped to the floor and removed her boots and socks, then took in the sight of her in the dim, flickering light, her pale skin irresistible, her little panties teasing me by barely covering the part my body throbbed for.

I drew those panties down her thighs and groaned once

she was completely undressed, letting the sight of her burn itself into my brain.

"Look at you," I whispered. "You're beautiful, Mags." I kissed her lips. "Worth the twenty-year wait just to see you."

She laughed quietly as her arms came around me. "I hope you want to do more than just see me, because I'm about to die from needing you."

I trailed my palms to the globes of her ass and steered her to the edge of the bed, then lowered her to sit on the mattress. Dropping to my knees, I spread her legs, took in the sight of her folds, and finally tasted her. She fell back onto her elbows with a moan as I licked her core and teased her with my tongue.

She lifted her feet to the edge of the mattress, opening up to me even more. I explored every forbidden inch of her with my mouth and fingers until she was bucking into my face, clinging to my head, moaning, whimpering, calling out to God and me in the same sexy gasp until she arched into me and shattered. Her orgasm went on, and I adjusted my touch to draw out as much pleasure from her as possible, my eyes on her gorgeous face that showed exactly what I was doing to her.

When she gasped like she couldn't take it anymore, I peppered her inner thighs with kisses as she came down from orbit. As her breathing evened out, I trailed those kisses slowly down her leg to her ankle, savoring every inch of her smooth skin. Grabbing my jeans, I stood, pulled out my wallet for a condom, and rolled it on.

Watching her come apart had tested my limits. I wanted to bury myself deep inside her so badly I ached.

I gently scooped her up from the mattress edge and set her the right way in the bed, then crawled over her, bearing my weight on my forearms. I gazed down at her, her cheeks pink, lids heavy, a satisfied grin stretching lazily across her irresistible lips.

"You look like the cat who ate the canary," I said.

She giggled. "More like the cat who got eaten by the canary."

I laughed at the innuendo, not expecting something like that to come out of her mouth but loving this updated version of Magnolia. She was less proper. More casual. More...real.

Back in the day, I was crazy about her. I liked this grown-up, sexy version even more.

She cradled me between her thighs, opening herself to me. The picture she made, lying there, willing and waiting and fucking gorgeous, undid me. All my finesse was gone, my ability to bide my time in the negative numbers. Twenty years I'd waited...

I pushed inside of her impatiently, moaning at the ecstasy of her tight channel. I tried to go slow. Wanted to stretch this bliss out for hours. It only took a few thrusts for me to feel as if my body wasn't in my control, as if I was compelled to pump harder, faster, deeper into this enthralling woman who must have cast a spell over me.

When she banded her legs around me as if to trap me in this heaven, I gave myself over to the need driving me higher, my every thought dissipating before I could catch it. I stopped trying to think, succumbed completely to the sensations, fighting to maintain enough awareness of her response so I could ensure she went over before me.

Working my hand between our bodies, I found her nub and ran my finger over it, receiving an immediate gasp as Mags arched up into me. Her head fell back as I continued to thrust into her and circled her clit with my finger until she cried out and contracted around me.

That was it for me. I careened over the edge after her, lost in a haze of euphoria.

Eventually my senses came back online as I caught my breath. My eyes still closed, I inhaled the sweet scent of Magnolia mixed with the earthy smell of sex. She let out a quiet, sensual moan of contentment as she trailed her fingers in a feather-light path over my back.

I opened my eyes to her mesmerizing blue-gray gaze and felt an instant ping of connection in my chest.

"That..." she said, still breathing hard, "was kind of incredible."

I growled, a grin curling my lips. "Kind of?"

"More than," she admitted, grinning back. "My brain can't come up with better adjectives, but it was those."

I rolled to the side of her so I wouldn't crush her, struggling to form full thoughts, then deciding full thoughts were overrated. "Stupendous," I muttered.

Magnolia laughed. "That's one." Her chest rose under my arm with her inhalation. "Spectacular."

"Mmm, yeah," I managed.

"Wow," she said, rolling onto her side, into me. "Was that, like, makeup sex?"

A laugh rolled out of me. "Seeing how we were mad for eighteen years, it's going to take more than one time to work it out." As soon as I said it, I realized I was assuming a lot with that statement. Maybe she was only in this for closure, or maybe it really was just her way of celebrating. For me, it was instantly clear I wanted more.

"I could get behind that cause," she whispered, running her fingers over my chest.

"Yeah? So this wasn't just you using my body to burn off the exhilaration of the evening?"

"That's just a side benefit." She grinned lazily, then went serious. "It's almost as if eighteen years of hating each other never happened. It's like we picked up right where we left off."

"Not exactly," I argued. "I didn't have the guts to get you naked back then."

"I'm glad you didn't. It set you apart, made you different. Special."

"Being a coward made me special?"

She shook her head. "Wanting more than sex made you special. At least that's what I thought until he who shall not be named ruined it."

At the reminder of all the bullshit that man must've put her through, I pulled her to me, kissed her forehead. "It's ironic," I said, holding her. "He tore us apart before. Tonight, in a way, he brought us back together."

"I'd like to think this would've happened even without his hateful existence."

I nodded. "Let's not give him credit for anything."

We went quiet, thoughtful, until she broke the silence with a question.

"Is this just for tonight?" she asked hesitantly.

"I hope not," I said, determined to communicate with her this time around even when it made me feel vulnerable. "I want...more."

"Me too."

"Good." I breathed out my relief. Those two words gave me hope. I didn't know exactly what I wanted from this, from her, but I knew I'd be crushed if this was the last time we were together. "It's tricky though," I continued. "My time is already spread thin, between tree season, working on the barn, and Addie."

She nodded. "I know. We'll just...steal time when we can."

"You're good with that?"

"It's perfect. I'm trying to build my business up and rebuild my life. We don't need to jump in too fast, right?"

"Mm-hmm," I said as I ran my hand over her curves, noticing at once the chill in the air and the stirrings of my body. "Would it be considered jumping in fast if we went for another round tonight?"

"I'd consider that...efficient. Smart. Making the most of what time we do have."

"I need to take care of the condom. Suit up again."

"You came prepared."

"Believe me when I say I had no idea where our evening was going before it started, but I'm liking it so far."

She kissed my lips, then looked into my eyes. "Me too, Luke. Hurry back."

Chapter Eighteen

Magnolia

Monday evening I went to Presley's house to work on her wedding. I was ready to tell her about Luke, but this was our first opportunity to talk in private.

"I brought refreshments," I said, holding up a box of llama-shaped sugar cookies when she let me in.

"I happen to know those pair extremely well with a Riesling I have on hand."

"Like peanut butter and jelly," I said as I followed her to the sprawling living area that looked out onto the lake.

I'd only gotten to know Presley recently, when she moved to town. Her story and mine were opposite, with her growing up poor, then making a killing in her previous career, and me growing up with unlimited money, then losing it all. Something we had in common though was that our father figures, if you could call them that, were manipulative jerks. That and we'd opened our businesses around the same time and bonded over every challenge and triumph.

"Is West joining us?" I asked as we made a pit stop in the kitchen.

Presley took out two wineglasses as I grabbed a plate for the cookies. "He's helping Luke tonight," she said, and my pulse kicked up at the mere mention of his name. "His mom and Thomas took the girls to dinner so I could meet with you."

"His stepfather's doing okay?"

"Other than complaining about the diet change, he's good."

We took our wine and cookies to the living room and relaxed on the sectional.

"How was your outing with Luke?" she asked before I could get settled. "Should we call it a date?"

I sank my teeth into the vanilla-frosted cookie with sprinkles before I answered. By the time I swallowed the bite, I couldn't wipe the grin off my face.

Presley's brows shot up, and she tilted her head. "That's a telling look."

"What is it telling you?"

"I could guess, but why don't you tell me?"

After another bite and some wine to wash it down, I said, "You're right. Perfect pairing. The wine and cookies," I clarified quickly.

"What about you and Luke?"

"We went to the Marks to see the wall, like I told you," I started.

"On a Saturday night. Date night."

I laughed. "He did convince me to have a drink and an appetizer."

I launched into the tale of running into Felix and did my best to retell our confrontation word for word.

"You said that?" she said, her voice climbing to a high pitch of delight.

I nodded. "I've been in counseling for two years now, but those five minutes of telling him off were the best therapy possible."

"And you told him to fuck himself?"

"With witnesses," I said proudly.

Presley leaned toward me with her palm raised for a high five. "It's the quiet ones who don't swear that you have to watch for," she muttered. "It makes the story all the more powerful. I'm so proud of you."

"The look on his stupid, smug face was priceless."

Presley let out a howl of joy. "So what happened next?"

"We went home."

Her shoulders sagged.

"To my place. Together," I said. "To celebrate."

She finished a sip and held her glass aloft, her eyes going wide. "Naked celebrate?"

"Mm-hmm," I said, my cheeks warming at the memories.

"Oh, my God, Magnolia. You and Luke...enemies to lovers. Bang!"

I laughed at the appropriate word. "Double bang."

"Wow. I was just hoping you two could call a truce for long enough to get through the wedding."

"Truce is in effect," I said.

"So are you a thing? Do you think it will happen again?"

"Judging by the dirty texts Luke sent me earlier, it's going to happen again. It's hard right now because we're both so busy."

"Right. Which reminds me, did the Earthly Charm girls commit?"

"The contract is signed," I said.

"Between the run-in with Felix the Fuck, sleeping with Luke, and landing another event, we should be drinking champagne. But cheers." She lifted her glass, and we clinked, then sipped.

"Thanks. It's sort of surreal to be on good terms with him after all this time, never mind sleeping with him."

"I'm so happy for you. Maybe your wedding will be the next one."

"Bite your tongue," I said, laughing. "It was one night."

"So far."

"So far," I repeated.

"That's how West and I got started. Isn't that how every couple starts? With one night?"

"You have to start somewhere, I guess. But you're way ahead of yourself. I'm only now getting the swing of running my own life, you know? I don't want to rush into something."

"I do. You're doing great. Your business is taking off. You're free from thinking you're Felix the Fuck's daughter. Your mom is trying to make peace. And you've got this hot farmer boyfriend who knows how to plow."

I laughed. "That pun is Chloe-worthy. He's not my boyfriend though."

"Yet."

I shook my head. "I'm not ready. I don't know how to do that. I've never had a real relationship, so we're just going to call it sleeping together for now."

"I was in those same shoes, my friend, just a couple of months ago. Besides, you've already survived your first fight."

"You mean the eighteen-year one?"

"Is there another?"

Shaking my head again, I said, "Just the one. On a serious note..." I glanced out the window, where the lake was dark except for the light at the base of Presley's dock. "I'm scared."

"What are you scared of specifically? Getting hurt?"

"Well, that too, but..." I took another cookie and broke off the llama's head to eat first. "I'm just figuring out this independence thing. Not relying on anyone. Not being accountable to anyone but me." I popped the llama head in my mouth, chewed, and swallowed it. "I'm kind of loving it, you know?"

"Preaching to the choir, my friend," she said. "Good news though. You can be in a relationship and maintain your independence. Look at me."

"What happens when West and the girls move in?"

"I can't wait," she said beaming. "The girls' rooms are almost ready."

"And you'll be a full-time stepmom."

"Slightly terrifying, but I love those girls," Presley said. "I'll still have my business and my friends and my nest egg and all the parts of independent me. I'll just be sleeping with my sexy husband at night."

Her expression told me exactly how she felt about that —overjoyed.

I wondered if I could ever find the same kind of balance she had. But that was getting ahead of myself. I might need a crash course in trusting someone. "For now I'll just worry about when we can sneak more time together."

"You're right. Baby steps." She set her wineglass down. "Before I forget, you're invited to Thanksgiving with us if you don't have somewhere else to go."

"Thanks. Loretta invited me to the Diamonds' dinner too."

"Because Thursdays are poker night," Presley recited, laughing. "You'll have a blast with the ladies."

"I will."

I was grateful for the invitations. When you were single, holidays could be tricky, but the Diamonds had taken me in for the past two years. I was grateful and yet ever aware of being the odd girl out. Always.

"Let's get to the wedding details," I said, having chomped down two cookies. They'd gotten me through the topics I was less comfortable about. I was more than ready to talk about the subject I was confident about. "Have you checked out those photographer websites yet?"

Chapter Nineteen

Luke

Wednesday night was the first opportunity I got to see Magnolia again. The week so far had nearly driven me out of my skin with wanting to see her, touch her, reassure myself that last weekend was real, but not surprisingly, my busy life had other things to say about that.

I'd kissed Addie good night, told my dad I was going out, and driven straight to Magnolia's apartment. I wasn't ashamed to admit I'd been here less than five minutes when I had her naked and under me. She didn't protest.

We'd both just come apart simultaneously, telling me we were perfectly in tune with each other. I rolled sideways and pulled her into me as I caught my breath.

"That was quite a hello," Magnolia said with a satisfied grin.

I laughed. "So how's your week been, since we skipped the small talk earlier?"

"Better now. Yours?"

"So much better now, and I've had a decent week so far as it is."

"Yeah?" she purred lazily, running her finger back and forth over my chest.

"West and I got all the drywall finished last night. Wiring's done. Water line is run. I need to paint and do a dozen other tasks, but we've got complete walls."

"That's exciting, Luke. How does it look?"

"Not like my old barn," I said. "In a good way."

"I can't wait to see it."

"Come out anytime."

"I just might. But does your family know about us?"

I shook my head. "Not yet. I didn't want to jump the gun."

She nodded. "I told Presley, because I tell Presley almost everything. She won't talk though."

"Are we a secret?" I asked.

"Not on purpose. It wouldn't take much for someone to see your truck outside and figure it out. It's different when it comes to your family though."

"Right. I'll have to figure out when and how to let Addie know. I haven't dated much."

"That's your call," she said. "I can handle being hidden away for a while if you want to protect her."

I shook my head. I didn't want to hide Magnolia away, not for any longer than necessary. I believed I could talk to Addie and set her expectations so she wouldn't jump ahead to me getting married or her having a stepmom. I'd let Jessie know I was introducing our daughter to someone I cared about, just to be transparent, but I didn't expect her to object. My bigger hesitation was Magnolia herself.

Though we'd texted every day since Saturday, we were in that awkward period where it was too early to call it a relationship. Not without a conversation first. As ready as I was to jump in with both feet, I was doing my best to take it one day at a time as we both made the mental adjustment from hating each other to sleeping together.

"We'll play it by ear," I said, determined not to overthink it. "I'll be right back."

I headed for the bathroom. When I came back, Magnolia had crawled under the blankets and held them up for me to join her, giving me another view of her body. That's all it took for me to want her again, but just like I could be an adult and enjoy dinner before jumping to dessert, I could spend time with Magnolia without ravishing her. Well, at least for a few minutes and after I'd had my way with her once, I thought with a grin.

"What are you smiling about?" she asked as I moved up against her under the blankets, soaking in her warmth.

"Just happy to see you," I said. "So tell me about your week. Busy one?"

"Not overly busy. I've only booked one new event, the one for Earthly Charm. I have a feeling I've hit that point in the season where I won't book anything else until the new year."

"You don't think you'll get some last-minute holiday parties?"

She shook her head. "Most of those are corporate, and they start preparing months in advance."

"I had an idea," I said. "I've had a couple inquiries for holiday parties in the barn."

"That's amazing, Luke. Congratulations."

"Thanks. I had to tell them it won't be ready in time this year, but what I was thinking is, what if I had a policy where people need to contract with you to plan their event if they want to use the barn?"

"So you'd force them to hire me?" she asked, frowning.

"That's sort of harsh phrasing, but we could work a deal."

She was shaking her head before I could say more.

"No?" I asked. "It might get you more bookings."

She propped herself up on her elbow, and I fought to keep my eyes on her face instead of her gorgeous breasts. "You're sweet, but I need to get business myself, Luke. I can do this."

"I never said you couldn't," I said quickly. "I was just trying to help you solve a problem."

She smiled and kissed me, and I got the impression that was her way of dismissing my idea.

"We could make it work both ways," I said in one last try. "Reciprocal agreement kind of thing."

She shook her head. "People don't want to be forced to work with certain businesses. Especially me in some cases."

"But if they come to me and I recommend you—"

"Luke." She kissed me again. "I appreciate the sentiment, but I need to make my own way. And I'm doing it. Every month my revenue increases. I've got this."

"Okay, okay. I wasn't saying you can't do it. I know you can. You're amazing."

"Oh, yeah?" she said, her voice going flirty. "Tell me more."

Somewhere in the apartment, her phone sounded with a notification. Magnolia glanced toward the love seat, where it looked like she'd been sitting before I got here, based on the half-full cup of water on the table and a planner and her phone on the cushion.

"I'll see who it is later," she said, snuggling back into me. The phone sounded again, two times in quick succession. She sat up and sent me a puzzled look, as if I would have any idea who it was. I shrugged.

"Go check it," I suggested.

"I've got this hot farmer in my bed," she purred, tracing my lower lip with her finger. "Do I look stupid?"

Shaking my head, I grinned and growled, "You look gooooood." I leaned in to kiss her.

Another notification came from her phone, then two more in rapid succession before we could say more.

"I hope nothing's wrong," she said, sitting up again and breaking out of the sexy haze we'd both been falling into. She climbed out from under the blankets and walked over to the love seat.

I was immediately sidetracked by the view even as there was another alert. There wasn't much that would prove worthy of pulling my attention from her exquisite body.

She picked up the phone. "Chloe. Oh, and Presley too. They both texted..."

She swiped and read for a few seconds. When she turned back toward me, her mouth gaped open, her attention still on the screen.

"What?" she said in an astonished tone. "No way." She hurried back to bed and slid under the covers as she continued to read.

"What's going on?" I asked, concern creeping in.

She let out a howl of laughter as she continued to read. "Look at the Tattler."

"My phone's in my pants."

Rolling to her back, she moved next to me, holding her phone up where both of us could see it. She pointed out an anonymous post in the community news thread that said Felix James had been fired from Lansford Development.

The poster claimed to be a friend of someone who worked for the company in Nashville.

"You think it's true?" I asked.

"It's almost unbelievable, maybe too good to be true. Except the timing... My mother intended to tell my grandfather everything, from my paternity to the fact she's filing for divorce. If anything could convince him to get rid of Felix, that would be it. He has a thing where he insists on the company staying in the family. A divorce and no blood ties would mean Felix is no longer part of the family in any way."

"But Felix has been with that company for years, hasn't he?"

"Since before my grandfather arranged for him to marry my mother."

I reared back mentally, trying to wrap my head around that. "Arranged? Forced?"

"The same way Felix attempted to force me to marry Rick."

I knew she'd been engaged to this Rick prick, and that when she'd broken the engagement, Felix had cut her off and kicked her out. Rumors had circulated suggesting the engagement had been *arranged*, but I'd not really believed that was realistic. "I wasn't sure if that was true or a rumor."

"It's true," she said. "Welcome to the James family. We put the F-U in dysfunction." She laughed dryly.

I thought about Addie and her future. My biggest wish for her was a happy, productive life, whatever that looked like for her. I couldn't fathom how a parent could manipulate and discount their child's life to that extent. For business? You built a business up to give your children the best life you could, not the other way around.

Magnolia continued to read the comments on the app

as I tried to grasp the difference between our families. Hers was more like the soap operas my mom had sunk into in her last few years when she wouldn't get out of bed. Crazy, unbelievable stuff. That was Magnolia's reality.

My family might've been stretched for money more often than not, but I wouldn't trade them for the world. A good family was worth a hundred times more than a huge bank account.

I noticed Magnolia tapping away on her screen.

"What are you doing?" I asked.

"Texting my mother to see if she knows whether it's true. I know it's late, but I need to know. If Felix was indeed canned, who knows what he'll do?"

"You don't think he'd blame you, do you?" I frowned, uneasiness swirling in my gut. I didn't trust that son of a bitch for anything.

"If anyone, he'd blame my mother," she said distractedly. "Or my grandfather."

I rolled toward her, my arm across her belly, content to breathe her in and hold her while she got to the bottom of the latest chapter of her family's drama.

"My mom told my grandfather everything a week ago," Magnolia read from a new message. "He told her he was going to 'make some changes.'"

I lay there listening to her periodic comments as she scrolled and texted, content to be a sounding board and a personal heater while she unraveled the truth. I couldn't help thinking how incredible it was that she was relatively normal considering her background. I knew when we'd been kids that lots of people called her a mean girl and talked behind her back. Others hadn't fully embraced her but accepted invitations to her parties because those were the places to be seen. Even back then, I'd seen beyond all that to the girl beneath the surface.

It had all started in sixth grade when I'd forgotten my lunch one day. I'd elected not to call home to see if my mom could deliver it, knowing she and my dad were hard at work and didn't have time to make up for my mistake.

I'd been out on the playground after the lunch break, and Magnolia had pulled a bag of chips out, smiled at me, and given them to me. They were salt-and-vinegar flavor, which she'd said she didn't like, but those chips had made an impression on me and helped fill my empty stomach that day. Allowed me to see beyond the rich-girl exterior to the kind gesture. As we got older, I wasn't blind to some of her antics, but I sensed somehow that there was a girl beneath all that who was hurting. I'd had a crush on her from that day in sixth grade forward.

By the time we were juniors, when one of our old family cars quit and was beyond repair, I was allowed to use my mom's car to get to and from school and football practice as long as I picked her up from her cleaning job each night. I remembered the first time I'd caught a glimpse of Magnolia driving her little sports car past me, up the long driveway and into the six-car garage. Instead of being intimidated, I'd been captivated. A few months passed before the opportunity to speak to her had finally arisen.

It had blossomed into a tentative, fledgling relationship. One that I'd fucked up, not her. Felix was the culprit and the liar, but I'd been the fool who jumped to wrong conclusions. I should've known Magnolia wasn't the bad guy. I'd gotten to know her, had started to think we might have a special kind of connection.

The firing of my mother had highlighted that we were from two different worlds and played on my every insecurity. I could see it clear as day now. She might've come from a toxic environment, but she wasn't to blame for our adolescent ending. I was. I'd stopped believing she was good and kind and succumbed to everyone else's opinion of her.

I couldn't fix the past, but I could try to give us a chance at a future.

"It looks like it's true," she said, her tone confident. "I found an article from a business journal dated today. 'Felix James Out as the Number Two Guy at Lansford Development.'" She laughed. "He must be losing his mind. What a glorious bit of long-awaited karma."

I kissed her cheek, sharing in her joy that the bastard had gotten what was coming to him.

"I have one question for you," I said as she sent Chloe and Presley a link to the business-journal article.

"Yeah?"

"How is it that you're so normal compared to the shit show you grew up in?"

She laughed again, quieter this time. "Normal? I'm far from normal. I was good and screwed up, but I'm working on it with my therapist every week."

She handed me her phone to set on the nightstand. I did so, then rolled on top of her, bracing my weight on my forearms as I peered down at her pretty face. "I think you're amazing," I said.

"Yeah?"

"Yeah."

"Could that be because I'm naked and under you?" she teased.

"I love it when you're naked and under me, but I'd think just as highly of you if you were on top, riding me into the sunset."

"Mmm," she said, grinning. "Maybe we should test that theory. See if it's true."

I rolled to my back, taking her with me, drawing more laughter from her and loving the sound. Loving the way she felt on top of me, particularly as she kissed me and ground her hips against me.

When she stretched over to the nightstand and took out a box of condoms, I watched her hungrily. Impatiently.

Once she had me sheathed up and we slid our bodies together, I caught my breath, then said, "Yep. I was right. Pretty fucking amazing."

Chapter Twenty

Magnolia

Thursday nights were poker night for the Dragonfly Diamonds.

Some people might not understand my deep affection for these ladies who were all in their sixties and seventies, but they were truly golden, no pun intended.

The night Felix had kicked me out, I'd spent it in my car, parked on a side street in town under the shadows of a grand, old, gnarled tree that seemed like a refuge through my tear-swollen eyes. That tree happened to be in Dotty's yard, though I didn't know it then.

Not only had she offered me the studio apartment above her store, but she'd given me a job when I had no work experience and only a burning anger and desire to prove to Felix I'd be fine without a penny from him.

She'd lent me a sympathetic ear and insisted I tag along with her to poker night to get out of my head for a few hours. I hadn't known what to expect from the weekly gathering of these much-older-than-me women, but what I'd found was kindness, humanity, empathy, and encouragement. They'd applauded me for standing up to both my former fiancé and my father.

I shouldn't have been surprised when I walked into Dotty's home this Thursday evening to discover all six Diamonds waiting for me with expectant grins on their weathered but beautiful faces.

"What's going on?" I asked slowly as I looked from face to eager face.

Loretta stood and hugged me. "We're having a quiet little celebration this evening."

"What are we celebrating?" I asked as Dotty took the bottle of gin from me. Normally I brought wine, but she'd suggested gin instead tonight because she had something special in the works.

"Karma," Nancy Solon sang out.

Rosy McNamara broke out into the Taylor Swift song, making me laugh.

"Whose karma are we celebrating?" I sat on the sofa between Kona and Darlene, who reached over and gave me a side hug.

"You have to ask?" Loretta asked. "As I understand it, one Felix James recently got what was coming to him."

I fell back into the cushion and laughed. "I love you, ladies. I should have known you'd be all over that."

"We've got your back, dear," Kona said.

"We always have," Dotty called out from the kitchen that was partially open to the living room.

"You ladies are the best," I said, feeling light and joyful.

"Normally we wouldn't like to celebrate someone's misfortune," Darlene assured me.

"But he's an evil man, and he deserves everything bad that comes his way," Loretta said.

"You won't hear any arguments from me." I leaned to the coffee table and helped myself to tortilla chips and salsa. "Is this your homemade salsa, Nancy?"

"You guessed it. I brought the mild for some of our weak-ass friends." She eyed Rosy, then laughed with the rest of us.

"Just because I have a weak stomach does not mean I am a weak ass," Rosy declared.

"I would say raising six boys mostly by yourself makes you anything but weak, Rosy," Loretta said. She stood and went to the kitchen, then came back with two glasses of a beautiful bright blue drink.

"What is this gorgeous cocktail?" I asked as she handed one of them to me.

"Tonight's special is the Karma Fizz," Loretta explained. "But wait for the rest of us so we can do a toast."

I took the drink and sniffed it. It smelled sweet and of lime, orange, and gin.

"They look spectacular," Kona said as Dotty delivered two more.

"Not as spectacular as it would've been to be a fly on the wall when Mr. James got his walking papers," Darlene said.

"Can you imagine?" Loretta laughed as she brought out the last three cocktails. "What I wouldn't do to see video of that."

Still standing, Dotty raised her glass. "To karma coming around."

"Hear, hear!"

"Cheers!"

We clinked and sipped. The cocktail was delicious and a little dangerous, as it would go down as easily as a juice box.

"I've got another one," Rosy said. "To our Magnolia, who has every reason to hate that man, but instead of wasting her energy on anger and hatred, she's focused on her new life and building it up."

"Yes," Dotty said amid another round of *hear, hear*.

"To resilience," Nancy added.

We all drank to both, me with gratitude and love in my heart.

"If we're being sappy, I've got one," I said. "To all of you, for building me up when I was at my lowest, for having confidence in me and helping me build confidence in myself." My eyes teared up out of nowhere. "I don't know where I'd be without you."

"We're going to be stewed before we get to the appetizers," Kona quipped.

"You keep drinking," Darlene said. "I'll win all your money at the card table."

"These karma whatevers might be worth it," Kona replied. "Maybe they should be our signature drink."

"Lord knows we've been around long enough to see a lot of karma served," Loretta said.

"Maybe none as sweet as Felix the Shit," Nancy said, making me laugh.

"We call him Felix the Fuck," I clarified.

"Better yet," Nancy cackled.

"Thank you, ladies," I said. "You're truly the best."

"To us," Rosy called out, raising her glass again.

"To soon-to-be-inebriated us," Kona added.

We all sipped again. Then Dotty said, "So if Felix is out, does that mean your grandfather's business will go to you, Magnolia?"

I set my glass on the coffee table. "Ugh. I hope not. I don't want it."

"No?" Rosy asked. "Even with Felix out of it?"

"You've got your own business now," Dotty said.

"Plus zero interest in property development," I clarified. "My business might be a newborn with an income to match, but I don't want that dirty money."

"You think they're dirty or just cutthroat?" Loretta asked.

I shrugged. "If they put their daughters up for marriage in the name of business, I don't think they stick to a strict moral code."

"Isn't that the truth?" Darlene emphasized.

"It's worth a lot of money though, right?" Dotty asked.

I nodded. "I assume so. I've never had a thing to do with it. Besides, I'd think it would go to my mother, not me."

"Is she interested in it?" Kona asked.

"I doubt it, but we haven't talked about it. I assume my grandfather will get the board to change the bylaws and allow him to handpick his successor."

"Well," Nancy said, "if he sticks you with it, you could always sell it and find a way to do good with that money. Start making up for the negative they've put out in the world."

"Or I could ignore it and let the company self-implode," I said, grinning.

"Or you could do that indeed." Loretta stood and said, "We better get the sustenance started. And Magnolia, wait till you see dessert."

Two hours later, after a round of bacon-wrapped dates, a delicious, hearty sausage and tortellini soup, and savory ciabatta bread, Dotty brought out dessert with much fanfare.

With her back to us so I still couldn't see what it was, she stood still while Loretta...lit a match?

"You know it's not my birthday, right?" I asked.

A high-pitched sizzling sound ignited. Dotty turned around, revealing a gorgeous midnight-blue and lavender cake with a single, lit sparkler jutting out of it.

"This is a karma cake," she proclaimed.

Rosy broke out into Taylor's song again, standing and swaying her hips.

We were on our third round of Karma Fizzes, and spirits were high even before the cake, but that cake got us excited like only sugar—and karma—could. The inside was a lavender sponge with honey buttercream and ribbons of edible gold glitter throughout.

"It's perfect."

"Wait till you taste it." Dotty beamed.

Once we all had a generous slice and had quieted down enough to devour it, Loretta said, "So, Magnolia, I've seen a manly pickup truck parked outside your apartment a few times lately."

I forked a big bite of culinary perfection in my mouth, considering how to answer that.

"A manly truck like maybe a farm truck?" Rosy asked.

Loretta nodded and winked. "Definitely something a farmer would drive."

"Maybe it's a Lily Pad customer?" I offered dryly. Luke was the opposite of Dotty's paper-store customers.

The round of laughter confirmed they all knew I was joking...and guilty.

"I don't mean to pry," Loretta continued, "but if you have anything you'd like to share with us, your secrets are safe."

I swallowed my food. "It's not exactly a secret, just not something we're not broadcasting."

"You and Luke Durham?" Kona asked. "I thought you were arch enemies."

"We were." I launched into the short version of our history and my mother's visit and Felix's part in the whole thing. None of it needed to remain a secret anymore. My conscience was clear. "The only reason I'll ask you to keep it quiet for now is out of respect for Luke and his daughter. I don't know how he plans to approach that yet."

"We'll keep it to ourselves," Loretta said, and though she had a rep for being the queen of the town gossip club, I trusted her to keep her word in this case. She wasn't a mean-spirited gossip, just...*involved*. She knew everyone, worried about everyone, kept track of everything.

"So is this serious, Magnolia?" Kona asked.

I let out a nervous laugh. "It's new. It's scary because we have a history. It didn't work out before, so I'd probably be crazy to think it could this time."

"You never know till you try," Darlene said. "He's a looker. Definitely worth trying, I'd say."

"I wish you the best, darling girl," Rosy said, and the others voiced their agreement.

"Karma can be good too," Nancy pointed out. "Maybe it's coming around in your favor after dealing with that small, insecure man for most of your life."

I liked that thought but knew there was more to Luke and me working out than karma. A lot more.

Chapter Twenty-One

Luke

The Saturday before Thanksgiving, Addie and I had another daddy-daughter date night planned. Our activity this time would be making friendship bracelets.

I'd been on time tonight, in no small part due to the weather. A cold, heavy rain had been falling for the past three hours, making work miserable. The crew had finished stringing thousands of lights along the gravel road, around the parking lot, on the nearby outbuildings, and around the sections of trees that would be for sale this season. There were so many lights out there you could probably see our place from space.

These last few days before Thanksgiving would be busy as hell, but if the weather cleared up enough, we'd get it all done.

When I came inside, I found my dad sitting at the table, reading a magazine. A red meat sauce simmered on the stove, and a bowl of steaming spaghetti sat next to it on the counter.

"Hey, Dad, you okay?" I asked as I wiped the water off my face.

"Just resting," he grumbled. "Was on my feet too much today, I reckon."

Cooking didn't help, I knew. I felt bad that my dad got stuck with most of the cooking, even though he'd volunteered to take it on once his doctor ruled out heavy farm work. Between meal preparation and Addie, he had a lot to handle on top of chronic pain.

He shoved his chair back as if to get up and finish putting dinner on the table.

"I've got this, Dad. You rest."

He muttered as he stood anyway, took stuttering steps to the counter as he regained his balance, and turned the burner under the sauce off. No one ever said he wasn't stubborn.

"Go get your shower, son."

I wasn't going to eat in wet, smelly clothes, so I hurried through a shower and returned to the kitchen as he was taking garlic bread out of the oven.

"Hi, Daddy!" Addie finished setting the table and ran over to hug me.

"Hey, doodlebug. Are you ready to make friendship bracelets?"

"We have to eat first," she said as if I was an idiot.

"Of course. We need fuel to power up the friendship bracelet factory."

Once we were all sitting down and had our plates full, my dad asked about what our crew had accomplished today. We talked trees for a few minutes.

"When are we getting our Christmas tree?" Addie asked.

"We'll see when we can find time. Probably one evening after all my work is done," I told her, making a mental note to keep an eye out for a tree that would work in our usual spot in the family room.

"That would mean you can't sneak out that night," my dad said.

"I don't sneak out." I shoved a bite of spaghetti in my mouth to hide my reaction.

"Where've you been running off to every night anyway?" he asked.

"It's not every night," I said, quibbling with the unimportant part of his question. I took another bite to buy time, my thoughts spinning.

Looked like it was confession time. I was aware of Addie's eyes on me as she nibbled her bread. Presenting this so that she could understand was vital.

"I've been dating someone," I told them both.

"Who?" my dad asked.

"Magnolia James." I took another piece of bread, trying to act as if I hadn't just dropped a bomb.

I hadn't dated anyone seriously enough for Addie to know about since her mom and I split up, which had happened when she was less than a year old.

"Are you gonna get married?" Addie asked.

"We only just started dating, bug," I told her. "People usually take a long time to get to know each other before they decide to get married."

The exception seemed to be all the guys in my dads' group. They'd each met their ideal person and jumped in with both feet pretty fast. Every last one of them except for Ben had fought their feelings up to a point, but then that point hit, and they were all in: engaged, married, what have you.

Now?

I was only a week into spending time with Magnolia, but I couldn't fathom letting something come between us again. It was as if the old feelings had never gone away, even though I'd buried them with anger, and we'd cared about each other for almost two decades. At least that's how I felt. I wasn't sure she was with me on that yet, but I could be patient.

"The James girl," my dad said. "How'd you manage that? She's not exactly in the same demographic as us."

I'd never told my dad about Magnolia and me in high school, so he didn't know about our past. He was removed from town gossip for the most part as well, unless Viola Berry, who cleaned the house for us every other week, got chatty. He didn't use his phone for anything other than texting and phone calls, so he missed out on all the news, legit or not, the Tattler spread. He obviously didn't know about Magnolia and her supposed father's falling out a couple of years back.

"Her family has money, but she's estranged from them," I said, trying to keep it simple, well aware of my daughter's little ears picking up everything.

He grunted. "That's a point in her favor then. That Felix James is a—"

"Dad," I interrupted. Whatever he'd been about to say, I'd likely agree with it, but I didn't need Addie to have all kinds of conflicting ideas before she even met Magnolia. "Magnolia lives in a studio apartment above The Lily Pad and works hard building her business up. She's not like her parents."

"Can I meet her?" Addie asked.

"I'd like that," I said. "I was wondering what you two would think if we invited Magnolia to our house for Thanksgiving dinner. She's not close to her family, and I'd hate for her to spend it alone."

My dad sipped his decaf coffee and eyed me. "Correct me if I'm wrong, but I was under the impression you didn't think much of this girl."

That was an understatement, as I hadn't ever hidden my opinion from him. He'd experienced the full power of my past anger toward the James family.

I'd thought about that a lot lately. What I'd concluded, I wasn't too proud of.

All these years, I'd blamed Magnolia for my mother's downward spiral. That had been wrong for two reasons: one, Magnolia had never accused my mother of stealing her ring; therefore she wasn't responsible for my mom being fired. Two, my mom was ultimately responsible for her own mental health and wellness. She'd been wronged without a doubt, but bad things happened in life, and it was up to each of us to come out stronger after challenges. If that meant getting extra help, then that's what we had to do. Sadly, my mom hadn't found a way to do that in spite of a family who loved her and tried everything to help her. She'd refused counseling and hadn't been good about taking her medications.

"I recently learned it was all her father behind Mom's employment issues." I glanced at Addie to find her paying full attention. "I was wrong about Magnolia."

"Gotta admit it's no surprise about the father," my dad said.

"So can she, Pops?" Addie said.

"Can she what?" my dad asked.

"Can Magnolia come for Thanksgiving?"

"I got no problem with it," he said, "as long as she understands that's opening night for trees, and our day revolves around that."

"Yay!" Addie's eyes sparkled as she scooped up another bite of spaghetti and sauce.

My dad narrowed his eyes at me. "Been a good bit since you brought a woman home for dinner," my dad said.

"Been a good bit since I've liked one enough," I answered.

The truth was, I hadn't ever had feelings like this. Even Addie's mom... There'd been attraction and chemistry and eventually love, but Magnolia was different. We'd grown up together, had a special bond that I'd been stupid enough to ruin, and now we miraculously had a second chance. I wasn't going to screw it up this time. I was all in with Magnolia James.

Now I just had to hope Magnolia would get there too.

Step one was convincing her to spend the holiday with us.

Chapter Twenty-Two

Magnolia

Something I'd never told a living soul before: little kids made me nervous.

As an adult, I hadn't spent much time with them. I'd never babysat as a teenager. Basically I kept my distance whenever possible.

But here I was, on my way to have Thanksgiving dinner with Luke, his dad, and his little girl. She was six, he'd told me. First grade.

As if that gave me any context.

If I was going to be involved with Luke, his daughter was part of the package. I needed to not only get along with her but also hopefully get her to like me.

I had no idea how to do that, so I'd asked Presley for advice. She'd suggested bribery.

I'd stopped in at A Novel Place and asked Maeve for suggestions. I'd come away with two Magic Tree House books—one about Thanksgiving and one about llamas.

Armed with the books wrapped up for Addie, a box of

chocolates for Luke's dad, a dish of corn casserole, and a pecan pie—my first ever—I drove out to the farm. My fingers were crossed that the pie was edible, but I had a can of whipped cream just in case I needed to mask anything.

I was nervous enough about spending time with Luke's daughter, but on top of that, his dad would be there too. His dad, who'd been married to his mom, who my *not*-father had fired because of a blatant lie. I'd never met Luke's dad, but I really hoped he didn't hold me accountable for Felix's actions.

I knocked on the door, shaking inside with nervousness. It was cold today, so I was wearing my winter coat. I regretted that decision as I waited, sweating hard.

The door opened, and to my relief, Luke stood smiling at me.

"Hey, Mags." He pressed a quick kiss to my lips. "Happy Thanksgiving. Welcome to our humble home."

"Hi," I said on an exhale. I tried to smile, but it more than likely came out as a grimace. "I have food in the car. Oh, and happy Thanksgiving."

"Let's go get the food," he said, smiling warmly, as if he understood I was halfway to basket-case state.

He took the gifts for Addie and his dad, set them on an entry table, and followed me out. He came up beside me on the walkway, wound his arm around my waist, pulling me to his side in an awkward, moving side hug as we headed to my car to get the food.

I started babbling about the pie and how I wasn't sure if it was okay and that I had whipped cream just in case and was his dad going to hate me.

"Mags," he said as we reached the passenger door. He pressed a kiss to my temple. "My family is happy you're joining us. They're going to love you."

Possibly a lie to make me feel better, but I grasped onto it.

"I"—I opened the door, bent in, retrieved the casserole and handed it to him, then picked up the pie—"don't know the first thing about family dinners. With a real family, I mean."

A frown flitted over his features so fast I almost didn't see it. "I suspect they're a lot easier than family dinners with assholes."

I laughed in spite of myself and felt some of my tension fade.

"Addie's excited to meet you," he said. "My dad is a crusty old farmer with a soft spot for his granddaughter."

"Does he like chocolate?"

"Does it have sugar in it?"

I took that to be a rhetorical question and followed Luke inside, nervousness inching up again.

We went through a dining room into the kitchen, which smelled like an incredible Thanksgiving dinner.

"You're the sole cook?" I asked.

"Giving my dad a break from the kitchen. He's great at the day-to-day stuff, but holiday dinners have been my responsibility since my mom died. Before that, actually, because she stopped cooking several years earlier."

"Well, it smells like you know what you're doing." I couldn't hide my surprise that this hardworking, rough-handed farmer could create such heavenly aromas in the kitchen.

"Born of necessity," he said as he set the corn casserole on the counter and took the pie from me. "Our family might be nontraditional these days, but I like to make holidays as normal as possible for Addie."

As if she'd heard her name, a little girl with a brown

braid down her back came into the room. "Daddy, are we eating soon?"

"The turkey has to cook for a while yet, doodle. But..." Luke opened the refrigerator and took out a store-bought tray of cheeses and sausages. "Wash your hands, and I'll get the crackers."

Addie shot a curious smile my way before she darted out of the room.

"I'll introduce you when she gets back," he said to me.

"Where did she go?"

"To wash in the bathroom. There's a stool so she can reach."

I heard a deep, quiet voice in the other room and guessed it was Mr. Durham, which served to pump up my nerves again and remind me their gifts were still by the front door.

"Come meet my dad," Luke said nonchalantly, as if I hadn't worried about that from the moment I'd accepted his invitation.

I nodded and forced a smile. "I'll get his gift."

I went back to grab both gift bags. Luke watched me return to the kitchen from the entry, extending his arm. We walked through the dining room into the living room, where his dad sat in a recliner and Addie sneaked in behind us, looking curious but shy.

"Dad, meet Magnolia. Magnolia, my dad, Dale."

I went over to the recliner and offered my hand. "Nice to meet you, Mr. Durham."

"Likewise. Glad you could join us, Magnolia."

"This is for you." I handed him the chocolates. "And Addie, I brought you something too." I handed her the bag with llamas on it.

The little girl's brown eyes went wide and lit up. "A present?"

"What do you say?" Luke prompted.

"Thank you," Addie said. "Can I open it?"

I glanced at Luke, who said, "Go ahead."

In the meantime, Mr. Durham had rustled in his gift bag and taken out the box of gourmet chocolates.

"Oh," he said, sounding pleasantly surprised. "Thank you kindly. I might have to try a sample before dinner."

"I hope you enjoy them," I said awkwardly.

"I can promise you I will."

"My turn," Addie said, climbing into her grandpa's lap with her bag. She pulled out the tissue paper on top and handed it to him. "It's books," she said in a hushed but happy tone. "Magic Tree House! My teacher reads us those." She read the titles out loud. "We haven't read these ones yet. Look, Daddy, a llama."

"You love llamas," Luke said to Addie. He sent a smile and a wink my way.

"Thank you," Addie said shyly to me. "I'm going to start the Thanksgiving one now because it's Thanksgiving today."

"Let me know how it is," I said stupidly. I didn't know much about how fast a first grader could read, or even whether Addie was a strong enough reader to tackle the chapter books on her own.

"Dinner will be ready in a half hour," Luke said. "Mags, want to come keep me company while I finish everything up?"

"Sure." My response was possibly a little overzealous because I wasn't sure what to talk about with Mr. Durham. He seemed kind but interested in the football game on the TV.

"Pops, will you read a few chapters to me?" Addie asked.

"You know how to read," he replied.

Luke gestured to me to precede him to the kitchen as Addie pleaded with Mr. Durham to read to her anyway. Luke's hand rested at my waist, which probably looked nothing but friendly to others, but his touch shot warmth through me.

Once in the kitchen, he said, "Those went over well. Thanks for doing that."

"Icebreaker," I said, then blew out my breath. "Sorry. I've never been introduced to a guy's family before."

"You did great." He maneuvered me so my back was against the cabinet, then braced his hands on the counter on either side of me, caging me in. His gaze dipped to my mouth. Then he slowly moved in for a kiss. "That's more like it," he said when we came up for air. "Now maybe I can finish prepping dinner."

An hour later, the four of us sat around the table, overeating an impressive dinner. I hadn't realized Luke could cook, let alone prepare an entire holiday feast. The house was cozy and comfortable, with a fire crackling in the living room and two taper candles casting a warm glow on the table.

We kept up a steady conversation, with Addie filling us in on the first three chapters of the Thanksgiving book, Mr. Durham updating Luke on the football game, and Luke answering his dad's relentless questions about whether he'd remembered this or that for opening night of Christmas-tree season.

Luke patiently went over the employees who were working tonight, which I gathered were some of their long-time workers who knew what they were doing. It seemed

Amy Knupp

tonight was a warmup for the season—not their busiest by any means but steady traffic from families whose tradition was to put their tree up Thanksgiving evening. He explained for my benefit that some of the families had been cutting down their tree at the farm on the holiday for thirty years straight.

"We've got some tried-and-true regulars," Mr. Durham said. "We're proud to be part of their traditions."

"Customer loyalty means everything, doesn't it?" I said. Not that I'd know from firsthand experience, but the day I booked my first repeat customer, I'd celebrate.

"I don't imagine you get lots of repeat wedding business," Mr. Durham joked.

I laughed. "Not so far. I'm new so I don't get any repeat business yet."

"I love weddings," Addie said.

"You love Disney weddings," Luke clarified. "You haven't been to a real wedding."

"Will I get to go to Mr. West's?" his daughter asked.

"I don't know if they're inviting kids. We'll have to see," Luke said.

"My dad said maybe I could help decorate when there's a wedding in our barn," she said to me.

"Decorating is hard work," I said, "but it's fun too." I switched my focus to Luke. "I was hoping I could steal a peek at the barn today before you get too busy so I can work out more details for Presley and West."

"We can probably arrange that," Luke said.

"Can I come too?" Addie asked.

"We have to kick off tree season, doodlebug."

Her shoulders slumped as she looked at her plate.

She was a cute kid and was warming up to me slowly, which I appreciated. Presley had told me how West's

188

daughters had glommed onto her the first time they met her. It was super sweet for her, but I wasn't sure I'd know how to handle a glomming child. Maybe Addie and I were similar in our need to get acquainted gradually.

"You keep pretty busy this time of year in your business?" Mr. Durham asked.

"I've booked a few holiday parties, but I got started a little late in the year to really be swamped," I told him. "I'm getting a steady number of inquiries for weddings for next year though. I have an appointment for late next week with a famous country singer who wants me to plan her wedding."

"Yeah?" Luke said, and I heard a thread of pride in his voice, which elicited an unfamiliar feeling in me. I wasn't used to the kind of man who supported me with no ulterior motive...or at least I didn't *think* he had an ulterior motive. It wasn't unpleasant, but it would take some getting used to.

"I can't share her name," I said, "but if you like country music, you've definitely heard of her."

"Good for you," Mr. Durham said. "That oughta bring in a pretty penny."

"I think so," I agreed, "and it could be a foot in the door with the country-music world in Nashville."

"Potential gold mine," Luke said. "They'd be smart to hire you."

"Thanks. We'll see what happens. It's just a preliminary meeting."

"I hope they hire you," Addie said, her eyes sparkling.

"Me too, Addie. I'll keep you posted." I smiled across the table at her, warming up to her more quickly than I'd thought possible.

"Dinner's delicious, Luke. You outdid yourself." His

dad reached for the turkey platter and helped himself to another round.

"Thanks, Dad. The corn casserole's good stuff too, Mags," Luke said.

"We'll see if the pie holds up," I said.

"I'm sure it will." Luke took a drink of his water. "Speaking of dinner, I talked to Mrs. Haines, Dad. She's going to start bringing dinner over three nights a week for us."

Mr. Durham set his glass down hard. "We don't need Mrs. Haines bringing us dinner. Cooking's my responsibility."

"Cooking's hard on your back, Dad. This will give you a break on Mondays, Wednesdays, and Fridays."

"I didn't ask for a break."

"That's why I did it. You won't ask for a break, but I'm trying to help you."

"I don't want help, son. I'm not a useless old man to be put out to pasture."

"Nobody said you were useless, Dad."

"You take care of me, Pops," Addie said.

"That's right, and part of that is cooking," Mr. Durham said. "Addie helps me sometimes, don't you, kiddo?"

"Mm-hmm."

"This'll let you spend time on things besides cooking, like doing homework and playing games and reading Magic Tree House books," Luke said.

"I don't need any charity," the older man grumped.

I was starting to wonder if I should excuse myself to the restroom so they could finish this heated discussion. As if he sensed my discomfort, Luke flashed me a half smile of apology.

"It's not charity," he said to his father. "Let's talk about this later. I didn't mean to make Magnolia uncomfortable."

"Can Mrs. Haines bring dinner to me?" I joked, hoping to lighten the tension in the room.

"You can come out and join us anytime," Luke said.

"I was teasing," I said, but I couldn't help thinking what it would be like if family dinners like this became my normal. I almost couldn't fathom it.

Chapter Twenty-Three

Magnolia

Two hours later, after all four of us cleaned the kitchen together, Luke, Addie, and I headed to the barn so I could see his progress.

The floor had been refinished, the walls painted, the restroom fixtures were in place, and the kitchen was more than halfway done.

"It's looking fantastic, Luke," I raved. "This is going to be such a great venue."

"You think so?"

I nodded. "It's spacious but cozy, rustic but classy. The ceiling beams are stunning. Twinkle lights are going to make it magical."

"We're gonna have more twinkle lights?" Addie asked her dad.

"Magnolia thinks we should hang some from every other beam up there. What do you think, bug?"

"Yes," she said, her neck craning to check out the beams. "Can we do them now?"

Luke chuckled. "We have to open tree season in a few minutes."

"Where else will there be twinkle lights?" Addie asked.

Luke raised his brows at me, as if deferring to my answer. Before I could say anything, his phone dinged with a notification. He pulled it out, swiped, and read a message. He typed an answer.

"Everything okay?" I asked, seeing his frown.

"It will be, but I need to go help Scotty with something."

"Would you mind if I stay a few more minutes and take some measurements?" I asked him.

"Stay as long as you like. If you're still here when we close up, I'll treat you to a hot chocolate."

"Can I stay with Miss Magnolia?" Addie asked.

The question that would've panicked me a few hours ago didn't seem as daunting now. Addie was growing on me quickly with her quiet but enthusiastic ways.

"She and I could figure out where else to put twinkle lights," I told Luke.

He studied me. "You're sure?"

"You want to do that?" I asked his daughter.

She nodded fervently. "Please, Daddy?"

"I should be able to get back here to get her before we officially open up."

"That's fine. We can talk weddings, right, Addie?"

"Right." Her eyes sparkled.

Luke met my gaze as if searching for a sign that I was really okay with this. I gave him a subtle nod.

"I'll be back in a few minutes, doodlebug." He kissed the top of his daughter's head, then caught my hand briefly and squeezed. It was a fleeting touch that made me want more. More time with him, more touching. But for now I could hang out with Addie and maybe even come up with new ideas for Presley.

"Text me if you need anything in the meantime," he told me, then jogged out of the barn.

Addie looked up at me expectantly.

"So," I said, nervous again. "Twinkle lights. The trick is to use just the right amount—not too many and not too few."

"So that's how come you want them on every other beam instead of every one?" she asked.

"Exactly. Let's go to the other end, and I'll tell you our plans for Miss Presley's wedding."

We started across the wood floors, with Addie at my side. I was surprised to feel her take my hand in her small one. When I glanced down and smiled, she said, "It's kind of scary in here at night."

"It'll be much better when it's full of happy people celebrating a wedding, don't you think?"

She thought about that for a second. "Yeah."

I hadn't bargained for a scared little girl and once again, or maybe still, felt out of my element. I'd spent a lot of time during my childhood alone and scared, particularly during storms. It always helped me when I had something to distract me, so that's what I set out to do for Addie.

"Miss Presley's wedding is going to be on Christmas Eve, and it's going to be beautiful," I told her. "It'll be a small wedding party, with two bridesmaids and two groomsmen."

"How many flower girls?"

"Three. I bet you know Mr. West's girls: Nova, Scarlet, and Sienna?"

She nodded. "They're the flower girls?" There was some low-key awe in her voice.

"They're the flower girls. I believe they'll be wearing sparkly silver dresses."

"Wow," she said in a hushed voice.

"The bridesmaids are wearing dark green, the color of Christmas trees."

"That will be beautiful," she said.

When we got to the wide end of the barn, I explained my idea for clusters of real trees with twinkle lights. We agreed that the windows should be outlined in twinkle lights as well.

I told her about the arch her dad planned to build and how that would be the spot where Presley and West exchanged their vows.

"Will it have twinkle lights too?" she asked.

I shook my head. "I was thinking bunches of white flowers. I want it to be pretty, but I don't want lights to take away from the bride and groom."

"Miss Presley's so pretty," she said.

"Yes, she is."

"So are you."

"Aw, thank you, Addie. You are too."

"I made a wish that my dad would get married so he could live happily ever after."

"That's sweet of you."

"I asked if he could marry you, but he said it takes a long time for people to decide who to marry."

"It's a big decision," I blustered, trying not to show any reaction even as I reeled inside.

Luke and I had been together for less than a month. We were a long way from getting married, but this was one of those damned-if-you-do, damned-if-you-don't topics. If I told her I wasn't thinking about marrying her dad, she might take that the wrong way. If I told her I might marry him someday, just to appease her, she might take it to heart and start planning *our* wedding.

Instead of answering either way, I made my reply about her. "I hope you get your wish someday."

I didn't allow myself to think about whether I wanted it to be with me. Marriage? I wanted it someday, but my focus right now was learning to stand on my own two feet, personally and in my business.

* * *

Luke

On Thanksgiving night, we were open from six to nine every year. We did enough business to make it well worth opening up on a holiday evening, and tonight was no exception.

At quarter till six, I'd been about to run over to the barn to get Addie when two of our regular families had pulled up. Since my skeleton holiday crew was out taking care of last-minute tasks, I'd texted Magnolia to bring Addie over whenever she was ready to go home.

She'd walked into the sales shelter holding my daughter's hand, and that vision had rocked me to my core and had me thinking about families.

That was premature, but something about seeing the two of them together made it easy to imagine a future with her. She might not believe she had any kind of knack with kids, but my daughter willingly holding her hand was proof otherwise. If Addie was drawn to her, that told me volumes.

Yeah, dude. Rushing it.

My premature fantasy had been helped along when Magnolia had asked if she could stay and help for a while. I got the impression she wasn't looking forward to heading home to her empty apartment, but I would've said yes no matter what. I loved that she showed interest in my family's business.

We ended up being short-handed due to the busiest Thanksgiving we'd had in recent years, so Magnolia's help collecting payment was appreciated. My dad showed up right at six, determined to defy his doctor's orders of no hard labor. Same story, different year. Having Magnolia there asking him questions as she learned served to deter him from helping me wrap trees and load them on vehicles.

Another reason it was good having her there was because he was still pissy about the cooking thing and snapped at me every time we were in close proximity.

At nine, we had two parties still out searching for their trees, so I'd asked my dad to take Addie in so she could get her pajamas on. That he'd agreed quickly told me he was indeed tired and had likely overdone it.

As Addie hugged Magnolia goodbye, my dad whispered to me, "Are we still putting the tree up when you're done?"

I nodded to make sure Addie hadn't heard since it was a surprise I'd engineered in the last two days. I'd marked the tree I wanted, and Scotty had cut it yesterday and put it in a stand in one of the outbuildings so it was ready for us to bring into the house and decorate.

My dad told Magnolia goodbye for show. I could easily tell he liked her because he was sugar sweet to her, in total contrast with his attitude toward me. That man could hold a heck of a grudge.

As soon as my dad and daughter were out of sight, I moved in on Magnolia and kissed her like I'd been dying to for the past three hours. Within seconds I had her pressed against the inside wall of the sales shelter as we waited for the last two stragglers to bring their trees up.

"Hello, sexy boyfriend," she said when we came up for air.

"I needed that," I said. "So I've got a question for you. Are you sick of my family, or would you like to stay and help us decorate our tree tonight?"

Chapter Twenty-Four

Magnolia

The difference between my family and Luke's was once again front and center as Luke and I made our way to the house, with him carrying a large Christmas tree and me opening doors for him.

In my family, we'd hired people to decorate our assortment of artificial trees so they'd be showpieces for my parents' holiday parties.

In Luke's family, decorating the tree was a special occasion that Addie was being allowed to stay up late for, the perfect ending to the very best Thanksgiving I'd ever had. Not that there was a lot of competition for that title...

We stopped outside the door to the house so Luke could text his dad to make sure he had Addie in the living room. As soon as he got a response, I opened the door and followed Luke and the tree inside.

"You're still here!" Addie said when I entered the living room first.

"I'm still here," I said, smiling.

The next moment was one I wouldn't soon forget. As Luke came through the doorway carrying the tree as if it weighed nothing, Addie's entire face lit up and she sucked in her breath, her mouth gaping open. In her earnest face I saw glimmers of the magic of the holidays. Excitement. Love. Anticipation. Pure joy.

"We're doing it tonight?" she asked in a hushed voice.

"We're doing it tonight," Luke confirmed.

"Miss Magnolia's staying?" she verified.

"Is that okay with you?" I asked her, hoping for her approval in a way I'd not known was possible.

"Yes!" Addie ran to me and hugged my legs.

My eyes inexplicably teared up as I bent down to hug her and hide the impact her acceptance had on me. I'd had no idea a child could affect me this way. I couldn't explain it other than...she was Luke's daughter. That meant everything.

"Are you too tired to do this tonight?" Luke teased his daughter. "We can wait till later."

"I'm never too tired for Christmas trees!" Addie said, jumping up and down.

"I hope your enthusiasm remains when you're old enough to work the tree farm with me," Luke said.

"She'll be the best worker we've had for years," Luke's dad said from his recliner.

I walked closer to Mr. Durham. "Are you okay with me joining your family tonight?" I asked him quietly as Addie helped Luke lug in the boxes of ornaments.

The older man chuckled. "Rather have you than my hardheaded son, to be frank."

"Well, lucky you, you get both of us." I squeezed his arm affectionately.

"You're okay, Miss Magnolia," he said, his eyes sparkling with kindness.

When Luke asked him if he was going to help with the lights though, his father grumbled, "You can handle it without me."

Between Luke, Addie, and me, we wrapped so many strings of colored lights around the tree that I wasn't sure how we'd fit on any ornaments.

While we'd been wrangling lights, Mr. Durham had sneaked out to the kitchen and popped popcorn for all of us. We took a few minutes to stuff some in our mouths. It'd been a long time since our huge Thanksgiving dinner.

"You must be famished," I said to Luke as Addie skipped over to the ornament boxes and started digging through them.

As he chewed, his eyes lit up, and he roved his gaze slowly down my body. "Famished. Yes, I am," he said in a low promise of a voice.

"Your muscles must ache too," I said, making sure the other two weren't paying attention to us.

His brows went up, and he nodded.

I moved even closer and said in his ear, "If you follow me home later, I'll give you a full-body rubdown."

Luke kissed me, tasting like salt and man, then raised his head and mouthed, "Hell yes."

That's all it took for my body to react, anticipating when we'd be alone in my apartment.

"I found it," Addie called out.

Luke wiped off his hands and went toward Addie and the ornament stash. "Your baby ornament?"

Addie held up a kitten with a little plaque that said Baby's First Christmas.

"That's so cute," I said, coming closer to look at it. "It must be getting pretty old if it's as old as you."

"Not as old as my daddy's," she said, giggling.

Luke pulled out one with a teddy bear in a Santa hat with a candy cane. It too said Baby's First Christmas, but it was indeed showing its age.

"I love that you still have those," I said. There'd not been any decorations in the James house celebrating *my* first Christmas, which was just as well. I didn't really want any family souvenirs from my childhood.

Addie attached a hook to her ornament, then carried it over to me. "Will you hang this up really high for me, Miss Magnolia? It has to go up first."

"Your ornament goes up first?" I repeated, glancing over at Luke.

"Tradition," he said. "Are you sure you don't want to hang it yourself, bug?"

"This time I want Miss Magnolia to do it. Real high up."

"I can't get it quite as high as your daddy can," I told her. "You want him to do it?"

She shook her head. "You."

"Okay." Again, I looked over at Luke, whose smile was swoony and full of affection.

I hung the ornament on the highest branch I could reach, earning applause from Addie.

"That looks real good," Mr. Durham said from his chair.

"Are you going to hang your favorite one, Dad?" Luke asked him.

The older man's face flipped to a frown. "Addie can do it this year," he grumped.

That there was friction between father and son was obvious. Still left from the cooking argument at dinner?

Luke shrugged and rifled through the ornaments until he found an antique-looking, breakable ornament of a bride and groom. He handed it to Addie.

"Where do you want yours and Gran's hung, Pops?" she asked.

"Wherever you think it would look nice," he told her, just as laidback as could be—in absolute contrast to his tone with Luke.

Luke didn't let it bother him as he unwrapped and unpacked the ornaments one by one and handed them to me and Addie to hang. She covered the lower branches, and I did my best to fill the top ones.

When we finished overstuffing the tree with years' worth of ornaments, most of them attached to memories, we turned out all the lights except the ones on the tree. Mr. Durham remained in his recliner. Luke and I sat on the sofa with Addie cuddled between us at her insistence, with instrumental holiday music playing quietly in the background.

I listened as the three of them reminisced about holidays past, from the time when Addie was three years old and Santa brought her a Barbie condo that was taller than her and had her in wide-eyed awe, to a Christmas from Luke's childhood when his mom had insisted on having a live Christmas tree in every room in the house. Even with the tension between Luke and his dad, there was so much love and care among the three of them.

This was how it should be.

This was what the holiday season should be about. Family, memories, love, togetherness.

I was too afraid to think about the future, to wish for something like this to be mine beyond right now, but I sure could soak it in while I had it.

When the conversation slowed down, Mr. Durham put his recliner upright and eased himself to the edge. "I'm gonna hit the hay, kids," he said, then slowly stood.

"Night, Pops," Addie said, sounding drowsy.

Luke and I told him good night as well.

"Good night, everyone." He shuffled off toward his room. His shoulders were hunched, but I could still tell he was extra worn out, probably from helping with trees.

"Pops is tired," Addie said as she leaned her head on Luke's chest. He brushed his fingers through her hair repeatedly in a slow, mesmerizing rhythm.

"He worked too hard tonight," Luke said.

"He loved being a part of it though," I said.

"Yeah." Luke frowned.

I was starting to understand the dynamics between them. His dad wasn't allowed to do the things he'd always done, and that had to be hard for the older man, but it was also difficult for Luke to watch. I felt for both of them.

A few minutes later, Luke stirred. I realized Addie was sound asleep.

"I'm going to put her to bed," he whispered, then picked her up and carried her off to her room.

I pulled my knees up and hugged them into my chest as I gazed at the tree. It was homey and beautiful in a very different way than the James household trees used to be. They'd been designer trees, with color schemes and themes and perfection.

This one was a hodgepodge of colors, Durham family milestones, love, and hundreds of lights. I stood to look more closely at the ornaments. Addie had mentioned one from Luke's childhood, something he'd made in preschool. I found it and grinned at the photo of Luke as a little kid.

He'd written *Ho, ho, ho* on the laminated construction paper and drawn a candy cane on each side of his pic.

"Hey," Luke said as he came back into the room. When he saw what I was looking at, he shook his head with an embarrassed smile. "Don't look at that."

"You drew a mean candy cane back in the day."

He came up behind me and wound his arms around me, peering at the ornament over my shoulder. "I was so proud to give that to my parents."

"I'm sure they loved it."

I didn't remember whether I'd had a similar project. If so, the ornament definitely had not been preserved and kept through the years. I knew now that was a reflection of my parents, not me. Their loss.

"So what was up with your dad tonight?" I asked.

Luke let out a slow, frustrated breath. "Pretty sure he's mad about Mrs. Haines cooking."

I frowned. "Why?"

"Because he's a stubborn old man who's still upset about his back."

"Which is why he can't work the farm anymore, right?"

"Right. He's in constant pain. Doesn't complain about it. I've wondered how many years he was uncomfortable before it got so bad he couldn't ignore it anymore."

"He's a tough guy," I said.

"He is. Typical farmer. He'd rather work the land until he keels over."

"So you're paying your neighbor to cook for your family?"

"Mrs. Haines is an old-school farm wife who cooks like a dream. She's actually the one who suggested the agreement. I had to argue with her just to get her to accept money to cover the ingredients. She wouldn't hear of me paying her extra for her labor."

"She sounds like a gem."

"She is."

I hesitated before asking, "Do you want my opinion?"

"Sure," he said, sounding anything but sure.

I turned around to face him, weaving our fingers together between us. "Your dad's whole purpose was taken from him when he had to quit farming. He still needs to feel useful though, and cooking might serve that purpose for him."

"Sure, but working in the kitchen is hard on his back too. He'd never complain about it, but he sits down to rest whenever he can."

"And then he gets back up and finishes?"

He nodded.

"So you're looking out for him."

"Yeah," he said. "Of course. I hate to think of him hurting all the time."

"I agree, but what if you think of it like he might be hurting in other ways besides just physical?"

"I can't help his emotional pain, and he won't see a therapist about it. I tried several times."

"Your intentions are admirable."

He raised his brows as if waiting for me to say more.

"Your goal is to help him, but what if cooking and caring for Addie are the purposes that keep him getting out of bed in the morning?"

"Maybe they are, but if he doesn't take care of his physical body, he won't be able to cook or look after Addie or get out of bed at all. Then where will we be?"

I took both his hands. "Luke, you're a problem-solver. A

fixer. Even back in high school, you wanted to help me find volunteer opportunities to show people I wasn't so mean."

He smiled. "Problem-solving is what I do. It's how I'm wired."

"And I love that about you. It's a wonderful trait to have. But this thing with your dad, it's not just about you, you know? Maybe this is one of the times when you have to reel yourself in and let him do what he needs to do. Cooking but not farming."

"Maybe," he said with a shrug.

"Will you think about it?" I asked.

He peered down at me, his eyes sparking with heat even as he said, "I'll think about it." Then he kissed me.

When we came up for air, I said, "Nice diversion tactic."

"I thought so." We kissed a few more times. Then he said, "How about if I follow your pretty little rear end to your apartment and divert you for hours? How's that for problem solving?"

My body responded with a telling ache deep inside. "In my opinion, that's the very best kind."

Chapter Twenty-Five

Magnolia

I guess you could say Luke and I had officially gone public with our relationship tonight.

"That was like a who's who of Dragonfly Lake," Luke said happily as we walked from Humble's Pizza to my business.

"I've never seen it so crowded." Ava, Cash, and Bronte were there with Holden, Chloe, and Sutton. Anna, Maeve, and Olivia had been sitting at the bar. Ben, Emerson, and their four kids had been in the large corner booth. We'd known more than half the customers, and we'd made it no secret that Luke and I were together.

"Buy-one-get-one pie night is a success, I'd say." Luke's arm was around me, his heat welcome in the cold December air.

He'd come over almost every night since Thanksgiving so we could spend a few hours together. He made a point of sleeping at home though, not wanting Addie to need him in the middle of the night and find him gone. He was burning the candle at both ends between tree season, the last projects on the barn, and spending time with his daughter. As much as I loved our time together, I'd told him I didn't want him to feel obligated to come over. He'd said our hours together were his favorite part of the day. Based on the fact we spent almost all those hours in my bed, I tended to believe him. The sex between us was incomparable to anything in my past, and he claimed the same.

Our hours together weren't just about the physical stuff. That was just where we started and often where we ended a night together. In between, we talked, we laughed, sometimes we cooked or baked a snack. He told me about his day-to-day. I shared what was going on in my business and life. So far we seemed to connect on a level I'd never known was possible. Did I worry that it was too good to be true? As much as I tried to just enjoy it, I couldn't deny it was hard for me to believe this was my life, and I was this lucky.

"So what the hell do you think your mom wants?" he asked me as we passed Earthly Charm. Though they were closed, the lights in the back room were on, telling me Cambria was probably making more candles in preparation for their upcoming open house and Presley's wedding.

"I've been asking myself that since she texted this morning. I have no idea. Maybe an update on her health?" I'd tried to get more information from her, but she'd told me she didn't want to discuss it through texts.

"You think it could be bad news?"

I shrugged. "I guess we'll find out soon enough."

"What if she doesn't want me there?" he asked.

"Too bad. She's the one barging into one of our few precious date nights outside of my apartment."

"Our only date night out of bed so far," he said, grinning like he wasn't too upset about any of it.

"We had Thanksgiving," I pointed out.

"Where we ended up in your bed."

"I'm hoping we end up in my bed tonight too."

He kissed my temple as we turned down the sidewalk to the Moments door. "Your wish is my command, milady."

I laughed and unlocked the door. Inside, the neon sign that burned twenty-four seven was the only illumination. The inner room was dark, and I kept it that way, deciding the best place for the three of us to meet was in this outer one, where there were a sofa and two armchairs. I flipped on the cozy floor lamp by the sofa.

"I'm going to need a glass of wine for this," I said, shedding my coat. "Would you like one?"

"If you still don't have whiskey." Luke seemed to have tensed up since we arrived.

I poured two glasses of red, handed him one, and stretched up to kiss him. "Are you okay?" I asked.

"I don't trust her."

"I don't either, but I don't think she intends to hurt me now."

"She'll have to deal with me if she does," he said, and I had to admit the caveman stance was hot, even if not necessary.

The door opened, and my mother stepped in, her gaze darting between Luke and me. "Hello."

"Come in," I said, noticing the shadows under her eyes. When she glanced at Luke again, I said, "This is Luke. Whatever you want to say to me, he can hear too."

She paused for a few seconds as if considering that, then nodded. "Hello, Luke." She shrugged her coat off.

"Ma'am," he said.

"You can call me Bianca."

His only response was a single nod.

"Would you like a drink?" I asked her.

"Just water. I started treatment last week."

"How's that going?" I asked, wondering again if her health was what brought her here. I pulled out a bottle of water from the minifridge and handed it to her as the three of us sat, Luke and me in the chairs and my mother on one end of the sofa.

"Not bad so far." She briefly explained her prognosis and treatment plan. They'd apparently caught it early, so her doctors were optimistic. "Thanks for asking," she said, "but that's not what I came to discuss." She scooted to the front edge of the sofa and set her bottle down. "Your grandfather had a heart attack Monday, Magnolia. They say he died instantly."

I sat back in my chair, not having expected that news at all. I said the first thing that came to mind. "Less than a month after he fired Felix? Are they sure it was natural causes?"

"You think like I do," my mother said, which I didn't necessarily take as a compliment. "I met with his lawyer today. They believe he'd been having small heart attacks for about a week beforehand, but he ignored them."

I could feel Luke watching me. I glanced over and made eye contact. His brows shot up as if asking if I was okay.

"No love lost for him," I explained, and he nodded, not seeming surprised at all.

"He wasn't an easy man to love," my mom said. "My conversation with him about Felix, however, seemed to propel him to make some changes. Dave, his lawyer, laid out everything during our meeting. Bottom line? You and I are now co-owners of Lansford Development."

"What?" I said, making a face. "I don't want it. I've never wanted it."

"Something else we have in common then," my mother said. "I don't want the godforsaken company either, but here we are."

"Uh, what did he think we'd do with it?" I asked. "I have my own business now. Even if I *was* interested, which I can't imagine being in this lifetime or the next, my responsibilities lie elsewhere."

"Dave said the second-in-command automatically slid to an interim CEO position, and he's got things handled for now. We've got time to figure it out. The lawyer's suggestion is to sell it. He says it's worth a fortune. For once in my life, I have no interest in or need for his money."

I eyed my mother, gauging her sincerity.

She met my gaze. "That man represents greed, misogyny, and a power complex."

"I agree completely. I sure don't want his money." I'd benefited from Lansford money for most of my life. Those were miserable years. What I'd learned was that I didn't need all the material things. People were more important. Good people.

"What if you sold it and did something good with the money?" Luke suggested, reminding me of Nancy's suggestion at the karma party. "To counteract all the bad crap. Money can do a lot of evil in the wrong hands, but you two seem aligned on this."

"What would we do with it?" I asked.

He shrugged. "You could donate it to a cause that's important to you or even start some kind of charitable foundation."

My mother and I looked at each other and shrugged.

"I guess we could," I said. "I'd have to think hard about what to support."

My mother nodded. "If we can't close down the

company or give it away, that might be the best option. I went to dozens of benefits over the years and volunteered for a handful. It was more about having something to do with my time than feeling a burning passion inside about whatever they stood for."

That and being seen and finding the perfect gown and being decked out in expensive jewelry, I knew. I wasn't casting stones, because I'd valued the wrong things too.

"What about Grandfather's estate?" I asked.

"He left everything else to me. I'm planning to sell his house."

"And money?"

"Same story, Magnolia. I know it's hard to believe, but I don't want it. What I want for the rest of my life, which I hope is a lot of years yet, is health, happiness, and peace."

"Did the lawyer tell you what the next steps would be if you decide to sell the company?" Luke asked her.

"He just said to call him, and he could guide us. He has a team he recommends to help us. People who specializes in that kind of thing." She shrugged. "We didn't go deep. I'm still shocked by all of it, his death included. I thought he'd be around forever, like a Twinkie."

"Except Twinkies are sweet," I said distractedly. "Do you have a favorite cause or ideas about what you'd want to do with the proceeds if we sell?"

She shook her head. "With the amount it would gener-ate, that becomes a very big question. Would we want to spread the wealth and support multiple good causes? Would we want to each choose one and split it?"

"That calls for a lot of thought," Luke said, "since neither of you have a particular organization in mind."

"Right." I leaned forward, ready to get back to my evening with Luke. My mind was swimming. I needed time to absorb this news, and I sure needed to consider all our options. "Is there anything else from the meeting with Dave I need to know?" I asked my mom.

"Those are the main points. I wanted to let you know as soon as I could. I didn't figure you were too attached to your grandfather—"

"You were correct," I interrupted.

"There won't be a funeral, per his wishes," she continued. "Thank God for that."

"I can't imagine many would show up. Only the butt kissers who want a piece of what he had." I stood. Luke and my mother followed suit.

"The vultures," Luke said, and I nodded.

"Thank you for meeting with me on such short notice," my mother said. "I'm sorry to interrupt your evening."

She looked exhausted. I wasn't sure if it was from her health situation, the news of her father's death, or both.

"Are you living here in town?" I asked her.

"In Nashville. I'm close to my doctor and treatment."

"Are you okay to drive back tonight?" I wasn't sure why I asked. Call me selfish, but I had no intention of letting her interfere with any more of our date. I didn't owe her a single thing, but I also didn't want her to fall asleep on the drive home.

"It's been a day," she said. "I planned to drive back home, but everything's catching up with me. I think I'll get a room and stay the night here."

"That's probably best," I said, starting toward the door to see her out.

"Where are you parked?" Luke asked her.

"I found a spot behind the hardware store."

"I'll walk you to your car," he said.

"That's kind of you, Luke. Thank you." My mom drank the rest of her water, then pulled her coat on.

"Just leave the bottle on the table," I told her. "I'll clean up while you're gone, Luke." I purposely didn't let her know he and I planned to walk to my apartment next. I'd made a point of not telling her where I lived, and I intended to keep it that way.

She could tell me she'd changed all she wanted, but it would take a lot for me to be able to trust my mother.

Luke

It was cold and dark out, but the sidewalks weren't deserted. Several stores stayed open late for holiday shoppers, and the bars and restaurants kept people coming and going.

"Do you know where you're staying yet?" I asked Magnolia's mother, just to make conversation.

"Maybe the Honeysuckle Inn."

"There's the Marks now too," I said, thinking the high-dollar hotel seemed more her style than the quaint, comfortable inn.

"Oh, I remember hearing about that opening a year or two back. That's a good suggestion. Thank you."

We walked in silence past Oopsie Daisies and the gym. As we turned toward the parking lot, she said, "What are your intentions with my daughter, Luke?"

The question caught me off guard for several reasons, not the least of which was I wasn't convinced she gave even half a shit about Magnolia's life.

"We're taking things one day at a time," I said curtly. "I could ask you the same."

Her step momentarily slowed, just enough for me to notice. "I guess that's a fair question," she said quietly. "I'm sure she's told you I'm a terrible mother."

"Not in those exact words."

"I don't want anything from Magnolia," she eventually said. "Well, that's not entirely true. I'd like very much to have some kind of relationship with her. I know," she said before I could tell her the odds of that. "I don't deserve it, and I'm not expecting it." We stepped off the curb into the parking lot. "I don't have a hidden agenda. I'm too damn tired for any more games in my life. But if I could have the chance to get to know her, that would mean the world to me."

Either she was one hell of an actress or that quaver in her voice was real emotion. It wasn't my place to soften toward this woman though. I only wanted to protect Magnolia.

"You're not going to lie to her or use her?" I asked.

"No."

"How do I know that's true?"

"I guess you'll have to trust me."

I shook my head. "That's not happening. If you hurt her again, Bianca, you'll answer to me."

We arrived at a Lexus SUV, where she hit the key fob and unlocked the door. She turned to face me.

"Look, Luke, I understand why you doubt me." She blew out a nervous laugh. "I was not a good person, let alone a good mother. I can't promise that I'll do much better now, but the one thing I can say is my *intentions*, to use my own word, are to do better. I might not have much time left on this earth. There's no way I could make up for the pain I've caused my daughter in the past. But I assure you my goal is to *not* cause her more pain."

I stared at her, looking for any kind of a tell that she was lying. She held my gaze steadily.

"I can tell you care about her," she said, burrowing deeper into her coat as a gust of wind blew through. "She needs someone who has her best interests at heart because God knows Felix and I failed at that."

"Yes, you did."

"Well, thank you for looking out for her."

I bit down on the shitty things I could say on the slim chance she'd genuinely changed. "Good night, Bianca."

"Good night, Luke."

As I walked away, it hit me that she wasn't the only one who'd caused Magnolia pain in the past. I was just as guilty of it. I'd apologized. Magnolia's mother had done the same. If anyone should be able to give her a second chance, it should be me. And maybe I would someday.

But for now, Magnolia needed someone in her corner, someone to look out for her. She'd never had someone to do that, but now she had me.

Chapter Twenty-Six

Magnolia

I'd been looking forward to Rowan's mini girls' night all day, but now that it was time to head over there, I thought hard about canceling.

It was going on seven o'clock Friday evening, and I was fuming. I wouldn't be good company. Rowan's three-month-old daughter would probably sense my emotions and fuss all night just from my energy being in the same room.

I had my phone out, ready to text Rowan, when it occurred to me that staying home would be a victory for Felix. His entire point was to ruin my life some more. So I didn't text Rowan. Instead I brushed my hair, pulled a thick sweatshirt on, grabbed my keys, and headed out.

In the Cordovas' driveway, I sat in my car for a few minutes, coaching myself to shake it off. I forced myself to smile, hoping it would lighten my tension, then climbed out.

"Magnolia, come on in," Rowan said when she opened the door for me. Lilah Rose was asleep on Rowan's shoulder, looking angelic and peaceful.

"Ahh," I breathed out. "I need this so bad." I smiled at Rowan, and it came out a little more naturally.

"Baby time?" Rowan asked. "Would you like to hold her?"

"I should probably calm down a little more before I try holding your daughter," I said. "But just seeing her precious little self so content is a good start."

No, I hadn't morphed into a big fan of kids and babies after a holiday and a couple of evenings with Addie, but something about the inherent trust and comfort of Lilah Rose worked its way into my heart. It was impossible to want to injure my *not*-father while watching the baby sleep.

"What's going on?" Rowan asked as she led me to the family room in the back of the house. "Are you okay?"

"As Presley would say, Felix the Fuck is at it again." I glanced at the baby. "Oops, sorry."

"Considering the fact that I've never heard you drop an f-bomb, you get a pass," Rowan said.

"Magnolia used the f-word?" Presley asked as we went down the single step to the sunken room. "What's going on?"

"Do you need a drink?" Chloe asked.

"More than air," I said. "If we're doing drinks." I glanced at Chloe, who was in her first trimester of pregnancy.

She held up a beautiful martini glass with a thick, creamy beverage and red, green, and white sugared rim. "Sugar cookie martinis. Mine's a virgin."

"Virgins for me too," Rowan said, pointing at her daughter, who I knew she was nursing. "But for you and Presley, full-strength vanilla vodka and amaretto."

"Sounds delicious. If you don't have whiskey," I joked, remembering Luke's same words.

Rowan put her daughter into the bouncy seat, then went to the kitchen, which had a cut-out to the room we were in.

"Sit down and start talking," Presley said, patting the sofa next to her. "This sounds serious."

"I didn't mean to come in and highjack the party," I said.

Chloe waved off my objection. "What's going on, Magnolia?"

I curled into the corner of the sofa opposite Presley, hugging a throw pillow to my chest. "So you can't mention the name outside of this room, just because it's business."

Chloe and Presley nodded as Rowan came back into the room with my festive martini.

"Last week I got a call from Ella McCabe's personal assistant to set up an initial consultation for her wedding."

"Ella McCabe? The singer?" Presley practically bellowed in surprise.

"That's amazing," Chloe said.

"I was stunned but so excited," I said.

"I don't like the past tense," Rowan pointed out.

"Our appointment was today at four. Her assistant, Allegra, left a message canceling it midafternoon."

"Why did she cancel?" Presley asked.

"She didn't say, and I didn't get the message until right at four because I had another appointment before that. So I called Allegra and left a message asking her the reasons, wondering if I could've done anything differently. She actually called me back at almost six o'clock and was super nice and understanding."

"So what was the reason?"

"Apparently Ella's father is a business associate of Felix. Felix warned him against me. It took me a bit to convince her to tell me more of what he said, but she finally did. He told her father I'm mentally unstable and that I miss deadlines and have no respect for budgets."

"What?" Rowan exclaimed. "Those are blatant lies."

I shrugged, even though I was anything but nonchalant. "Her dad forwarded the lies to Ella." I swallowed, fighting back the urge to cry. When I'd hung up with Allegra, I'd gone straight to screaming mad.

"What did you say to the assistant?" Chloe asked.

"I was so stunned I kind of faltered, then told her Felix James has it in for me. I didn't think it was appropriate to lay all my family drama on her."

Chloe nodded. "That would come across as unprofessional."

"Exactly," I said. "It's one thing to want the people of this town to find out the truth, since they've known my family all along and lumped me in with my jerky parents. It's quite another to have a complete stranger who wants to do business with me learning the craziness I was raised in."

"I agree with that. Felix the Fuck is the unprofessional one but he's trying to bring you down with him," Presley said, then looked at the baby, whose eyes were now closed. "I'll stop swearing before she turns one, Rowan, I promise."

"I have faith in you," Rowan said, shaking her head and grinning. "So what are you going to do?" she asked me.

"I'm going to drink this pretty cocktail and buy a voodoo doll with Felix's name on it," I said.

"I support all of that," Presley said. "I'm so sorry, hon."

"That man needs to burn in hell," Chloe said, "sooner rather than later."

"I'm for it," I said. "I really thought this could be a foot in the door with the country-music world, you know?"

"It could've been," Chloe said.

"Is there really nothing you can do?" Rowan asked.

I lifted my drink. "Drink heavily?"

Presley lifted hers too. "I'm here for you." We both sipped. "I'm sorry, Magnolia. I'm furious on your behalf."

I nodded, taking another swallow of my drink that turned out to be absolutely delicious. "Subject closed. No more talk about that worthless worm who is *not* my father, thank all the gods ever in existence."

"Yes, I'm glad you vented to us, Magnolia. He's a piece of dog doo who doesn't deserve any more of our girls' night," Rowan said. "Presley, The Bean Counter was packed the other day when I stopped by before work."

"Same thing every time I went this week," Chloe said, "which, come to think of it, was pretty much every day. You're killing it, my friend."

"It's going better than I even hoped for," Presley said. "And thank you for supporting us."

"It's not out of the goodness of my heart," Chloe said. "It's just good coffee. I don't know how we lived before."

"My favorite is the gingerbread latte," Rowan said. "With real whipped cream."

Talk shifted to Presley's wedding for a few minutes, and then when Luke's name came up regarding the barn, Rowan said, "Speaking of Luke..." She turned her head very deliberately to me. "Word on the street is that you and he are an official thing. Like, out in public, seen holding hands, all the things. You've been holding out on us."

"Luke and I...are an official thing," I said, shrugging but unable to keep a big smile off my face. "It's early days, and he's so busy right now that our time together is never long enough, but...yeah. It's good so far."

"I never thought I'd see the day," Chloe said. "There was *so much* tension between you two."

"You know what they say about love and hate," Presley said.

Rowan grinned and nodded. "So you can put all that pent-up emotion for...how long did you hate him?"

"We had a falling out when I was seventeen," I said.

"That's a *lot* of pent-up emotion to put into sexy times," Rowan said.

"And a lot of time to make up for," I said. "And we're trying." I told them how he invited me for dinner a few times and how he visited me several nights a week after Addie went to bed.

Rowan brought out a tray of finger foods—mozzarella-stuffed pretzel bites and ham-and-cheese biscuit bites—and we covered a bunch of topics, like where their guys were tonight, Chloe's Thanksgiving with all the Norths and all the Henrys at Faye and Simon Henry's new lake house, and Presley's soon-to-be stepdaughters' brand-new bedrooms in her home.

"How's your mom doing, Magnolia?" Rowan asked. "Have you heard from her?"

"Oh," I said, sitting up straighter and taking a large gulp of martini number two. "Are you guys sick of my drama yet? Because there's more."

"Not sick of it at all," Presley said. "There's more since Felix got booted?"

"You're looking at the new owner of Lansford Development."

"Uh, Magnolia? You didn't lead with that?" Chloe asked. "What the hell?"

"You own a bajillion-dollar company? Right now?" Presley asked.

"Well, half of it," I said flippantly. Because I might be the owner, but I hadn't taken ownership of any of it, and I had no intention of doing so. "My grandfather died of a heart attack Monday. He apparently changed everything in his will and in the company after my mom told him she was divorcing Felix."

"To make you the owner of a company you have no interest in," Presley clarified.

"With my mother who I have no relationship with." I drank more, craving the thick, creamy sweetness.

"Does she want it?"

I laughed. "Not even a little bit."

"This is so out there," Rowan said. "If you made it into a movie, people would say it's too farfetched."

"Welcome to my family," I said.

"So what does this mean for you?" Chloe asked. "Are you going to get involved in the day-to-day?"

I shook my head. "We're going to sell it. I don't even know how that works, but that's what we're doing. Anyone want to buy it?" I joked.

Presley was on her phone, typing in a search window. "Estimated worth is in the nine-figures range. You're well on your way to being a billionaire, Mags."

I made a look of disgust. "I don't want his tainted money. Luke suggested we sell it, take the money, and put it into something good in the world to counteract all the bad mojo my grandfather and Felix have put out there."

"I love that idea," Rowan said.

"How do you prevent Felix from buying it?" Chloe asked.

I sat forward in alarm. "That's a very important question. I don't know the answer."

"You should be able to approve any sale," Presley said. "It's your company."

"Right," I said, relaxing back again. "We'll just have to

screen anyone hard to make sure there's no connection to that snake."

"So what are you thinking you'll do with the proceeds?" Rowan asked.

I shrugged. "I haven't come up with anything yet."

"It should be something pro-women," Presley said, still clicking around on whatever website she'd looked up.

"Definitely," I agreed. "I don't really want to run a nonprofit myself, but I was thinking... Something my mother and I have in common is that we got away from a controlling man, which meant starting over. Which was really hard. I spent almost two years not knowing how I was going to rebuild my life."

"You did it step by step," Chloe said.

"Thanks to Dotty," I said. "She happened to find me when I had nowhere to live and no income to pay rent. The only half plan I had at that point was selling the two designer bags I'd brought with me. So many women who get away from controlling men don't have ridiculously expensive bags to sell or a good Samaritan finding them in their car the first day. A lot of them don't even have a car. I honestly don't know what I would've done if Dotty hadn't taken me in."

"What did your mom do?" Chloe asked.

"She went straight to another guy."

"Because honestly, what do you do in that situation?" Presley said. "Unless you have a nest egg like I did."

"Nobody has a nest egg like you did," Chloe said.

"I had to start over, but my baggage didn't have anything to do with a controlling asshole," Rowan said. "It was hard enough, so when I think of what a woman must go through who's been abused, either physically or emotionally, who has no money, who might be scared to death..."

"I'd think it takes a lot of courage just to get out of the situation," Presley said.

I nodded. "I'm not proud to admit I had to be forced out of it."

"But you got out of it and look at you," Rowan said. "So what would help women in that position?"

"There are shelters they can go to," I said. "Those are so important, but I don't want to do the same thing. My most pressing problems were housing, income, and practical things like learning to cook and budget. I previously had never had to do any of that."

"Just one of those could be enough to keep someone from leaving," Chloe said.

"So what if there was a campus," I said. "A place where women could live in their own apartment without worrying about rent at first. They get access to whatever they need. Job skills? They can learn them. Resume help? Check. Lessons in budgeting, financial goal-setting—"

"Counseling," Presley said.

"Absolutely," I said. "There could be work opportunities on the campus for those who just arrive, until they're ready to spread their wings."

"I'm loving this," Rowan said. "It's a big, formerly manipulated-by-assholes girls' survival club."

We spitballed for the rest of the evening, to the extent I made Rowan get me a notebook and pen after she put Lilah Rose to bed. I set aside my drink and took pages of notes, feeling optimistic and excited for the first time about my impending inheritance.

"Are you going to need your mom's agreement on this?" Presley asked. "Or will you just split the proceeds, and you do what you want with your half?"

"I have no idea. She might actually go for this. The

bigger problem is that I'm already way out of my element. I don't know the first thing about building this, never mind running it and keeping it going. I don't want to give up my event-planning business. I've put blood, sweat, and tears into it, and I love it."

"You don't have to run this," Presley said. "I'd need to look up some nonprofit information, but you can hire people to run it, and you could be on the board of directors."

"That's a board of directors I'd like to be on," Chloe said.

I looked at Presley, and she nodded.

"I'd love to be in on this too," Presley said.

"Can my mom and I choose the board?" I asked.

"It's your organization," Presley said.

"I'm interested," Rowan said. "Depending on how old Miss Lilah is and whether I'm getting sleep yet."

"You guys would seriously be interested?" I asked.

"One hundred percent," Chloe said. "There's a need for it. I think it could be life-changing for the right women."

"I'm absolutely interested," Presley said.

"I'm about seventy-five percent," Rowan said. "Ask me again when I've slept for more than two hours at a time."

"Oh, girl," Chloe said, her voice oozing with empathy. "We need to go so you can get ready for bed. Will Chance be home soon?"

"He texted five minutes ago that he and Luke were nearly done working for the night."

"Ooh, almost time for Magnolia's booty call too," Presley said.

I laughed and maybe blushed a little, because that was my hope. "We'll see how tired he is. He's been working way too hard."

"Well, if you're here, you're definitely not getting lucky," Presley said, standing.

I stood too. "True, but Rowan needs chill time even more than I need sexy times."

"Yes." Chloe gathered glasses, and we forced Rowan to go upstairs and get ready for bed while we cleaned.

Twenty minutes later, Rowan came down in her pajamas with her daughter in her arms.

"She woke up already?" Chloe asked.

"Every two hours," Rowan said, kissing the baby's sweet head. "Oh, my God, you guys. My kitchen is spotless. Thank you."

"Thank you for hosting us with a newborn," Presley said.

"It was easier to have you guys here than go some-where," Rowan replied. "I needed a dose of girlfriends."

"Who knew you'd get seventy-five percent snookered into being on the board of directors of a nonprofit organiza-tion?" I said, laughing. "I need to educate myself, and my mom and I will have to agree about everything, so I'll keep you posted."

"I'm going to research too," Presley said. "I'm excited about this."

"Thank you," I said. "All of you. For being a sounding board and a support system, not to mention brilliant women."

"Plus a three-woman cleaning crew," Rowan added, "and the very best of friends."

The four of us went in for a group hug.

"I feel the same," Presley said. "Weird that three years ago, none of us lived here. Now we're all here, making our new lives. I'm so fucking glad mine includes you girls."

"Same," I said.

"Amen," Chloe added.

"We're doing this again soon," Presley said.

We all agreed, said good night, and took our leave.

I walked out thinking my night couldn't have gone better. And then, as I climbed into my car, I got a text from Luke saying he was on his way to my place. Some nights were so good it was hard to believe this was my life now.

Chapter Twenty-Seven

Luke

Myth: Christmas tree farmers loved Christmas and were the most festive guys out there.

Fact: Christmas tree farmers were usually tired, grumpy, and ready to not see another tree for a few months. Often our houses were the least decorated of anyone's because we didn't have time to do anything but sell Christmas trees to other people.

Every year I promised myself I'd take some time to slow down and appreciate the season more. Every year I failed to varying extents.

Having Addie helped. She wasn't jaded or extra tired or overworked yet. Christmas was her favorite holiday. She still believed in magic and Santa, and I wanted to help her hold on to that for as long as possible and maybe soak up some of her wonder in the process.

This year, everything seemed different.

I should be more worn down than ever, what with the barn project and the late-night visits to Magnolia's, preventing me from sleeping more than four or five hours a night, but I felt energized. Superpowered. And filled with more Christmas spirit than I could remember having for years.

A large part of that was due to the woman by my side. Magnolia had finished putting on a baby shower for a client just in time to join us.

Tonight was my dad group's Christmas party, but instead of just us guys, this year it was us and our immediate families—twenty-four of us in all, soon to be twenty-six once Harper and Max's and Quincy and Knox's babies were born.

Ben and Emerson were hosting all of us in their recently expanded home. They'd doubled the size of their living room, so some of us were at a folding table in there, with the rest of the adults at the dining-room table. The kids had their own table in the kitchen. It was a little crowded but cozy. Maybe next year I'd host in the barn.

Addie loved playing with Ben and Emerson's four kids and West's three daughters, so she was having the time of her life. I was savoring every moment with the prettiest woman in the room.

Since hooking up, Magnolia and I had been stealing whatever private moments we could, and I wouldn't trade my alone time with her for anything. But having her with me in public, going to a party as a couple—as a pseudofamily, really—had ideas lodging in my head and making me wonder if I'd found a woman worthy of becoming my real family.

We'd only been together a few weeks though, and I sometimes got the impression Magnolia wasn't as ready to commit as I was. I knew she was working through a lot, figuring out who she was, building a new business, dealing with parental baggage, and now pondering an entire nonprofit foundation with her mother, so I understood.

I could be patient.

We were sharing a table with Ben, Emerson, Chance, and Rowan. We'd devoured a potluck meal, then taken a break for a white elephant gift exchange. Now we were back to the food scene, digging into an array of desserts, including divinity, peppermint brownies, gingerbread bars, and llama-shaped sugar cookies from the bakery, when Ben blew into Ruby's karaoke microphone.

"Testing," he said, standing between the living and dining rooms so we could all see him. "Don't be alarmed. I won't be singing."

"Even the livestock would take off running if you did," West bellowed.

"Unless he shares the cookies with them," Chance called out to a round of laughter.

The eight younger kids and Chance's teenage daughter, Sam, came out of the kitchen and crawled onto laps or settled next to their parents. Addie snuggled against my side, her eyes full of life and excitement.

"Did everybody get what they wanted from the white elephant exchange?" Ben asked, grinning like a bandit. He'd managed to walk away with the toilet night-light, which was the coveted prize of the evening that had been stolen multiple times.

"I heard Emerson's happy with her hot-dog pen," Knox said. "She finally has a hot dog that's a full six inches."

"I love my heart-shaped waffle iron," Scarlet, West's oldest, announced.

"I love my Lego set," Xavier called out.

"My yodeling pickle is up for grabs," West said.

"Harper, are you sure you won't trade your chocolate penguins?"

"I'm sure!" Harper said.

"She's already eaten half of them," Max reported.

Harper laughed and said, "More than half."

"If you're smart, you know better than to take chocolate away from a pregnant woman," Chance quipped.

The teasing continued for another couple of minutes, filling the house with laughter and love.

Eventually Ben tapped on the microphone to get us to shut up. Quieting this group was a chore, but it gradually worked.

"I just wanted to say a few words," Ben said, "into my high-powered microphone."

"It's *my* microphone, Daddy," Ruby informed him. "But I said you could borrow it."

"Thank you for letting me borrow it, Ruby Tuesday," Ben said. "Anyway, it was close to two years ago, I think, when Max, Luke, Chance, and I decided single dadding wasn't for the weak at heart and that we should start an informal group that met every week to talk dad stuff, or sometimes talk nondad stuff."

Low-voiced agreements arose from both tables.

"Along came Knox and West, rounding out our group of dudes stumbling through parenthood, with drinks and sports along the way."

West raised his beer in acknowledgment.

"All I can say is," Ben continued, "thank God for you guys. I don't want to get too sappy, but I think I speak for all of us when I say we've been through some rough times that our group helped us get through. Of course, half of those challenges revolved around falling for the beautiful women at our tables who we now call our families."

More laughter ensued, mostly because he was spot on. These guys had been hardheaded when it came to love. They'd each needed to be smacked upside the head. Meanwhile here I was the whole time, wanting to find a wife to share my life with, and I was the only single guy left.

I glanced at Magnolia and brushed my hand down her arm.

"This year, we've evolved, gentlemen," Ben said. "Look at us tonight. None of us are alone anymore. We're all lucky enough to have found some damn fine women, and yes, Ruby, I'll put money in the swear jar for that when I'm done. Luke and Magnolia, I know you're a new thing, and I'm not putting pressure on you for long-term, Magnolia. We're just happy you're here with us tonight."

"Happy to be here," she said, meeting my gaze with affection in her eyes.

"Does everyone have a beverage?" Ben asked. "Kids and pregnant ladies, grab your juice boxes. Anyone else need a refill? I'd like to make a toast." He waited while Emerson poured herself more wine, then passed the bottle to Presley.

"Okay, we're ready," Emerson told her husband.

"A few years ago, it was just me and the kids, as you know, and we did okay. We bought this property so we could get horses and dogs, and we did. But then I kept on going, taking in animals like it was my job—"

"It sort of is your job," Max called out, making Ben laugh.

"You all know I love animals," Ben continued, "but I think part of that was me searching for the final piece of our family. It turns out that was not, in fact, yet another four-legged creature but a gorgeous single mom and her two kids."

After a round of aahs, Ben raised his wineglass and said, "Here's to the single dads we once were. As hard as it was, it brought us together into this tribe that's become an extended family. Here's to the women who've brightened our lives and made our families complete. And here's to you kids who've made us crazy at times, prouder than we ever thought was possible, more patient than we realized we had the capacity for, and who've filled us with learning opportunities and so much love. To friendship and family. Thank you all for being here tonight and for being an important part of my family's lives."

"Hear, hear," rang out around the room as we clinked our glasses and cans and juice boxes.

Ben started to head back to the table, then lifted the mic again. "One more time, though, seriously, Magnolia. No pressure."

I laughed along with everyone else, then leaned over and kissed her.

"Thanks for having this rowdy group over tonight," Knox said.

Emerson stood and said, "Please stay for as long as you want, everyone. The party's not over."

"Well, not *too* long," Ben joked.

The place became loud and chaotic again. Chance and Sam came around with bags for trash. Ben and Xavier took down the folding table to open up more space. Apparently some of the women were organizing a round of karaoke, and they needed room to move.

"Daddy, can we go look at the llamas now?" Addie asked me. She'd been excited about the animals since we'd arrived. I'd promised we'd check them out after dinner.

"Go get your shoes and coat on," I told her. "I'll be right there."

Addie zipped off, and I turned to Magnolia. "Would you like to go to the barn with us?"

With her attention on Quincy and Presley, who were setting up the karaoke speaker, she said, "Trust me when I say nobody wants me singing. It would frighten the children. So as long as Esmerelda doesn't assault me again, I'll go with you."

"If she does, I'll rescue you," I said, grinning as I remembered the night we first kissed. "Again."

"I'll hold you to that."

Ben came out to the barn with us, saying he wanted to check on a pregnant barn cat who was getting close.

"Are you sure those kittens aren't going to wind up inside with the rest of the herd?" I joked, referencing the three dogs and five cats who were closed in on the second story of the house for the evening.

"If I want to stay married, they're staying out here," he said, laughing. He headed up the stairs to the hayloft, where he'd last seen the pregnant cat.

Addie ran ahead of us, stopping off at each of the three horse stalls and quickly greeting the horses. Then she skipped ahead to the llamas.

"Esmerelda!" Addie called like it was a celebrity sighting.

"I wouldn't mind meeting Betty," Magnolia said.

"You're not scared of a little llama love, are you?" I asked.

"Esmerelda is a menace," she said with conviction.

We said hello to Betty, the brown-and-white llama, then backtracked to Esmerelda, the pure white, long-haired llama who looked at us with so much judgment as we approached.

"Look at her," Magnolia said. "I swear she has it in for me."

"Esmerelda is a sweet girl," Addie said, closing in on Esmerelda's stall door.

"Come here, doodlebug," I said. When my daughter came up to me, I lifted her so she could see over the wall.

She cooed at the judgmental llama, but Esmerelda barely gave her a second glance.

Instead the white barn queen strode in her slow llama way toward Magnolia, who stood three feet from me, toward one side of the stall.

"Hey, Esmerelda," Addie sang. "You're such a pretty girl."

Esmerelda didn't even blink at my daughter, who wanted her acknowledgment so badly.

"Go visit Addie," Magnolia said to the llama, pointing. "She loves you."

Ben came up to us then. "No kittens yet but the mama cat told me in no uncertain terms to back off. Hey, Es."

The llama turned her big eyes on him for a moment, then looked back at Magnolia, who raised both hands.

"I'm not your person," she said, laughing. "What is her deal? Why is she staring at me?"

"Addie, we're playing tag!" Xavier yelled in the barn doorway. "Come on!"

Addie forgot the llama and galloped toward the exit.

"Guess I better go see what's going on out there," Ben said and followed my daughter out.

I tried to get Esmerelda to come to me so I could pet her, but now that it was just the three of us, she beelined over to Magnolia, whose brows shot up as she looked at me in disbelief.

"What?" she said rhetorically.

Then Esmerelda nuzzled Magnolia's neck, making her

laugh. She hesitantly ran her hand down the llama's frizzy neck.

Esmerelda nuzzled her neck again, then lowered her llama snout and stuck it right between Magnolia's breasts.

Magnolia took a step backward. "Are you seeing this? I'm not kidding about an assault."

I grinned and moved to Magnolia's side, putting my arm around her, pulling her into me. "Esmerelda, we could've been friends, but you just touched what's mine."

The llama snuffed, then turned away, as if she couldn't care about the fallout of her poor decisions.

"Are you okay?" I asked Magnolia, who was still laughing.

"I'm okay but ready to exit the barn."

"Good night, Betty," I said toward the end stall. "Good night, Esmerelda. Pervert."

As we walked out of the barn, Addie ran up to us. "Daddy, can I have a sleepover with Sienna and her sisters?"

Sienna and Nova followed a few feet behind Addie, their eyes on me.

"Did your dad say that's okay, Sienna?" I asked.

She nodded, and Nova said, "We can all sleep in our playhouse bunk bed!"

"If Mr. West approved it, you can go," I told my daughter. "You don't have any pj's with you though."

"She can borrow some of mine," Sienna said.

"Okay then," I said. "But Addie? If the other kids aren't invited, you need to be mindful of their feelings."

"I will, Daddy!" My daughter ran off with the others, who were organizing a game of capture the flag in the open area on the other side of the house, by the chicken coop.

I pulled Magnolia into the shadows against the house,

gently pressed her body against the wall with mine, kissed her, and said, "You know what that means?"

"What?"

"It means we can have our own sleepover."

"Mmm, I'm in," she said.

"Good." I kissed her again. "Because I have plans for you all...night...long."

"We should probably show our faces for a little longer inside first."

I put some space between us, recognizing that the longer I kissed her, the harder it would be to not sneak away from Ben's. "Not only is she sexy, she's smart," I said. "What more could a guy ever want?"

Knowing that was true, I ushered her inside while I still could.

Chapter Twenty-Eight

Magnolia

The party at the Holloways' was the kind of party I'd only ever dreamed of being at.

Every single person there had welcomed me into their group without question or hesitation. The bond between Luke and his dad friends ran so obviously deep it was enviable, and the women seemed just as close even though some, like Presley and Rowan, were relatively new additions. There'd been so much genuine affection and love in their house that I felt blessed to be a part of it, whether my relationship with Luke became long-term or not.

Right now though, I was all about alone time with my handsome, sexy date.

We'd managed to stick around at the party for another forty minutes after Addie asked to stay at West's, which I thought was admirable. On the way to my apartment, we'd talked about surface stuff—the party and the presents and how well all eight kids between five and ten years old got along. Even Xavier, the only boy among them, fit right into the group. But beneath our benign conversation, a tension and anticipation pulsed between us.

We ascended the stairs to my apartment in silence, with Luke's hand on my waist and my body buzzing with need for him.

Once inside, Luke ducked into the bathroom, which was exactly what I'd hoped would happen. As soon as he shut the door, I switched on the light on my nightstand, then whipped my dark green party dress off as fast as I could, which left me in the special Christmas lingerie I'd bought for tonight. It was bright red, a color I normally shied away from because of the red in my hair, but it was all about the theme. The top part was a bow that concealed my breasts as a present. The rest was sheer and connected to my sheer stockings. I left my heels on, prayed everything was in place, and hopped up onto the kitchen counter. I crossed my legs and waited for Luke to emerge, feeling like it was our first time.

The bathroom door creaked open, and I sat up straighter, my body aching for him.

When he came around the corner, his gaze went toward the bed first. When he didn't find me there, he turned his head and spotted me.

His brows went up, and his mouth fell open.

"Merry Christmas," I said. "I have an early present for you." I held out my arms, presenting myself.

"God, Magnolia," he said as he approached, his eyes roving over me from head to toe, appreciative heat in his gaze. "I must be at the top of the good list if this is my present."

"You're definitely good," I purred as I uncrossed my legs.

When he reached me, he braced his hands on either

side of me and leaned in to kiss me, his body hovering close enough to mine that I could sense it but not touch it, as if he was prolonging the moment when we finally came together.

After he'd kissed me thoroughly, our bodies still not touching, he stepped back enough to take in the closeup view. My body thrummed with need and impatience.

"Are you going to unwrap your present?" I asked.

"You better believe I am." His voice had gone rough and husky. "I might have a present for you too. Is this a real bow?" He picked up the trailing end of the red ribbon and tugged.

I didn't need to answer because the bow came undone, baring my breasts to him. He nuzzled into my neck and nibbled his way down.

"You smell good enough to eat," he said.

"Then by all means..." I left the invitation hanging, grinning down at him as he raised his gaze to mine. "You know you're killing me with your slow, careful approach to your present. I pegged you for a guy who'd rip into it with enthusiasm."

"Oh, trust me, I'm enthusiastic." He closed his lips around my nipple and sucked, sending a shock of need straight to my core. Then he released it and said, "I'm taking my time to appreciate every single inch of my present." He took my other nipple in and swirled his tongue before sucking and sending another zing of heat deep inside me.

I hooked my legs around him and drew him closer, then reached down and unbuckled his belt.

"Don't I get to unwrap my present all the way first?" he asked, a devilish glint in his eyes.

I unsnapped and unzipped his pants and said, "You took too long."

As if he took that as a challenge, he went after my

breasts, taking one into his mouth and teasing the other with his talented fingers, kneading, pinching, drawing a moan from me. I let his pants go, braced my hands on the counter behind me, and sought out a place to support my feet, finding the door pulls of the lower cabinets.

"You smell like vanilla cookies," he said, then licked between my breasts and over to the other nipple.

"It's my lotion," I said on a gasp.

He pulled away to meet my gaze. "Vanilla cookie lotion?"

All I could do was nod as I focused on how to get him to have his way with me and fill this aching neediness.

Instead he grinned and said, "Well, it's no wonder Esmerelda wanted to devour you."

My eyes popped open and met his. I laughed breathlessly and said, "I need new lotion."

"Maybe we'll shower yours off after a while. Or I could just lick it off."

"You should definitely try that."

He got busy doing exactly that. My lingerie was down to two thin straps that connected to the sheer part and snapped between my legs. I waited for him to discover that, which took another five minutes because he was obsessed with my breasts. Which worked for me, because the things he was doing to them had me close to orgasm.

As he continued working my nipple over with his mouth, I felt his fingers on my upper thigh, trailing toward the edge of my teddy. His thumb scooped beneath the mesh material and down to the apex of my thighs.

He groaned, lifting his mouth from my breast to look lower. "Snaps?" he asked rhetorically, then whipped them open. "God, that's hot."

He touched my folds and dipped his finger inside me,

eliciting a gasp from me and making me arch into him, my head falling back.

"You're ready for me, aren't you?" he growled.

"I've been ready," I said in a breathy, needy whisper.

"As much as I'd like to lick your vanilla cookies off from head to toe"—he took his wallet out, flipped it open, and removed a condom, then lowered his pants—"I need to bury myself inside you in the next twenty seconds."

"Please."

As he rolled the protection on, I shoved his shirt up his chest until he lifted his arms so I could remove it and toss it to the floor. He slid me to the edge of the counter and guided his dick to my opening as I wrapped my legs around him. Then he pushed inside, filling me, making me gasp with the suddenness of his glorious invasion.

I moaned at the friction as he slid partway out, then thrust home again, my breasts jiggling with every stroke until he palmed one of them.

"Yesss," I said, winding my arms around him to hold on for the ride of my life.

Between his manipulation of my nipple and the bliss of his thick cock pumping into me, faster now, I succumbed to an overload of sensations. My thoughts went offline as I merely held on and *felt*, my body fully out of my control as it climbed, reached, stretched toward release.

"Luke...God...*yes*...harder."

He gave me what I asked for, and my body crashed into ecstasy, stealing my breath away. I clung to him, arched, keened, riding it out for long, blissful seconds. Finally I gasped for breath and collapsed into him, summoning control over my arms to hold on more tightly as he thrust harder, working for his own climax.

"Fuck, Mags," he ground out.

The next thing I registered was his hands scooping me up by my butt. He held on to me, turned, stepped to the empty wall by the refrigerator, and pushed my back against it, pumping harder into me as if his life depended on it. All I could do was hold on and let him use my body however he needed to.

He pounded into me for a while longer, and I was stunned to feel my body come alive again out of nowhere. As Luke's thrusts became even more intense, I climbed with him, reduced to gasping and needing and clinging to him. I came at the same time he did, thankful he pressed all his weight into me as he released, because there was no way I'd be able to stand on my own two feet. Possibly not in the next twelve hours.

We stood there, or rather he stood there holding me up, both of us panting as I tried to process what he'd just done to me.

"That's never happened before," I said when I could get enough air to speak.

"What? Sex against the wall?"

I laughed lazily. "That too but two orgasms so fast."

"Told you I had a present for you. And now I need to get you to the bed before my legs give out."

He pushed away from the wall enough for me to slide my feet to the floor, then leaned in and pressed a tender kiss to my lips. "You okay?"

"I think my entire cellular makeup was blown apart and rearranged."

Grinning, he said, "We're damn good together, Mags."

"Mm-hmm."

We kissed again. Then he stood back enough to shed his pants the rest of the way. He kicked them and his shoes off, making me laugh.

"Oops," I said. "We forgot to get all the way naked." My teddy still hung from my shoulders.

"Seemed to work out just fine." He took my hand, and we crossed the floor to my bed, ignoring the discarded clothing and the condom wrapper.

When we got to the bed, I took off the teddy, pulled back the bedding, and crawled under the blankets. Luke followed me in, reached back to turn the lamp off, then pulled me into his arms.

I'd never felt so satiated, content, and taken care of in my life. I drifted off within seconds.

The next morning, minutes after Luke left at quarter till six, I stretched out in my warm bed, my body pleasantly sore from multiple rounds over the course of the night. The sex had been incredible, creative, and infused with laughter and conversation, which was yet another thing I'd never experienced before.

We'd talked for hours about deep topics and silly ones. We'd even managed to catch a little bit of sleep, though I worried about how he'd get through his full day of work.

He was so good to me. It was like he'd said. We were good together.

As I started to get drowsy, a thought popped up in my mind: *When it has seemed too good to be true in your life, it always has been.*

I forced myself to dismiss the thought and succumbed to another hour or two of slumber.

Chapter Twenty-Nine

Luke

The evening of the Earthly Charm open house, a light, fluffy snow fell gently on downtown Dragonfly Lake. The temperature hovered around freezing, but the ground was warm enough that the snow wasn't sticking or becoming a nuisance. Even though I wasn't much of a shopper, I could admit it was the ideal effect to put someone in the mood for holiday shopping.

"Can I get a present for Miss Magnolia?" Addie asked me as we walked down the sidewalk toward the store.

"That might be pretty tricky tonight," I told her. "Miss Magnolia will be here the whole time since she's the party planner."

"Maybe we could do it in secret?" my daughter asked.

"If not, we can come back when she's not here, so keep your eyes open for what you want to give her."

As we approached the door, I could see lots of people inside through the festive window displays, exactly as

Magnolia and the owners had hoped for. I took Addie's hand and opened the door.

"Welcome to Earthly Charm, guys," Harper said as we entered. "Hello, Addie. I love your llama hat."

"Thank you," my daughter said. "It's white like Esmerelda."

"It looks exactly like Esmerelda," Harper said. "Thanks for coming to our party. Help yourself to any of our goodie stations, you two. We've got a hot cocoa station, hot cider, a cookie station, and candle making."

"Cookies!" Addie said, looking up at me.

"We'll get there," I told her. "This looks like an early success," I said to Harper.

She nodded, her eyes sparkling. "Lots of people so far. Be sure to hit the photo op area and take a pic with the reindeer."

"Is it real?" Addie asked.

Harper bent down to her level. "It's just a statue. We couldn't bring a real reindeer inside, so you have to pretend."

"Can we, Daddy?"

"We'll get a photo with the reindeer," I said, grinning at her wide eyes. "After cocoa?"

"Yes!"

Harper pointed us toward the cocoa station, then greeted Loretta and Dotty, who came in behind us.

As we headed for the cocoa setup in the corner, I scanned the room for Magnolia. When I spotted her near the checkout counter overseeing the raffle basket, my heart pumped faster, more like a teenager with a crush than a man who'd been sleeping with her for several weeks and knew her inside and out.

Tonight she wore a plum-colored party dress with sheer sleeves, a deep V-neck that teased me with her cleavage, and sparkles everywhere. I wondered if it concealed another brain-scrambling lingerie surprise beneath it. If I was lucky, I'd have the chance to find out.

I watched her until she glanced my way, enjoying the zing of connection when our gazes met. She smiled and waved before turning her attention to Ava Henry, who looked to be entering the raffle.

"Daddy!" Addie called.

I caught up to her at the hot-cocoa stand, where Dakota, Max's sister and one of the owners, stood over a large Crock-Pot of cocoa, ladling it into cups.

"Hey, Luke," Dakota said warmly. "Addie told me she wants every single topping."

I eyed the array of toppings and laughed. "Of course she does. Why don't you pick three, bug? I've never seen so many choices."

Different sized jars, all with a red-and-white ribbon and a handwritten label, contained chocolate chips—white, milk, and dark—peppermint sticks, caramel drizzle, marsh-mallows, two kinds of sprinkles, and more.

My daughter lobbied for four. I gave in because I was having as much trouble limiting myself.

Addie shrugged and said, "It's Christmas," as if that excused any gluttony.

I decided she had a decent point.

Addie and I got a quick selfie with the reindeer, then browsed the store as we sipped our cocoa, chatting with everyone we knew along the way. Several from my dads' group were here with their families. Rosy McNamara and Nancy Solon joined the other Diamonds at the cider station. I even spotted Magnolia's mother talking to some guy I didn't recognize. I knew Magnolia and her mother had been in frequent contact now that they were trying to sell the company they'd inherited and making plans for their nonprofit, but I hadn't expected Bianca to dip into Dragonfly Lake life on a social basis. She looked a little pale as she talked animatedly to the guy. I wasn't ready to trust Bianca entirely yet, but Magnolia seemed to believe she'd evolved. I supposed a cancer diagnosis could do that to a person.

When we reached the candle-making station, we ran into West with Nova, Sienna, and Scarlet, who were choosing their candle scents. My daughter burrowed right in among the sisters as West and I greeted each other. A flicker of a thought went through my head about how much Addie would love to have sisters. I wasn't sure if that was in the cards, but... I glanced in Magnolia's direction, caught her eye again, felt that zing, and savored it like an addict getting a fix.

Once the girls were engaged with Cambria as she explained how they would make their candles, I asked West, "Are you going to be here while they finish their candles?"

He nodded. "I'm keeping track of them while Presley shops."

"Would you mind watching Addie while I say hi to Magnolia?"

"Course not."

I made my way through the people toward Magnolia, wishing I could sneak her out the back and kiss the hell out of her for an hour or two. When I reached her, I stood to the side while she answered a question from Kemp's sister, Natalie, who was apparently back from college for the holidays. I checked out Magnolia's party dress from closer up, looking for a hint of what might lie beneath it.

I was rewarded when Magnolia turned to me, planted a quick but fervent kiss on my lips, smiled up at me, and said, "Hello, sexy farm boy."

God, she was pretty. I wanted to devour her, but instead I just smiled back and said, "You look gorgeous, Mags."

"Thank you. How's the cocoa?"

"Just the sugar shot I need to ensure I'll be awake for hours." I gave her a look intended to convey that I'd like to spend those hours in her bed.

Glenda Thomas asked Magnolia a question, and I backed away so she could do her thing.

I spotted Seth Henry standing to one side with Anna Delfico, who was holding Seth and Everly's infant son.

"Hey, guys," I said, sidling up next to Seth. "How's this little man doing?"

"I'm thinking of stealing him," Anna said. "He's the sweetest little chunk."

"He doesn't miss a meal," Seth reported.

I brushed my finger under Beckham's chin. "Hi, handsome guy. Look at you in your Santa cap."

The baby peered up at me, his chubby cheeks bunching up with a big baby grin.

"What a cheerful baby," I said.

"He's the best," Anna confirmed. "Aren't you, Beckham?"

"He's pretty easygoing," Seth said. "I'm told this is how the first baby lures you into having more."

"Sounds like a distinct possibility," I said. Jessie and I had never gotten to that stage. We'd decided shortly after Addie was born that we'd be better off as friends instead of a couple.

"I didn't know you and Magnolia were together," Seth said. "That's a big turnaround, right?"

I chuckled and shook my head. "That's me coming to my senses and realizing I was a putz all those years ago."

"Is it serious, Luke?" Anna asked.

I glanced at Magnolia again, allowing an image into my mind of her with our own little baby. Fuck, I liked the thought. "Just between us? It's getting that way for me, but I don't know if she's there yet."

Truth be told, I shied away from asking her, not wanting it to feel like pressure. I knew how much she had going on, so my objective was to honor that and not hurry her.

Kemp rushed up to us, seeming upset or in a hurry.

"Hey," Anna said to him, frowning. "What's going on, Kemp? Are you okay?"

"Fuck," he said on an exhale. He swallowed, looking like he'd seen a ghost or maybe an entire alien spaceship. "I just got this call..." He chuckled, but I got the impression it was not out of humor in the least. Shaking his head, he said, "I don't know if I'm being pranked or what. God, I hope I'm being pranked."

"Tell us what happened," Anna said. "What call did you get?"

"I met this girl last year. She came here for a weekend trip, and we hooked up. Her friend just called." He looked around desperately, as if searching for an out. "Fuck, I don't even know where to start."

"What did the friend say?"

"Valerie—the girl I hooked up with—was killed in a car wreck."

"Oh, no," Anna said.

Kemp nodded. "Her baby wasn't in the car with her, so

he's okay." He rubbed his fingers over his eyes, then dropped his hand. "Her friend says it's my kid."

"What?" Anna blurted.

"She said I'm on the birth certificate," Kemp said, becoming paler by the second.

"You didn't know about the baby before now?" I asked.

He shook his head. "Not a thing. We didn't keep in touch. I don't know if any of it's real."

"Why wouldn't the mother tell you that you have a kid?" Seth asked, clearly disturbed. "Especially if she put your name on the birth certificate?"

"I don't know," Kemp said. "We didn't discuss that. It was more about... I'm a fucking father? Is this real?"

"So...does she want you to take the baby?"

"She's working with children's services to figure it out. I guess Valerie's mom wants the kid, but Valerie didn't get along with her parents and would never want them to get custody of her child."

"So Valerie's friend thinks you should get the baby?"

Kemp let out a hollow laugh, bent over with his hands on his knees, then straightened, shaking his head. "Sounds that way. What do I do? I don't know what to believe."

"What did the friend say to do?" Anna asked.

"She told me she'd call me as soon as she knows more. What if it's my kid?" Kemp ran both his hands over his face, clearly distraught.

"You need to get involved and find out," Seth said. "You'll want a paternity test ASAP."

Kemp nodded at him as if he was still in shock. Hell, I would be.

"What can we do?" I asked him.

He cackled semihysterically. "Hell if I know. What should I do? Should I drive to Nashville to see the baby?"

"I think I'd want to be close by while things shake out with children's services. Assuming you want this kid if it's yours," Seth said.

Kemp made a who-the-fuck-knows look. "I mean, I'm having a little trouble wrapping my head around any of it. I keep going back to, is this a big, giant joke someone's playing on me?"

"I doubt it," Anna said. "You wanna go back to your daddy?" she cooed to Beckham, then held him out to Seth, who pulled the baby into his chest. To Kemp, she said, "Let's go call the friend back and tell her we're coming in. I'll drive you."

"What do I tell my sister?" Kemp asked. "I'm supposed to be shopping with her."

"Tell her you have to help me with something," Anna said. "I wouldn't mention the baby until you know more."

"Think about a lawyer," Seth said. "Who knows what you're looking at, but you might want one."

Kemp nodded distractedly, and he and Anna left us to look for his sister. I looked at Seth in disbelief.

"Crazy times," I said.

He shook his head. "I can't imagine. That makes my life look boring and sedate."

"In a good way," I added.

Everly came up to us then, holding out her hands for her son, whose attention was on her. "Come here, jellybean. What's going on?" she asked us. "You guys look serious." She traded her shopping basket for the baby.

"I'll tell you later," Seth said. "Pretty sure it's not for public consumption. Are you ready to check out with this stuff?"

"Sure. I wasn't sure if you'd found anything."

"I've been staying out of the way," her husband said. "I'll go get in line."

"Thanks, hon. How's it going, Luke?" she asked.

"I can't complain," I said. "How about you? Are you working on new music?"

"Always. I just recorded a duet with Bryan Covington about a week ago. We had fun collaborating."

"Cool," I said. "You'll announce on the Tattler when it's available?"

"Of course." She pressed a kiss to Beckham's head.

A thought popped up in my mind. A memory. "You did a duet with Ella McCabe a couple of years back, didn't you?"

"I did," Everly said. "'Stone Cold.'"

"I know it well. Are you still in contact with her?"

"Frequently. We hit it off, and we've been friends ever since."

I glanced at Magnolia, then made up my mind. "She recently got engaged, right?"

"Yes, to Jonathon Metzger. I met him a few months ago, and they're perfect together."

"Do you have any sway over Ella?" I asked.

"About her fiancé?"

I shook my head. "About her wedding planner." I stepped closer and lowered my voice. "She apparently had an appointment with Magnolia to discuss hiring her, but then Felix James went to Ella's father and told a bunch of lies to lose her the potential business. He apparently convinced Ella to find a different planner."

Everly narrowed her eyes. "I recently read that whole crazy thing about Felix losing his job."

That and the truth about Magnolia's paternity had recently been leaked on the Tattler. Magnolia had been

relieved her broken ties to him had become public knowl-
edge. She'd declared she was finally free of him, but then
the fucker had done this.

Nodding, I said, "He is pissed and vengeful, so he's
trying to ruin Magnolia's business. She hasn't done
anything to him. She's just trying to make her own
way."

"I like Magnolia. She was the planner for Harper and
Max, right?"

"That was officially her first wedding."

"It was gorgeous," Everly said. "Very personalized to the
couple."

"Magnolia's the planner for Presley and West's
Christmas Eve wedding, among others. That one's at my
barn. Anyway...she's put up with Felix's BS her whole life.
She thought she was finally free of him."

"It's not easy to break out from powerful parents."

Everly would know. I remembered hearing about her
breaking away from her dad's big-label production for her
music and going indie.

"You seem to be thriving now," I told her.

"A lot of people don't understand, but I'm so happy
with the changes I made. But back to Magnolia. I'd be
happy to recommend her to Ella. I don't know anything
about her dad or how controlling he is, but I can put in a
good word."

"That's all I can ask for. I appreciate it. Not only does
Magnolia deserve the chance, but Ella will get the best
service and attention from Magnolia. She's working to prove
herself and build up her business. Nobody will work harder
than Mags."

Everly smiled as she studied me, making me a little
nervous. I didn't know her all that well, which made it a

stretch for me to ask any favor of her, but if it would help Magnolia...

"I'll ping Ella this evening before it gets too late. No promises it will change anything, but she should know Magnolia's a great planner."

"Thanks, Everly."

She squeezed my arm. "She's a lucky girl to have a good guy like you in love with her, supporting her goals," she said, taking out her phone and holding it up, as if she was going to contact Ella now.

I was unsure what to say to that, so I merely nodded as Seth came back to her, and we went our separate ways.

Was I in love with Magnolia?

I let the words roll around in my head for a few seconds, waiting for some kind of alarm bell to sound. None did.

I wasn't afraid to fall in love. I just never had before. I'd thought I loved Addie's mom, but I questioned that now.

Standing out of the way of all the shoppers, I watched Magnolia as she listened to something her mother said. Magnolia's expression went from shocked to glowing, and then the two women hugged. Magnolia's eyes fluttered shut, and I saw so much emotion beneath the surface. A thread of caution. Relief. Hope.

I wanted nothing more than for the woman to finally do right by Magnolia. So far she'd heeded my warning not to hurt her daughter. I'd do anything to ensure Magnolia didn't get hurt, by her mother or anyone else.

The truth crept in and enveloped me like a comforting hug. If this wasn't love, then what was? I wanted Magnolia's success. I wanted to be by her side for every joyful moment, but I'd also fight every battle I could for her. If her mother— or anyone—hurt her again, they'd answer to me, and I'd be there to support Magnolia in whatever way she needed.

Hell, I'd imagined having babies with her tonight. You didn't think long-term family without being in love.

I realized I was grinning as I nodded to myself, still watching the strawberry-blond bombshell across the room. The bombshell I absolutely could imagine living happily beside for the rest of my years.

Everly was right. I was utterly, completely in love with Magnolia James. Now I just had to figure out how and when to let her know.

Chapter Thirty

Magnolia

I 'd spent more time with my mother in the past week than I had in the previous twenty years.

Things were happening fast with the sale of Lansford Development and the creation of our nonprofit, faster than I ever could've imagined. I hadn't asked for this project, and I still had less than zero interest in Lansford, but I was surprised at how invested in the nonprofit I was becoming.

When I'd shared the ideas from girls' night with my mother over lunch last week, she'd been enthusiastic about them, agreeing a women's campus with multiple kinds of support and resources was a fitting way to use the proceeds. I'd told her about the night Felix had kicked me out and how I'd managed to get my feet under me afterward. She agreed I was lucky to connect with Dotty. Most women didn't have a Dotty.

Our first step was to find a buyer for Lansford, and as if it was meant to be, we now had one.

My mother had surprised me when she'd shown up at the Earthly Charm open house, saying she wanted to become involved in Dragonfly Lake life again and start making connections for our project. Like me, she hadn't really fit in before, being the wife of a tyrant and having practically more money than the entire rest of the town combined. In the past, her social life had been more wrapped up in Nashville's high society. That was where the galas were, the benefits, the organizations she'd chosen to volunteer for back when she still lived with Felix and me.

She was starting over here, just like I had.

Somehow, as if some higher power was making things happen for us, she'd ultimately found our buyer at the open house when Dakota had introduced her to Ian Finley, Dakota's grumpy billionaire roommate. Long story short, Ian was more than qualified to purchase Lansford, and he'd been looking for a business opportunity now that he'd walked away from Wall Street. Lansford was in his wheelhouse.

Over the past week, our lawyers and his had worked nonstop to forge an agreement that would work for all of us. It wasn't finalized yet—we were told that could take weeks —but Dave, my grandfather's estate attorney who'd sat in for most of the negotiations, said he didn't foresee any problems cropping up.

In the meantime, we were working on plans for our nonprofit. We'd lined up the assistance of more lawyers and a nonprofit consultant my mother had met years ago through her volunteer efforts.

Today my mother and I were at the Dragonfly Diner for a late lunch work session to organize our ideas before we had our first official meeting with the consultant. Presley's wedding was only two days away, so my plate was overflowing, but now that my mother and I had our purpose, we were both impatient to get the ball rolling.

"You ladies look like you've got some serious business going on here," Patrick, the server, said, making a circle with his hand to indicate my mother's notebook and my laptop on the table. "Are we ordering lunch today or just having beverages?"

"Definitely lunch," I said.

We put our orders in, then got down to business.

The consultant had sent us some materials with an overview of topics we needed to address.

"The first question is where we want to locate," I said, glancing at the list. "I think we'll have to build."

"I agree," my mother said. "Finding a property that would work for everything we want would be a long shot."

"We'll need apartments and a headquarters for offices. Classrooms, community center, a workout facility..."

"What do you think about a medical clinic?" my mom asked. "Maybe we could get doctors to volunteer their time for a few hours each month. These people likely won't have health insurance at first, so what do they do for health care?"

"Good idea. We could do the same for counseling. Why don't we start a wish list of all the things we'd like. A dream list with no budget restrictions for now. That'll come later."

"I like that. Our pie-in-the-sky list," she said.

I opened a new document on my laptop and added the items we'd already mentioned.

"What if we had a community kitchen where residents could apply their lessons in cooking and nutrition?" I asked. "Kind of a cooperative setup."

"That would cut down on paid staff if residents had some responsibilities like cooking, cleaning, landscaping..."

"I love that," I said. "We could even turn these into hourly jobs so people can begin earning a paycheck right away. If we'd have to pay someone to staff the kitchen anyway—"

"It might as well be a resident who needs an income."

"Exactly." I typed in some notes. "Are you thinking Nashville or Dragonfly Lake or somewhere in between?"

Patrick dropped off our lunch, so I pushed my laptop to the side but kept it close enough I could type. My stomach growled at the aroma of the juicy cheeseburger and fries on my plate.

"I'd forgotten how good simple diner food can be," my mother said.

I didn't imagine a diner was someplace she'd ever frequented. When I was growing up, we'd had a cook, so we hadn't dined out often. When we had, it was often to some high-dollar, fine-dining establishment in Nashville.

"We might have more options in Nashville," my mom said, going back to my question about location, "but I'd prefer Dragonfly Lake. It's a lot more peaceful, more of a respite."

I agreed. "Maybe we could start a program with local businesses to help residents get entry-level jobs," I suggested.

"That would certainly be easier here in town where nearly everything is a mom-and-pop."

"And we know a lot of the owners," I added. "The trick will be finding suitable land. We'll need a real estate agent to start the search soon."

We spent the next forty-five minutes talking about the rest of the list—our mission statement, researching similar organizations, and what we needed to set up legally, financially, and staffwise.

"Speaking of staff..." I switched my now-empty plate with my laptop so I could get back to typing easily, "as I understand it, we'll need a board of directors—"

"I've got that covered," my mom interrupted.

"Uh, what do you mean, you've got that covered?"

"I had lunch with several of the ladies I've volunteered with for years. People are excited about this. I've got six solid commitments plus two maybes for the board."

I frowned, my gut tightening. "I hope you didn't promise them anything, because I have friends here in town who are interested."

"These women are experienced in nonprofits and running large events and big-city foundations, Magnolia. They're the best."

There was a thread of steel in her words, as if this was nonnegotiable and a done deal. For our *joint* project, of which, last time I'd looked, the original idea was mine, and the decisions were supposed to be agreed upon by both of us. I was all about working *together*, but to have her swoop in and take control of something we hadn't agreed on?

"Hold up," I said. "You can't just form a board of directors without my input."

"I didn't set out to do that, but these women will be stellar. We couldn't do better."

I thought of Chloe, Presley, and Rowan. "Don't be so sure. I've got three powerhouse friends who are interested."

"I don't think we want our board to get too big," she said. "We might not need them."

"It's not a matter of needing them. It's a matter of creating a diverse, effective board. *Together*. If we're going to work together, I need to be included in decisions."

"We need to be willing to split the workload, Magnolia. I might not know as much about operations, but I've been volunteering for many years. If there's one thing I know, it's women who've been involved in large, important nonprofits."

"And I'm sure their input is valuable, but the women I'd like to present for the board are experts in business and in caretaking."

"Well, I'm sure they'd be good, but I've got it handled. These women are committed."

"You're going to have to uncommit them until we can make the decisions together, Mother."

"How am I supposed to do that? They volunteered, Magnolia. When someone offers to help, I know to get them locked in. This is good. It's one thing we can check off our list. You should be happy for one less thing."

"This is a *critical* thing," I said. "A board of directors isn't just about who volunteers. It'll determine the direction this entire organization will take. I want our board carefully curated. It's possibly the biggest decision we face."

"But it doesn't have to be a difficult one," she insisted. "The people I promised positions are good, solid folks."

"But *you can't promise them positions,*" I said through clenched teeth. "Do you see how you basically just walked all over me by doing that?"

"I was embracing opportunity, Magnolia. What did you want me to say? No?"

"You're going to have to call them and walk back your promise."

She shook her head. "I can't do that."

"Well, I can't work with someone who takes action behind my back. You and I agreed, Mother. We're equals in this endeavor. We agree on everything, or it doesn't happen."

"And I fully intend to honor that, but I can't go to these women and take it all back."

"You'll have to find a way. If you can't, we'll split the money from Lansford, and you can do what you want with your half."

"There's no need to threaten that," she said. "Let's not let emotions ruin this."

"I might be emotional, but that's not what this is about. This is about working together, about you not going behind my back and making big decisions *for* me. I've had enough of people disregarding me and making decisions for me for a lifetime. If we're in this together, we're making the decisions together, or I'm out."

I didn't want to fight with her. I wasn't a fan of confrontation. But I wasn't going to quietly accept someone taking away my autonomy over my life, my business, or this endeavor.

My mother gazed out the window, her jaw visibly tight. My heart pounded as I waited for her response, because I meant what I said. If she didn't relent, I would walk.

Finally she said, "Fine," through clenched teeth. "I'll tell them we'll be making our final selections in the coming weeks."

"Thank you," I said tensely. I glanced at the time and closed my laptop. "I think we're done here today. I have a wedding to pull off."

I threw enough cash on the table to cover my half of the bill, then slid out of the booth. "I'll call you next week to continue the discussion."

"Have a merry Christmas, Magnolia," she said, her tone only a little softer.

"Same to you." That was all the holiday goodwill I had

in me at the moment. I needed to get to the barn and get a jumpstart on the decorating for the wedding.

Chapter Thirty-One

Magnolia

I'd known we were cutting it close for time with Presley's wedding in general. It wasn't a small-budget affair, and to have only two and a half months to pull it off was a big task. One I was absolutely up for, but right at this moment? After the frustrating meeting I'd had with my mother? My mood wasn't great, and my energy level was in the cellar.

Both Luke and I were sleep-deprived, short-tempered, and stressed to the hilt as we worked on our separate projects in his chilly barn.

His most pressing concern was the barn's new heating system, which was currently not working right. We'd need to pass out parkas at the wedding if he couldn't fix the problem.

My project at the moment, one of a long list, was assembling the remaining centerpieces. Cambria had been swamped with candle orders, including ours, and had finished the last batch for the wedding late last night. I was nearly done when my phone rang in my pocket.

"Hello, this is Magnolia," I answered, not recognizing the number.

"Hello, Magnolia. This is Allegra, Ella McCabe's assistant."

"Yes," I said, standing up straight to stretch my aching back as I wondered why the heck Ella's assistant was calling. "I remember. What can I do for you?"

"Ella would like to reschedule that appointment if that's possible. She wanted me to apologize on her behalf—"

"She's fine," I said, my curiosity growing.

Luke came out of the barn kitchen, his attention on me as he pulled a chair out from a table and sat down tiredly. He was due to go help with tree sales, I knew, but he looked about to fall over.

He raised his brows at me as if asking what the call was. I shrugged as Allegra continued.

"She said to tell you she received incorrect info and that she's so glad your boyfriend went out of his way to set her straight."

"Wait," I said. "What?" I frowned at Luke.

"She had no idea the person who warned her father about you was your estranged father or that he was trying to hurt you."

My stomach sank at the mention of my embarrassing family drama. "He's...not actually my father," I said stubbornly.

"Felix James is—*was* with a company that Ella's father has done business with for years. Her father didn't realize Felix was no longer employed. Her friend Everly filled her in on the truth."

"Everly?" She had to mean Everly Ash, but I didn't know her well.

"Apparently your boyfriend tracked Everly Ash down at a party and asked if she knew Ella. He remembered they'd done a duet and was hoping Ella and Everly were friends. Everly told her everything about the spurned Felix and his vendetta against you."

"There's some history between us, yes," I said, striving to stay professional.

Why the hell did Luke interfere? Did he think I couldn't do this on my own?

As I paced out of the room, into the preparation room, I did my best to maintain my end of the conversation as we set a time and date to meet right after Christmas.

When I ended the call, my gut was roiling. I didn't even want to meet with Ella. I would, because it was potential business, and as the new planner on the block, I needed every last event I could book, but I wasn't sure I'd ever feel comfortable sitting across the table from her, wondering if she'd hired me out of sympathy or pity.

Between my mother and now Luke, I felt as if nothing was under *my* control. As if someone had swooped in and taken away my autonomy and made decisions about *my* life without my input. Just like when Felix had decided I would marry his stupid, philandering underling, Rick. Or in high school when Felix had pulled strings to make sure I made the cheerleading squad even before tryouts because it would look better for him if his daughter was a cheerleader.

"Hey," Luke said from the doorway behind me.

I didn't turn around.

"Magnolia? What's wrong?" he asked.

"That was Ella McCabe's assistant," I said, my voice low and monotone. "She wants to meet with me."

"Yeah?" His tone was cheery, animated. "Mags, that's great."

I pressed my lips together and pivoted to face him. "Luke, it's not great."

His smile faded. "What? Why?"

"You went behind my back, made a decision about my business without my permission."

He ran his fingers through his hair. Maybe I'd have handled this better if I hadn't just had a similar argument with my mother. Unfortunately we weren't going to find that out today, because I wanted to scream.

"It's *my* business," I emphasized. "Nobody else's. My successes and my failures. I don't need a man thundering in and saving the damn day for me, Luke." My voice had climbed in volume and pitch.

"I wasn't thundering in or saving the day," he said tiredly. "I just wanted to help."

"You have to understand that sometimes people don't want help. Sometimes they want to prove themselves. *Need* to prove themselves."

"Magnolia, you don't need to prove anything. You're doing fantastic with your business."

"Then why not stay out of it?" I asked.

I was wound up. Exhausted, stressed, and a touch hysterical with the emotions storming through me. Maybe I was being a raging stubborn idiot, but I didn't care. I was sick to death of people who thought I wasn't capable of running my own life.

"Ella McCabe is huge," Luke said. "If she signs with you, it's all you. I just wanted you to have the chance. You said yourself planning her wedding would be a foot in the door with the country-music scene."

"It might be, but how can I feel good about it *if* she signs with me and *if* it leads to more business? Don't you see? It'll always be thanks to you."

That truth made me feel like vomiting. In that moment, I couldn't see how it would ever feel like *my* success—if I did someday find success. There would always be a kernel of doubt.

My entire business felt tainted. I'd started it by myself because I needed something that was all mine. It was supposed to be my fresh start after escaping Felix's control.

Luke was only a couple of feet away from me now, but I was too upset. I needed to get out of here before I said something I couldn't take back.

"I need to go," I said abruptly. Without waiting for him to respond, I marched out of the prep room, grabbed my bag, left the centerpieces right where they were, and headed to the door.

"Magnolia," Luke called out just before I reached it. "Come back here. Can't we talk about this like adults?"

My answer was a big, fat hell no, but I didn't bother to say it. I smacked the barn door open, stormed to my car, and managed to get off Luke's property before my eyes filled with tears.

* * *

Luke

I stood there staring at the door Magnolia had exited through, trying to wrap my head around what had just happened.

"What the fuck?" I asked nobody.

She was pissed that I did something nice for her?

Something that had worked out to her benefit?

She'd gotten a meeting with a famous country star. If she landed Ella's wedding, it would be because of what Magnolia said and the impression she gave during the meeting, not because I'd put a bug into Everly Ash's ear.

All I'd done was try to help her with one little action. It'd been a serendipitous moment, not premeditated, just a random long shot for me to ask Everly if she knew Ella.

Now I was the bad guy?

Fuck that.

I was dead-fucking tired, battling the fear that this barn venture was a huge waste of time and money, and I had another six or seven hours of work ahead of me yet tonight. I couldn't let my outrage derail me, not with two days left to finish tree season strong, to get the barn heated, to make sure every detail was ready for West and Presley's wedding, and to somehow find the will to celebrate the holiday with my family.

I wasn't feeling any damn holly-jolliness at the moment. Tomorrow wasn't looking good either.

On the bright side, I would not be visiting Magnolia tonight, so maybe I'd be able to catch up on sleep.

Chapter Thirty-Two

Magnolia

I was a hot mess as I drove off from Luke's.

While my dramatic exit had been fueled by anger, I actually did need to get to Presley's house to work on the guest favors. I had to hold it together for a few more hours before I could go home and collapse and give in to my stormy feelings.

In the meantime, I tried to drown out my thoughts with loud music. It was enough to get me the ten minutes from the farm to Presley's. I parked in her driveway behind Chloe's car, climbed out, slammed my door, and sucked in the crisp, cold lake air, trying to get a grip.

The sun had set while I was at the barn, even though it was barely after five. The evening was cloudy, but the briskness in my lungs made me believe I could forge through the next few hours of wedding prep without losing it.

Presley let me in and hugged me, which I kept short and surface level because if I sank into her comfort, I knew the tears would come.

"Hey, Mags," Chloe said from the farm-style kitchen table where the favors would be assembled. Her smile faded as she looked closer at me, so I made my smile brighter.

"Hey, ladies," I sang out. "Let's get this tree factory going."

The favors were one-year-old evergreen saplings from Luke's farm, potted in a little silver bucket. Tonight we were wrapping the buckets in cellophane, tying them with raffia and a tiny pinecone, and adding stickers, one that said Let Love Grow and had the bride and groom's names and the date, and one on the back that had planting and care instructions for the spruce tree.

"You just sapped the romance right out of the favors," Chloe joked.

"I see what you did there, punny lady," Presley said. "Would you like a drink, Magnolia? I've got wine, seltzer, beer, water, lemonade, or soda."

"Just lemonade," I said, eying her wineglass and Chloe's water. "Alcohol would knock me out at this point."

"You look exhausted." Chloe was eying me again. "Is everything okay?"

Presley came up to the table with my drink, scrutinizing me as she set it down. "Magnolia?"

That was all it took. I crumpled into tears that quickly evolved into blubbering. I would have been mortified if I had any energy left for it, but I didn't.

"Sweetie." Presley pulled me into another hug, and just like I'd feared, that made me lose it further.

All I could do was hold on and let my body try to purge the emotions that had taken over.

"Hey," Chloe said, coming up to us and putting her arms around both of us. "What's going on?"

I couldn't speak if I wanted to. Not yet. They seemed to understand, and we just stood there in a group hug, with me soaking them with my tears.

When I could finally get it out, I said, "I'm so sorry. This is the happiest time of your life, and I didn't want to do this."

Presley grabbed my shoulders and forced eye contact. "Stop that. Welcome to life. Nothing is all joy all the time. What happened? Did your mom do something? Did you and Luke fight?"

"Yes to both," I said and collapsed into sobs again. "These are angry sobs," I insisted, because dammit, I was so flipping angry. And hurt. And frustrated that I couldn't just shove everything in a box for three days and deal with it later.

"Let's go sit by the fireplace and talk," Presley said.

"We need to do trees." I used the cocktail napkin she'd put under my drink to blow my nose.

Chloe made a sound that said I was being dumb. "We'll do trees eventually, but we don't want them snotted on by the wedding planner. Come on." She wove her arm with mine and guided me into the living room, where the gas fireplace glowed and the lights were low, making it warm and cozy.

We all settled on the sectional, the two of them flanking me.

"Tell us everything," Presley said. "Who are you mad at?"

I sniffled, and Presley produced a box of tissues from somewhere. After blowing my nose, I took another to dry my eyes, a futile action because the tears were still falling, which only fueled my frustration and anger.

"Is it your mother?" Chloe asked, knowing I'd had a meeting with her today.

"She was first." I told them how she'd promised her society friends positions on our board of directors without asking me.

"You even told us you'd need to get her agreement," Presley said.

"Exactly. It's a partnership, not a dictatorship."

"That would piss me right off," Chloe said.

"Yes," I hissed. "I finally got her to back down. She's going to call her friends and tell them we have a lot of candidates and we'll finalize the list soon."

"That's good," Presley said. "What was she thinking?"

"I imagine she meant well," Chloe said. "But she went about it wrong."

I nodded, wiping my eyes again, noticing my jaw was tight enough I could crack my skull. "She completely disregarded me, just like she and Felix have done my whole life. Like I can't make a decision myself. I thought I got away from that."

"You did," Presley said. "You just had to remind her you're partners in this project."

"Who was second?" Chloe asked, frowning. "You fought with Luke?"

Tears poured out again. "It was Luke, and the stupid thing is, I think he probably meant well." My composure slipped again, and I buried my face in my hands, my anger mixing with doubt and shame because the more I thought about it, the more I knew that was true. He had my best interests at heart.

"Tell us what he did," Presley said, her hand on my forearm.

Chloe handed me another tissue. I told them the latest

chapter in the Ella McCabe wedding-planning story. "He apparently asked Everly Ash to run interference, taking advantage of her friendship with Ella. I would never do that on my own behalf."

"Knowing Everly the way I do, I'm sure it didn't bother her at all," Chloe said. She would know, as they were sisters-in-law.

"But I completely understand why that would bother *you*," Presley said.

"And to have Everly go to Ella and explain Felix and my over-the-top family drama... I'm so embarrassed."

"Felix is the one who should be embarrassed," Presley said.

"If he had any decency whatsoever," Chloe added. "Which, as we know, he doesn't."

"So I made the appointment with Ella, but now I have to figure out how to act like I'm not the product of a train wreck."

"Magnolia, you're not," Chloe said. "You've overcome your unfathomable upbringing to be a well-grounded, competent event planner and businesswoman."

"Thank you," I said between sniffles. My next thoughts pulled me under with another wave of sobs.

"Hey, what is this?" Presley asked. "It's going to be okay in the end. You can meet with Ella and keep it professional and pleasant. She won't say a word about Felix the Fuck's antics—unless it's to apologize again for believing his lies."

I couldn't answer, couldn't get any words out for several minutes, during which both women held on to me and let me get it out. When I could finally manage it, I said, "I was so mad at Luke, and he was just trying to do something nice for me. All I could think in that moment was someone else was trying to control me."

"And that's a trigger for you," Presley said.

"Apparently a big trigger." I pressed my lips together, so tired of being hysterical.

Chloe made a sort of aha sound. "And if you're like Presley, who also had a controlling father, who also hadn't had a healthy romantic partnership before, you tend to snap defensively before seeing the true motivation behind something that was done out of love."

"Because you're used to having someone try to control you," Presley said, raising her hand as if to own it. "I completely understand your reaction, Magnolia."

I leaned my head on her shoulder. "It doesn't make it okay though. I screwed up everything."

"You didn't," Presley insisted. "You're entitled to your feelings."

"I made him feel terrible."

"Maybe some quieter communication would've been more effective, but you're human," Chloe said with a half smile. "And, hey, communication is important. Now he knows that helping you behind your back might not land right."

"What if he doesn't want to be with me anymore?" I asked in a high-pitched voice.

"He will," Presley said.

I wasn't sure he would, and honestly I wasn't sure I could blame him if he didn't. "You don't know that. He acted out of kindness and caring. I reacted with anger and frustration."

"He knows you're under a lot of stress right now, right?" Chloe pointed out.

I massaged my temples, wondering how I could ever make this up to him. "He's under just as much if not more. Probably more."

"So he should understand you weren't at your best," Presley insisted. "If you apologize and he doesn't accept it, he's not the guy I thought he was."

"I think he is, and he will," Chloe said quietly. "That night you guys were at Humble's together, I watched the way he was with you. Caring, loving, happy to have you at his side."

"I wasn't being irrational or easily triggered that night," I said before blowing my nose again.

"All you can do is apologize," Presley said, "but I'd advise going big."

"Oh, for sure." Chloe pulled one leg up and faced me. "You're going to need to grovel."

Something about that made me laugh. "Is there one step beyond a grovel? Because I need to do that."

"Do you want us to help you come up with something?" Presley asked.

I took in a slow, shaky breath as I thought about how I could ever convince Luke to give me another chance. "I've got the start of an idea," I said. "And tonight is supposed to be about you, Presley, Ms. Bride to Be."

"You were there for me in my time of need," Presley said, undoubtedly referring to the night not that long ago when West had broken her heart.

"And you've been here for me in a big way now, but I'll ponder my grovel when I can't sleep later tonight." I clasped both girls' hands in mine. "Thank you for letting me vent and for understanding me, even when I mess up spectacularly."

"Happens to the best of us," Chloe said. "Someday maybe I'll tell you how I screwed up with Holden."

"But you got the guy in the end," I said, taking hope from that.

"I got the guy in the end." Her contentment and love shone on her face.

"And you're marrying the love of your life in two days," I said to Presley, whose face also lit up. "We've got a lot of work to do, and you're my number one client, so I officially pronounce it wedding time."

Chapter Thirty-Three

Luke

half hour before West and Presley's wedding, I couldn't begin to sort out the shitstorm in my head.

The last two days had put me through a goddamn wringer. The last two months actually, but now that it was Christmas Eve, everything was culminating at once, both good and bad.

The barn was finished on time, and with a functioning furnace, thank all the fucking things, just in the nick of time. We'd finally gotten a working unit installed last night after the rehearsal, and now, twenty-four hours later, the temperature inside was right where we wanted it to be.

West was on top of the world. His daughters were so excited; it was a tangible force that swirled around them. I was elated for him and Presley and their girls. He'd found exactly what I wanted.

Well, not exactly. I'd had my heart set on a strawberry blonde instead of a brunette.

Unfortunately it appeared that desire was one-sided and based on a delusion, because Magnolia hadn't said one single fucking word to me about our disagreement two days ago. We'd been reduced to polite remarks only when necessary in the company of others. *Luke, you'll stand here. Luke and Chance, you'll enter from here at this time. Wedding party, your table is there.*

Not one word of regret about blowing up at me for trying to do something nice for her.

Silence could convey a lot. Hers told me I'd cared a whole bunch more than she did.

I was in the mens' getting-ready room of the barn with West, Chance, and Thomas, West's stepfather, when my phone buzzed with a notification. I pulled it out of my pocket to read the message from my father.

> Dad: Addie and I are here. She's itching to show you her dress.

> Luke: I'll be right out.

I shoved the mental shitstorm aside, told the guys I'd be right back, and walked out to the main room. I paused for a moment and took in the scene before me, letting myself really see what I'd done here with the help of my friends and employees.

I'd practically lived in the barn for the past week, and especially the past two days as I'd dealt with the heating issue. The rehearsal had been here last night, followed by dinner at Henry's, which I'd been late for because of said heating issue. We'd already had the first look and taken care of all the wedding party photos, the formal ones here in the main room in front of the altar. So yeah, I'd spent a hell of a lot of time in here, but only now did I really *see* the place.

It looked fucking incredible, if I did say so myself.

It was even better than I'd envisioned now that all the soft touches had been added for the wedding.

That was Magnolia. I could fully admit she had a special talent. She'd transformed the barn into a beautiful, magical winter wonderland, with loads of greenery from our farm, fairy lights, silver ornaments, ribbons, and accents, and cozy LED candlelight. It smelled of pine, wood, and now the savory dinner the caterers were busily prepping in the kitchen. I couldn't see them from here, but I could hear their clinking and sense a hive of activity beyond the opposite wall.

I'd held on to hope for the months this project had taken, and now, being able to see it all fall into place, I believed I had a winner here. This humble barn would serve as a gorgeous venue for weddings and whatever else anyone wanted to hold here far into the future. I felt sure of it now.

"Daddy!" Addie's voice drew me out of my thoughts, and I spotted her and my dad just inside the double entrance doors. She waved frantically, holding my dad's hand.

I waved back and headed toward them, through the few guests who'd already arrived and were being seated for the ceremony at the opposite end.

"Wow," I said as I approached them. "When did my doodlebug turn into an actual princess? You look stunning, Addie."

She let go of my dad's hand, held her lacy burgundy dress out to the sides, and spun around for me to admire her. Her hair had big curls held back by ornate clips on each side, thanks to Emerson and Willow, who'd styled hair for the bride, her bridesmaids, West's daughters, and had kindly included Addie in the mix. My dad was damn good with her, but his hairstyling skills left a lot to be desired.

"I told her she might outshine the bride," my dad said.

"Wait till you see Miss Presley," Addie said, her eyes wide with awe. "She's beautiful."

"Snow's coming down pretty good out there," my dad said.

I glanced outside as the door opened and saw there was maybe a couple of inches of snow on the ground.

Then I realized it was Ben who'd opened the door. He entered with his four kids. They all stomped snow off their shoes.

"Addie!" Ruby hollered even though they were just feet away from us.

"Can I go see them?" Addie asked.

I looked to my dad for the answer.

"You go say hi to them as they take off their coats, but come back to me before it gets too crowded," he said. "Maybe we can sit next to them."

My daughter ran off, calling out to her friends about sitting together. I met Ben's gaze, and he nodded, as if to say he'd keep an eye on her.

When I turned back to my dad, he was facing the length of the barn, looking toward the altar, taking it all in, from the majestic beams above to the beautifully set tables in front of us and the white-fabric-covered chairs in rows at the other end.

"Luke, I have to admit, this is downright astounding," he said.

I whipped my head his way to interpret whether he used that word in a good way or a negative one.

He nodded repeatedly as he continued to take it all in. "I've been a naysayer from the start, but I finally under-

stand. What you've done to this old barn is extraordinary."
He slapped me lightly on the back. "Well done, son."

I let that compliment sink in, maybe waiting to see if he
took it back because it was such a turnaround. When he
didn't say more, I said, "Thanks, Dad." Two little words that
didn't begin to express what was going on inside me at
hearing him say something positive about the project, never
mind praising it.

Addie came running up to me. "Daddy, can I go show
Miss Magnolia my dress?"

"Miss Magnolia is very busy today, bug. I haven't seen
her for a while."

"She's right there!"

I looked where she was pointing and saw the back of
Magnolia in the doorway to the kitchen.

"She might be busy," I told her, still taking in the back of
the woman I was pathetically in love with.

At that moment, Magnolia turned around and looked
straight at me, as if she'd felt my stare on her back. Then she
shocked me when a smile slowly lifted her face—a real smile
that went all the way to her eyes.

"Miss Magnolia!" Addie called, waving.

My decision as to whether to let Addie go bother her
was taken away when Magnolia made her way toward us. I
stood there unsmiling, watching her every step, admiring
the way she looked in her long velvet dress that hugged her
curves and dipped low between her breasts. Her hair was
down in back, with waves flowing over her shoulders and
portions of it in a twist on the sides. She looked gorgeous.
When she got closer, I noticed the exhaustion in her eyes.

I knew damn well she was beyond tired and stressed,
and I suspected that was part of her lashing out two days
ago. I understood her condition well because I'd been going

through similar pressure and overwork. But it didn't seem like too much to ask for her to take two minutes to text me before she went to bed at night and say she was sorry.

"Look at you," Magnolia said, her attention fully on my daughter. "Your dress is beautiful, Addie. *You're* beautiful."

"Thanks," Addie said, suddenly shy. "So are you."

"We look very fancy, don't we?" Magnolia put her arm around Addie in a side hug.

"Addie, we're getting seats!" Ruby announced as the Holloway family walked past.

My dad was following them and held out his arm to his granddaughter. "Let's go if you want to sit by Ruby and her siblings."

"I'll see you at the reception," Magnolia said to Addie as she skipped away toward my dad. She raised her gaze to me. "You look good, Luke."

"We need to talk," I stated, trying to keep my anger out of my tone since people milled about nearby.

"I agree. Tonight? Afterward? Once you get Addie to bed and I finish cleanup?"

"Text me when you're ready. I need to get back in there." I pointed to the guys' room.

She looked at the time on her phone. "Yes. You and Chance go up in five minutes."

She was back to business. The only thing for me to do was nod and walk away, unsure how we'd be able to mend our relationship in a few hours.

* * *

Magnolia

.　.　.

After sending the breathtaking bride down the aisle, I took a seat in the back row and watched West meet Presley at the altar.

The chairs were nearly full, telling me the snow hadn't kept anyone away.

Putting my personal life out of my head took effort, but I forced myself to pay attention to every moment while staying aware of the vendors in case any of them needed me.

As West took Presley's hands, my eyes teared up and spilled over. I made a mental note to always have tissues with me during a ceremony from now on.

West's face radiated love and a dose of *I can't believe how lucky I am*. When I looked at Presley, hers said the same. These two were so perfectly in love.

Along with the sheer joy I felt for them was a poignant ache in my chest. I wanted what they had so badly. I wanted a man to look at me the way West looked at Presley. I wanted someone by my side for the rest of my life.

I wanted all these things, but was I capable of accepting them?

As terrifying as it was to put all my trust into someone else, I was ready with every fiber of my being to try with Luke. But I was worried sick that I might've done irreparable damage.

During the thirty seconds we'd talked right before the ceremony, he hadn't given me any indication that he was open to trying again. Anger had radiated off him, even though he'd been doing his best to keep it inside. I'd been able to feel it.

I knew I deserved his anger, but I also hoped he could find it in him to give me a second chance.

I tuned back in to the ceremony and realized I'd zoned out during the vows. The bride and groom were about to kiss. As they locked lips and the kiss went on, a dreamy sigh escaped me. When the bride and groom finally came up for air, the expression on West's face was a mix of mischief, love, and happiness, eliciting laughter from the guests.

As the string quartet began the processional music, I hopped up. Back to work for me. I had to get through the next three plus hours before I'd know whether my planned grovel was enough to win Luke over.

Chapter Thirty-Four

Magnolia

Despite the state of my personal life and an underlying nervousness about my upcoming talk with Luke, I was riding a bit of a high as Presley and West's wedding and reception ended, even though the only sip of alcohol I'd consumed was for the champagne toasts hours ago.

We'd sent off the ravingly happy bride and groom earlier, and the guests didn't linger for long after their departure since it was Christmas Eve. We'd had enough food but not too much, the music had been on point, the barn was honestly a fantastic venue, and an atmosphere of love and joy prevailed.

My second successful wedding was in the books, and it felt tremendous.

The catering staff had done a thorough cleanup of the kitchen and all the tables while I'd packed up the lion's share of Presley's decor. Luke didn't have a cleaning crew yet, so the plan had been for us to clean the rest after Christmas. The big question was, would there still be an us after Christmas?

Everyone else was gone now. The chairs from around the tables were stacked neatly along the wall near the door so they were ready to go into storage. I'd swept the entire main room and tidied up the getting-ready rooms to make sure no one had left anything behind. Now I was setting the scene for my talk with Luke.

Self-doubt set in deeper with every LED candle I moved to the far end of the barn, which had served as the dance floor during the reception. I kept moving them according to my plan though, with the goal of setting up a romantic backdrop.

Please let us get to the romantic part. Please let him hear me out and forgive me.

The very thought of tonight ending badly made me want to throw up, because I'd admitted it to myself—Luke was the one for me. If I couldn't have him, I didn't see how I'd ever want anyone else.

I'd moved two armchairs out from one of the rooms and situated them in the middle of a ring of more than two hundred candles from the reception. Presley had enthusiastically given her blessing for me to repurpose them for my mission, as she called it. I'd set up a Bluetooth speaker with romantic piano music in the background. It was a fine line between overdoing it with romance and making the barn feel homey and comfortable for the most important discussion of my life.

When everything was in place, I curled into one of the chairs, pulled my legs up under me, and texted Luke.

Magnolia: Come out to the barn?

> Luke: Do you want to come inside to talk instead?

> Magnolia: I have something for you out here.

He didn't reply, leaving me to hope he was on his way out and not blowing me off. He'd been the one to bring up talking before I'd had the chance. If he wasn't here in five minutes, I might break down and sob—again.

I was so tired of crying.

The barn door opened three minutes later. Hurdle one cleared. Only a dozen or so to go.

I turned to watch him cross the floor toward me, trying to read his mood. His face gave nothing away, but his body language conveyed fatigue and a hardness I hadn't seen in him since we'd ended our eighteen-year cold war.

Not exactly encouraging, but it didn't deter me.

"Hey," I said, offering up a smile as he approached.

"Hey. What's going on?" He glanced at the candle display in confusion and stopped between the two chairs but didn't sit.

"Have a seat?"

He lowered himself to the front half of the cushion, as if he didn't intend to stay long.

I sat up straighter and smoothed the soft velvet of my dress, gathering my thoughts even though I'd gone over what I wanted to say a dozen times since the barn had emptied.

"Thanks for coming out here." I sought out eye contact and barreled forward. "Luke, I'm sorry for my reaction the other day. My overreaction."

"Your explosion?" he asked.

"Yes. Whatever you want to call it, I'm sorry. Now that

I've had time to cool down, I can see your only motivation was to do something kind and caring for me, not to control me. Not to embarrass me. Instead of thinking it through, I jumped to my old way of thinking. I was completely in the wrong, and you didn't deserve my wrath."

He nodded once. "Thanks for apologizing."

I kept my eyes on him, hoping he'd say more, but he didn't.

So I did.

"It came right after my mother steamrolled me, which doesn't make it okay, but I was already in defense mode. I'm not making excuses. I was in the wrong." I studied him, silently urging him to say something.

Eventually he said, "I can't understand how you could find out someone did something nice for you and jump straight to outrage. I don't know how to handle that, Magnolia."

"I know. I don't know how you could handle it either. I'm sure my reaction didn't make any sense." I gathered my hair at my nape and pulled it to one side, a nervous tic. "Trust is hard for me, Luke. I haven't had many people in my life who had my best interests at heart, especially not men."

He leaned forward, propped his elbows on his knees, and ran a hand over his hair, seeming deep in thought. "On the surface, I know that," he said, "but I don't think I understood how much that could crop up between you and me. I'm not your father, Magnolia. I'm not your grandfather. I hope like hell I'm *nothing* like either of them."

"You're *not*. If you were, I wouldn't be with you. I wouldn't be in love with you."

His head popped up, and his gaze snapped to mine.

I swallowed and gathered my courage. Then I slid off

my chair and kneeled in front of his, needing to be closer to him. "I love you, Luke. I've never said those words to a man before."

My eyes teared up for the seven thousandth time in the past three days, but this time it was different. An overflow of the love I felt for him, the hope I had for us. And yes, I was also terrified he wouldn't reciprocate.

He straightened and held out his hand. I put mine in his, relishing the feel of his fingers clasping me, holding me there. As if my declaration of love mattered.

Tears overflowed from both my eyes at the same time, dropping down my cheeks.

"Mags," he said, his voice softening, his whole body softening, as if I'd broken down his rigidity with my vulnerable confession.

I exhaled fully for the first time since he'd entered the barn.

He brushed his finger across my cheek, wiping away my tears. "I love you too."

My relief rushed out of me in the form of more tears, even though he wasn't pulling me into his arms and running off with me into the proverbial sunset.

"I want to make us work," I said, "and I'm so afraid I'm too messed up. I'm working on this trust issue with my therapist, but it's a lot of years to deprogram, and I might screw up sometimes."

He squeezed my hand, blew out a breath, and stood. I sat back on my heels in alarm. When he paced slowly toward the speaker I'd set up near the altar, I tried to calm down, noting he wasn't stomping toward the door.

At the altar, he craned his neck back and looked up at the decor high on the wall, above the small window, a cluster of large metal stars. My heart pounded as I waited for him to say something, to look at me, anything to make me think he wasn't about to throw his hands up and leave.

"Luke?" I said quietly.

He finally pivoted, came back toward me, and sat on the thick arm of the chair. "It occurs to me that I added to your trust issues when my mom was fired. You should've been able to come to me. I broke your trust." Again he craned his head back, this time with his eyes shut. "*Fuck*." He held out his hand again. I stood and took it as I stepped closer. "I'm so sorry for that again, Mags."

"It's in the past," I said.

"Yes, but isn't that the point? Your past made you who you are. Well, some of who you are. I refuse to credit any of the good parts to that asshole who raised you."

"I'm glad you think I have some good parts."

He stood, pulled me tightly into his arms, and held me. I hugged him back, rested my head against his chest, and took comfort in the feel of his arms around me and his heartbeat in my ear.

"You have so many good parts," he said. "But I love all your parts. Good, bad, sexy, stubborn."

"I love all your parts too."

We stood like that for a while, both of us seeming to soak up the feel of the other, as if Luke had missed me as much as I'd missed him the past two days.

"I have something for you," I eventually said, pulling away enough to look at his handsome face.

He looked puzzled. "A present? Christmas isn't until tomorrow."

"Two presents, and you're getting them tonight."

"You're getting yours tomorrow."

I smiled up at him, taking it as a good sign he'd gotten me a gift. I couldn't care less about the present itself, but you didn't give Christmas presents to someone you were planning to break up with.

"Sit," I said, pointing at his chair again.

I hurried over to where I'd set his gift bag out of sight and took it to him.

"This is heavy." He went for the handles, but I stopped him.

"Before you look inside, this is part one of your Christmas present. It's for when I screw up again, because I probably will even though I'm going to do everything in my power to try not to."

He looked at me with amusement in his eyes. "Are you trying to tell me you're not perfect?"

"Not quite yet," I said lightly, then went serious. "I'm trying my best though."

He grabbed my hand and tugged me down close enough to kiss me. "That's all any of us can do."

I kissed him again, reveling in the taste of him after two horrible days of no kisses. I managed to pull myself away, straighten, and gesture to the bag.

Luke reached into the folds of tissue paper and drew out the bottle of whiskey. A grin broke out across his face. "You think I'm going to need this, huh?"

"I think we'll have some champagne moments but probably some whiskey ones too."

"Sounds about right," he said, grinning. Then he pulled me onto his lap. "I'm here for both kinds, Mags."

"So am I. Let's hope there's more champagne than whiskey though."

I put my arms around his neck and kissed him again. It was sometime later that we surfaced and he said, "You said there's a part two? Does it include sexy lingerie with a bow for me to undo?"

I laughed. "This didn't seem like the time or place for that, but maybe later?" I sat up straighter on his lap. "It turns out you're really hard to buy for. All we've done since we've been together is work and sneak out so we could spend some time together."

"That's the truth."

"My second gift is time for you and me to spend together. I talked to your dad and Scotty and arranged for you to take three full days and two nights off around New Year's Eve. We're going to a quaint little inn in the Smoky Mountains where we can focus on us and nothing else. Your dad will take care of Addie, and the Holloways are going to have her out for a sleepover for one of those nights to give him a break. Scotty's got the farm covered. There will be no working for either of us."

He closed his eyes as if savoring the thought of some time away. "That's literally the best gift you could ever give me," he said, his voice husky. "Time. With you." He pulled me closer. "I can't wait. Thank you, Mags."

"You're welcome," I said, hugging him again. "Confession: It's not exactly a selfless gift. I want you all to myself for as long as I can have you."

He pulled me in for a kiss. "You've got me, Mags. I'm all yours."

I repositioned myself so that my legs straddled his lap. "I'm all yours too. But probably not right here in the middle of the barn. Any chance you can get away to my place?"

He laughed. "Have you looked outside lately?"

"It's snowing. I know," I said.

"When I came out from the house, there were five or six inches on the ground, and it was still coming down in big, fluffy flakes."

I frowned, thinking the drive home with my worn tires would not be fun.

"Tomorrow's Christmas," Luke said. "We've been careful around Addie, but I want to wake up next to you on Christmas morning. Here, in my bed."

"Are you sure?"

He gave me a knowing look I didn't quite understand until he said, "There're six inches of snow out there, Mags. I believe you're officially snowed in."

I smiled, my whole body going hot imagining spending a full night with him and waking up beside him. "I didn't bring any pajamas with me. What ever will I do?"

With a sexy growl, he said, "You'll have to sleep naked, I'm afraid."

"Won't I get cold with no pajamas on?"

"I promise I'll keep you warm."

"That's a really good offer," I said, my temperature already rising.

"In the morning, I'll lend you some sweats, and we'll do Christmas morning the Durham way. Casual, with lots of presents, lots of food, and lots of love."

Tears filled my eyes again. Who knew one person could produce so many freaking tears? This time they were from utter joy. "Tomorrow will be my very first true, love-filled, family Christmas. There's no one in the world I'd rather experience that with than you. I love you, Luke."

"I love you, Mags."

We disentangled ourselves and stood, left the dozens of battery-operated candles glowing, and ventured out into the snowy night together.

Epilogue

Luke

We hadn't had a Christmas like this since I was a teenager, when my mom was healthy and seemingly happy.

Our old farmhouse was warm, cozy, and brimming with love, family, and holiday spirit. The whole main floor smelled of the cinnamon rolls we'd devoured as we'd opened presents and the ham I'd put in the oven once the rolls were out.

Waking up with Magnolia in my bed had brought me a peace like I'd never felt before. A sense of completeness, rightness.

This had always been my home, but it'd never felt quite like this.

Making love to Magnolia until the early-morning hours didn't hurt either. I didn't even care that my body was tired. My heart was full.

And my nerves were buzzing with anticipation and—I could own it—fear.

"I still can't get over these," my dad said, sitting in his recliner and studying the gifts Magnolia had given him. She'd presented my dad with three framed, color sketches of his favorite tractors with their names, Matilda, Dolly, and Jane, underneath. She'd come up with the idea after being here for Thanksgiving and had hired one of the artists at the art studio outside of town to bring it to life.

"Even on the coldest days when you don't have to go outside," Magnolia, who was curled up on the sofa next to me, said, "you'll be able to see your workhorses."

"And you'll have a piece of Mom too," I pointed out, since she'd been the namer of tractors.

I did a double take as my crusty old father wiped a tear from the corner of his eye.

"I just love 'em, Miss Magnolia," he said. "I'm going to hang 'em on that wall over there so I can see 'em all the time."

"Your 'ladies' will look great on that wall," Magnolia told him. "Thank you all for my presents. I love everything so much." She held up the thick sweater Addie had picked out for her with an appreciative grin, then brushed the soft yarn against her cheek. "This is the softest sweater ever, Addie."

In addition to the physical gifts, Magnolia had heard from her mother earlier. Bianca had apologized for their argument the other day and acknowledged Magnolia's point was valid, so they'd made a tentative peace. Then she'd revealed that Felix's house was on the market. The asshole was leaving town.

There almost wasn't a better present than that, except...

"There's one more thing," I said, working my way out of the nest she and I had made among all the presents. "Be right back."

As I headed to my bedroom, Addie closed in on my spot, already wearing the heart pendant Magnolia had given her and carrying the horse from her pet salon. The pendant was silver with Addie's birth stone in the middle. My daughter adored it and Magnolia's suggestion that she could always touch her necklace and remember how much she was loved by everyone in this room.

Once in my room, I tuned out their conversation, my heart pounding and my mind drowning with what I was about to do.

Was it too soon? Had we known each other for two months or eighteen years—or nearly our whole lives? All were true in different ways, of course, but for me it felt like a lifetime so far.

I wanted more.

I opened the top drawer of my dresser and took out the little cloth bag. Without giving myself more time to worry, I closed my palm around it and headed back out to the living room.

As I entered the room, Magnolia's gaze met mine, hers curious and so damn pretty, even with her drowning in my too-big sweatshirt and some leggings she'd remembered were in her car. Her hair was uncombed, her face bare of makeup, her cheeks like pink apples, and I'd never felt half as gaga about a woman as I did for her.

Instead of joining her back on the sofa, I headed toward the Christmas tree, making eye contact with my dad. He nodded, his eyes gleaming.

"Mags," I said, then gestured with my index finger for her to come join me.

She looked over at Addie, who I hadn't let in on my plans.

"Did you get Miss Magnolia another present, Daddy?"

"I sure did." I reached out for Magnolia's hand as she approached me.

Without blinking, she placed her smaller, softer hand in mine, filling my heart with hope. I closed my fingers around hers.

"You already spoiled me," she said, grinning wide.

I hoped she felt spoiled by the spa gift certificate and the brand-new knee-high boots. I also hoped she nearly forgot all about those gifts when I presented the next one.

Letting go of her hand, I pulled the cloth bag out of my pocket, reached into it, and removed the first item.

"Hold out your arm and close your eyes," I told her as my dad and Addie looked on.

Magnolia tilted her head, closed her eyes, then held her arm out. I rolled a friendship bracelet onto it, making sure it faced the right way.

After a quick glance at my father, who winked at me, I said, "Open your eyes."

Grinning, she looked at the colorful bracelet I'd made using Addie's beads. "Oh, pretty colors," she said.

I'd gone with forest green, midnight blue, and silver, but the colors were hardly the point.

I waited as she twisted her arm to see the whole thing.

"Will you...marry me?" she read, her voice going high-pitched at the end of the question. Her gaze popped up to mine, her eyes wide and questioning. "Is this...?"

In answer, I took her hand and lowered to one knee.

"Luke..."

Still holding her hand, I lifted the other item I'd stored in the bag—a vintage white-gold engagement ring with a transitional-cut diamond flanked by three smaller diamonds on each side of the band. "I heard a rumor you're looking for a new last name. Would you do me the honor of a lifetime by becoming Mrs. Durham?"

"Daddy!" Addie hollered, jumping up and down on the sofa. "You have to say, 'Will you marry me?'"

I laughed and gazed up into Magnolia's beautiful, damp eyes. "My bad. Will you marry me, Magnolia?"

"Yes!" She laughed and watched as I squeezed my eyes shut on the dampness threatening, then slid the ring on with shaking hands.

It fit as if it was made for her.

Magnolia gasped as she looked at the ring. "Luke, this is beautiful."

I swallowed down on my emotions so I could explain, "It was my mother's and my grandmother's before her."

She looked back at me as that sank in, then let out an awed, "Ohh. It's absolutely perfect. I'm the one who's honored."

She tugged me to my feet, placed her hands on each side of my face, and kissed me hard. Then she threw her arms around my neck and hugged me, bouncing on the balls of her sock-covered feet. "We're getting married!"

I pulled her into me and breathed her in, overcome by bliss and happiness and, not going to lie, relief. She wanted to be mine. Forever.

"Thank God," I said, pressing my forehead to hers. "It took us a long time to get here."

"But we made it."

At that moment, a wrecking ball crashed into our sides. I laughed at my daughter, picked her up, and pulled her into our hug.

"You're okay with me marrying Miss Magnolia, bug?"

"Yes, yes, yes!" Addie yelled. "I'm getting my wish, Daddy!"

My dad had shuffled over to us. As I set Addie back on the floor, he came up to Magnolia's side with his arms spread. "Welcome to our family, Magnolia."

"Thank you," she said as she hugged him. "I'm..." She shook her head. "I'm blown away. Did you know about this?"

"I did. I dug out his mother's ring. She'd be thrilled for you two."

Magnolia examined the ring again, holding it up at every angle, watching how the light hit it.

"Wait till you see it in the sunlight," I told her.

It wasn't the largest stone, but I knew very well that Magnolia would treasure this family heirloom a thousand times more than something that cost, well, a thousand times more.

"We get to have a wedding!" Addie sang. "Can I help decorate again?"

Magnolia laughed and bent down to her level. "You can help with more than decorations. Your daddy and I have a lot to discuss, but how would you feel about being a flower girl?"

My daughter's eyes went huge. "Will my dress be sparkly?"

"It just might be," Magnolia said. "We'll have to find something beautiful."

Addie threw her arms around Magnolia, making my heart damn near explode.

The Facetime ringtone sounded from Addie's tablet, which she'd set out on the coffee table for her mom's planned call.

"Mommy!" Addie yelled. "I have to tell her we're having a wedding!"

"Let's go out to the kitchen and set you up at the table for that call," my dad said. "Let your dad and Miss Magnolia have some time together."

Addie grabbed the tablet and sprinted to the kitchen table with my dad shuffling after her.

"Are you okay with your ex being the first to know?" she asked.

"Jessie will be cool. She's been seeing a guy for over a year and always asks me if I'm ever going to settle down."

Magnolia held her hand out again, admiring the ring on her finger. I moved next to her and admired it too.

"I love it so much, Luke. I love that it was your mom's and your grandmother's. I don't know about your grandmother, but your mother left some big shoes to fill."

"She had her share of challenges, but she had a good heart," I said, wishing my mom could've known Mags as my girlfriend and wife instead of just as her employer's daughter. I turned her to face me, pulled her into my arms again, and kissed her slowly, thoroughly, the kind of tongue kiss that would have my daughter yelling *gross!*

When we came up for air, I said, "I have another big question for you."

"Nothing could be as big as this." She held the ring up again, as if checking to make sure it was really there.

"What do you think about moving in?"

"Here?"

I chuckled. "Your apartment is cute and all, but I don't think it'd fit both of us, let alone my kid and my dad."

"Before the wedding, you mean?"

"Hell, tomorrow if you can make it work."

"Really? You think Addie would understand?"

"We're committed. You're going to be my wife."

She closed her eyes and smiled, as if savoring that idea. I sure as hell was.

"And your dad?" she asked.

"Already talked to him. He's all for it. We've got years to make up for, Mags. I want to be with you as much as possible. I want you in my bed every night, your toes curling, your head buried in your pillow to keep from screaming my name too loud."

She kissed me then looked me in the eye. "It's another yes from me, Luke. I want that too."

"I just realized the flaw in my plan," I said. "I'm dying to whisk you away to my bed right now and spend the next twelve hours making love to you."

"Mmm, that sounds amazing...and impossible."

"Yep. Dammit."

"It just means it'll be extra sweet when we finally get there later."

"I hope you're not planning to get a lot of sleep tonight."

"I'm hoping you won't let me."

"I won't. Promise."

We kissed again, with Addie and my dad talking to Jessie in the background.

Magnolia ended the kiss, took my hand, and pulled me to the sofa. "I actually have one more surprise for you."

"You gave me my gifts last night," I said.

"This one isn't Christmas-specific, and it's not entirely for you."

She picked up her phone from the table, unlocked it, and swiped several times, then showed me a photo of some kind of document.

"What's this?" I asked, trying to puzzle it out.

"I sold the emerald ring."

"The heart ring?" I asked.

"The very one my mother stole and returned."

I looked at the photo again and my eyes nearly popped out of my head. The dollar amount at the bottom was damn close to six figures. "Congratulations, Mags. That was some ring, huh?"

"Historical significance, blah blah, nothing I wanted weighing me down, so yeah, I sold it. At first I swore I didn't want anything remotely connected to Felix, but I changed my mind. I want to put it in a college fund for Addie if you're okay with it."

My mouth fell open. I hadn't priced a college education lately, but this would go a damn long way toward covering it. Further if we invested it wisely.

"If you don't want it because of the source, I get it, but here's where I landed on that. Felix did everything he could to come between us, and this ring was at the heart of it. But guess what? It didn't work. We won. We're together and happy. He's alone and miserable. There's a kind of poetic justice for us to use the proceeds for good, for our family. For Addie. Because I get a sick pleasure from turning what he did out of evil intent into something joyful and full of love."

Hell. I couldn't seem to find my voice because I was so overcome with love for this woman.

"You know what?" I said as soon as I could speak. "A few weeks ago, I swore to myself he'd never come between us again. And like you said, we won. He didn't. It's a perfect ending, Mags."

"So you like the idea?"

"No. I fucking love the idea. This could be life-changing for Addie. And I agree about poetic justice. While he rots in his personal hell—in a different town—we'll be building a life and a family full of love. It's the best revenge in the world."

"The very best."

We sealed our lips again, a promise of a future full of love.

Bonus Epilogue

August, one and a half years later

Magnolia

The smell of pizza could make a pregnant woman act possessed.

By the time I got home to the farm, I was ready to harm anyone who came between me and the Humble's pies I'd picked up for my family fifteen minutes ago. Their aroma had been torturing me ever since.

As I ungracefully slid my eight-months-pregnant body down from the driver's seat of my SUV, my handsome husband appeared out of nowhere. Luke took my hands and pulled me into him for a kiss.

"Hey, gorgeous," he said, then bent to kiss my ready-to-pop belly. "Hello, Truett Ander. You been kicking your mama today?"

"He's been calm actually," I said, lovingly cradling my abdomen.

"Must be exhausted like his mom."

"Entirely possible. Even more than tired? I'm famished."

"We better get those pizzas inside then," he said, eyeing the two boxes on the passenger seat.

I stepped out of the way, and Luke reached over the driver's seat to grab the food and my bag. Slinging the bag over his shoulder and balancing the pizza boxes in one hand, he took my hand in the other. We walked to the door of the farmhouse.

"How's your day?" I asked.

"Batshit. So right on track for the start of pick-your-own."

This weekend marked the opening of a promising apple season. According to Luke, our yield would likely be the highest ever. Mother Nature had smiled upon our farm for both berries and apples this year. On top of that, the barn was booked every single weekend, mostly weddings with a handful of family reunions and birthday parties. Luke had added multiple outdoor areas, including one that overlooked the apple orchard. We'd exchanged our own vows last year when the apple trees were in full blossom, then held our reception in the barn. I couldn't imagine a more perfect day for our little family.

This weekend's event was a small wedding of about seventy-five guests for a couple in their fifties. The bride had hired me as her planner and chosen the barn for the venue. My assistant, Celia, was handling many of the details for it since I was up to my eyeballs with the public open house at the Lotus Collective, our nonprofit women's community.

After more than a year and a half of planning, developing, building, learning, and chaos, not in that order, we were four days away from our very first residents' move-in. In spite of my bone-deep exhaustion, I was buzzing with excitement and pride for what we were creating. I'd never set out to lead a nonprofit organization, but the fulfillment this giant project gave me was unparalleled. Our mission to help women who'd come from ugly places and harmful relationships like my mother and me had lit a fire inside me. As the president of the board, I felt like this was my baby even though, thankfully, we had a compact but highly competent staff who'd be in charge of the day-to-day. I'd continue to run Moments by Magnolia.

We'd purchased a large plot of land on the northwest edge of town. Over the last sixteen months, we'd constructed a thirty-six-unit apartment-style residence and a headquarters that housed the offices, a community center, areas for education, fitness, healthcare, and mental health, and a dining center. The next construction phase would be our equine therapy center and our nature retreat, both of which promised mental health, exercise, and healing benefits for our residents.

The board—made up of Chloe, Presley, Rowan, three of my mother's acquaintances, plus my mother and me—and a handful of other volunteers were busily prepping for tomorrow's event. The open house was from four to seven, and our hopes were to get as many on the property as we could, to familiarize the townspeople with what we were doing and build connections with the community.

We were already forging partnerships with local business owners in a program that would assist our residents in finding jobs. If they needed help with resumes and interview skills beforehand, we planned to provide that, along with other life skills like goal setting, budgeting, organizing, planning, cleaning, cooking...whatever people needed to become independent and successful.

"Are you going back after dinner, or are you done for the day?" Luke asked as we walked into the kitchen.

"I'm going back," I confirmed. I didn't even need to ask whether he still had work to do after dinner. "We've still got so many finishing touches and lots of tidying to do."

"Hi, Daddy. Hi, Mags." Addie pranced into the kitchen. "Pizza, pizza, pizza."

"You're telling me," I said, grinning conspiratorially. "Where's your pops?"

"Right here," Dale said. "Following my nose." He headed to his place at the table, moving a little more easily these days thanks to regular acupuncture treatments that helped his pain.

Once we were seated around the table, we dug into our dinner, the room going quiet. I was three bites in when my abdomen hardened in what I could only imagine was a contraction. It didn't hurt so much as surprise me. Since we were still about a month out, I knew it must be those practice contractions. It wasn't remotely strong enough to keep me from my dinner.

I was nearly done with my first slice when another fake contraction tightened my belly. I put my hand on it and frowned.

"You okay?" Luke asked.

I smiled and held up my pizza crust before taking another bite. "I'm good. The pizza's delicious."

"Always is," Dale said as he helped himself to another piece.

As I took a bite of my second slice, I felt a sudden gush

of warm liquid between my legs. I froze, trying to make sense of the situation. Still not chewing my food, I met my husband's gaze, my eyes surely bugging out.

"What's wrong?" he asked, concern threading his tone.

I glanced at Addie, then Dale, then back to Luke. I chewed my food, trying to find a way to break this news without causing an uproar as liquid continued to soak my legs, my chair, maybe the entire kitchen. After swallowing, I said, "I think my water just broke."

Luke leaped out of his chair faster than I'd ever seen him move. "We need to get to the hospital."

I knew he was right, but I couldn't help a mournful glance at the cheese-laden Meat-astic not-even-half-gone pizza.

Dale pushed his chair back, looking stern. "It's early, isn't it?"

"Almost a month," I said, fear gripping me as reality sank in that this baby was on its way.

I was about to *give birth*. Today.

"What is happening here?" Addie asked, her gaze darting from one grown-up to the next.

"Baby Truett is on his way," Luke told her.

Addie's eyes went saucer big. Then she slipped out of her chair and darted off, on a mission I couldn't figure out, mostly because I was distracted by the incredible mess I was sitting in the middle of. "We need towels."

"I've got the mess," my father-in-law said in a tone that left no room for arguments. "You two get outta here."

Another contraction gripped me, this one harder and inching toward painful. Boom. Another reality check. I was terrified of childbirth, but I'd managed to put it out of my head lately, what with the insanity that was planning a large event at our brand-new, sparkling campus.

"I don't want to do this," I said quietly as soon as the contraction ended.

Luke grinned and kissed my temple as Dale came into the room carrying a stack of old towels.

"You don't have to do that," I told my father-in-law. "It's...ew." Bodily fluids. Embarrassing.

"I'm a farmer, my dear. This is nothing." He tossed the towels down one by one as Luke led me out of the puddle.

Addie sprinted back into the room carrying the bag I'd packed less than a week ago at Luke's urging. I'd done it to relax him, believing I had weeks before I'd need it.

The joke was clearly on me.

* * *

Luke

I finally got my wife into the truck and settled on a waterproof pad after we'd changed her into dry clothes. She'd been about to bring a slice of pizza with her until another contraction struck, making her realize she had bigger things to focus on.

The drive to the hospital in Nashville was about an hour on a normal day. I intended to cut that by at least a quarter. Thank fuck we'd be missing rush hour as it was nearly seven p.m.

The first five minutes of the drive, as we got through town, were silent, with me trying to summon a calm facade in spite of my rampaging nerves.

It was early—thirty-six and a half weeks—but once the water broke, that baby was going to be born. Today was the day. Or possibly tomorrow. I didn't care what birthday our son had as long as he was healthy.

Addie's birth had come after Jess was induced, so this emergency, water-breaking situation was new territory for me. I reminded myself it was Magnolia's first child, and chances of it being a quick delivery were slim. Her contractions were still five or six minutes apart, which was borderline for when her doctor had advised us to head in—*if* her water hadn't broken. Magnolia's pain level didn't seem too bad so far. I knew it would likely get a lot worse, and I was dreading that part.

Once we hit the highway, I squeezed her hand before turning my focus to getting us the hell to the hospital. I shot her what I hoped was a reassuring smile, but she didn't smile back.

"You doing okay?" I asked. "How bad is the pain?"

"Not very bad," she answered. She turned her head and watched out the passenger window. Eventually she said, "Maybe if he comes quickly I could still make it to the open house."

My mouth fell open, but then I realized this was her way of compartmentalizing and blocking out her fear, which she'd previously confessed was nearly paralyzing.

"Mags, you're having a baby. Even if he's born before midnight, you'll be exhausted, and what are you going to do? Pack up a brand-new little guy and tote him around on your chest as you make sure everyone has a beverage?"

Her shoulders fell as that truth sank in. "You're right." She went silent again as the truck ate up the highway. A few minutes later, she said, "I'm a planner, Luke. I planned this event carefully, deliberately. Almost four weeks before our due date. What were the chances that he'd come today?"

I couldn't hold in a grin as I reached over for her hand

again. "I'd say about fifty-fifty between today and tomorrow."

Again, she didn't smile.

"Hey," I tried. "You've planned all the details. You have a solid team in your mom, your board, and your volunteers. They've got the event handled for you."

She nodded. Her head bobbed until her expression turned to a grimace as another contraction gripped her.

"Keep breathing," I told her. "You're doing great. Just a few more seconds and you can rest."

Magnolia made a point of taking in air, clasping to my hand. This one seemed to last longer than the others. I pressed my foot down on the gas pedal, glancing in my rearview to ensure there were no flashing lights behind me. Eventually her grasp on me loosened, and she exhaled.

"I'm scared, Luke," she said quietly.

"Childbirth is scary," I said, hoping to be reassuring, "but you're a superstar and you're going to do great. I'll be by your side every second."

She nodded and exhaled audibly.

"Keep doing that and thinking good things like who's Truett going to look like? Me or you?"

At that, she did crack a faint smile. "You. He's going to be a mini Luke."

"God help us," I said with a laugh, thankful for the tension-disrupting moment.

She breathed through another contraction. Once it passed, I called her mom to let her know what was happening. Bianca's emotions came over the connection in a burst of surprise, excitement, and concern. When Magnolia secured her promise to oversee the open house and visit her grandson afterward, I could almost see my wife finally letting go of that particular worry.

The two women had had their differences over the course of the project, but overall their relationship had deepened. My trust in Bianca—and I think Magnolia's too—had grown. I believed she was as invested in the collective as Magnolia.

When we reached the outskirts of the city, contractions were closer to four minutes apart. After a particularly intense one, I put in a quick call to her assistant, Celia, and put her in charge of this weekend's wedding. The woman had never handled one solo, but Magnolia had been grooming her for nearly a year. I had every bit of confidence she'd handle everything competently. My dad would be there onsite the whole time and could answer any questions and help solve any issues that arose.

"The open house is handled," I said after Magnolia's next contraction. "The wedding is handled. Now let's go meet our son."

* * *

Magnolia

Truett Ander Durham was perfect.

Okay, okay, go ahead and accuse me of mama bias. It was true. I was in love.

Our son had dark hair, blue eyes, a round, adorable face, and a stubbornness that would carry him through whatever challenges he faced, as proven by the number of hours he'd clung to his warm, comfy home in my womb. Twenty-one and a half hours, to be exact.

Though he was three and a half weeks early, he was

doing well, his lungs fully developed, his first cry a healthy, strong one.

I was immeasurably, irrevocably in love.

Truett was going on two hours old. The nurses had done their tests, cleaned him up, and helped us with our first attempt at breastfeeding. That would take some getting used to, but my little guy had attached after a few tries. Lauren, the nurse, had proclaimed him a champion in the making, assuring me he'd done better than eighty-five percent of newborns.

She'd left us with Truett in my arms, my bed mostly reclined, and the lights low so we could all rest. Luke had climbed into the hospital bed and curled up next to us. True to his word, he'd been by my side every second of my long labor, encouraging me the whole way, massaging my back, giving me crushed ice, and advocating for whatever I needed. He was truly my hero and had gotten me through it.

"Did you want to get something to eat?" I whispered to him.

Luke shook his head. "This feels good," he said sleepily. He opened his eyes, suddenly more alert. "Unless you're not comfortable. Want me to give you space?"

"Don't you dare. We love it, don't we, Truett? Your daddy is the best cuddler."

Luke burrowed back into my side. As sapped as I was, I couldn't close my eyes, couldn't stop gazing down at our beautiful boy in wonder.

My life had changed in a heartbeat. It now centered around this six-pound-seven-ounce bundle.

"The ceremony should be over by now," Luke said.

"What ceremony?" I pulled my gaze from Truett to my husband.

Looking amused, he said, "The ribbon-cutting?"

"Oh!" I glanced around for a clock but found none. "The open house. What time is it?"

"A little after five. Did you really forget?"

I grinned and shrugged one shoulder. "I've got more important things on my mind." I kissed Truett's beanie-covered head.

"So you don't want to pack up our boy and trundle off to catch the last hour?" he asked, amusement in his tone.

"I'm not going to hear the end of that anytime soon, am I?"

"Probably going to come up at Truett's wedding rehearsal dinner."

"Or his first therapy session," I said, only half joking.

"For sure his first therapy session." Luke nuzzled my cheek.

A notification buzzed somewhere nearby, and he rolled slightly to remove his phone from his back pocket. I momentarily wondered where my phone was. My friends were all at the open house, either as board members or volunteers or for a tour and a free meal, but they'd be demanding photos any minute now. I couldn't wait to show off our son.

"Presley's live-streaming the remarks," he said, reading from a text message. "She says you need to watch."

I let out a teasing scoff. "As if. I'm momming right now."

He chuckled. "You'll be momming for the rest of your life officially."

He tapped on a link, then held up his phone so we could both see it. Eventually I heard Janice's voice, one of the board members my mom had brought on, introducing my mother. In spite of my motherhood bliss, I perked up, curious what she'd put together since I was supposed to be the one welcoming the community and talking about the project. I'd had my remarks laid out on notecards, but I couldn't tell you where those cards were to save my life, and frankly, I didn't care.

We watched as my mother thanked the vendors one by one, the builders, the entire team that had contributed in any way. She looked good, her color healthy again, her hair grown out to a pixie cut that looked great on her, and her outfit professional but approachable. Somewhere along her journey to beat cancer, which she had, her values had truly seemed to shift. She often wore sweats and leggings from big box stores and shoes that cost under fifty dollars instead of more than five hundred.

What was more, she'd been going to counseling weekly and working on herself, and it showed. We'd had more than a handful of deep conversations about Felix, the damage he'd done to both of us, and how we were moving past it and reinventing ourselves in big and small ways. They were among the first valuable, real conversations I'd ever had with my mother.

Whoever was recording the video—Presley was my guess—made a point of panning across the outdoor area that was currently lined by ten food trucks and filled with what looked like at least two hundred people. I spotted familiar faces throughout the crowd

After several minutes of thank-yous and rounds of applause, I figured she'd close quickly, but she seemed to settle in as she said, "As exciting as this is"—she gestured to encompass the entire campus—"maybe I shouldn't say this?" She exchanged a look with Chloe, who stood closest to her and gave her a knowing smile. My mother nodded. "Yes. I'm saying this. As excited as we are about the Lotus Collective and our objective of helping women recover from controlling relationships, I'm even more excited to announce the birth of my first grandson, Truett, just hours ago."

My mother beamed as another round of applause rose, louder this time and with calls of congratulations and cheers.

I kissed Truett's head again and whispered, "You are so loved, my precious boy."

Luke switched hands to hold the phone with his other one so he could put his large palm on Truett's little tush as he pressed another kiss to my cheek.

"Now, my daughter's an event planner, as many of you know, and she's very good at what she does. Very dedicated," my mom continued. "And rumor has it she was more than a little distressed that her carefully planned event"—she again motioned to her surroundings—"was spoiled by what turned out to be twenty-one-plus hours of labor leading up to Truett's birth."

A collective laugh arose from the crowd.

"Once this is over, I get to meet our little pumpkin and hug my daughter," she said.

There were awws and more clapping from the gathering.

"My daughter, Magnolia, has been open about this, so I know she won't mind me sharing some of our history with you all. I was married to a controlling man for more than forty years. My daughter was raised by us, if you can call it that, but I'll be the first to admit we were terrible parents."

The crowd listened in silence as my mom paused, letting that sink in.

"I'm deeply ashamed of that," she continued, "but I've come to recognize that I can't change the past. I can apologize and learn how to do better. So that's what I'm doing.

It's my path of recovery from my own marriage to a controlling man."

As the crowd reacted, she nodded. "My daughter... She's stronger than me. Smarter. When my ex-husband tried to manipulate her into a marriage of convenience, she stood up for herself and refused. When she told me this, I was stunned, because, well, in my experience, you didn't stand up to the bully. Magnolia is my hero, because she did. In spite of his threats, which he did follow through on, she took her power back and started her journey to healing and forging her own path."

There was more applause, and my own eyes filled with tears. Luke moved his hand from Truett's rump to clasp my hand.

"Not only am I so stinking proud of my daughter and the woman she's become, but I'm in awe of her. Every single day. Seeing her strength, her determination, it's what made me believe I could have a different life too. So when I tell you that there's no one more qualified to lead this endeavor than my incredible, brave daughter, I mean it with my whole heart and soul." Her voice cracked as emotion overcame her, which made my tears spill over the rims of my eyes and cascade down my cheeks.

"It's true," Luke whispered before kissing me again. "All of it."

My mother carefully wiped her eyes. "I didn't mean to cry my eyes out." She let out an embarrassed laugh. "Anyway, it's been quite a day. A brand-new grand baby and a brand-new collective to support women who need a chance to become who they're meant to be, just as my daughter has. We couldn't do it without every single one of you, from the curious neighbor who wanted to learn what we're doing while enjoying a street taco, to the business owners who've already signed up for our employment initiative partnership, to the city folks who helped us through the construction phase, to the men and women who literally built this place brick by brick. Thank you to you all. And now I have a date to meet a much younger man."

The people laughed and clapped as my mom blew a kiss to them and handed over the mic to Janice. Luke muted the volume as the event broke up into people filling up on food truck fare and signing up for tours of the campus.

"That was quite a speech," he said.

I nodded, overcome by...everything. "When she came back into my life almost two years ago, I didn't think we could ever get past our history. Of course, there was also a time when I didn't believe you and I would ever mend our past. And look at us now."

With a lovestruck grin, he gently squeezed Truett and me closer. "Look at us now."

"I wasn't sure I'd ever have a real family," I said. Tears continued to stream down my face. Good tears. Happy tears. My heart was bursting with so much love it was as if the tears were the overflow. "I didn't think I'd find someone who could love me with all my flaws and my crazy-pants background."

"I love you even more because of your background and the woman it's made you. I'm with your mom. I'm in awe of you. I was already in awe of you, and then you did this." He cradled Truett's little head, bent down and kissed it, then trailed his big, gentle hand down our son's back. "I didn't know I could love this hard."

He leaned in and kissed me, gently but with so much adoration and love it made my heart dip in my chest.

"I can't wait for Addie and your dad and my mom to

meet our son," I said. "I love you, Luke. I love our family. I love our life."

He let out a low, satisfied growl. "Our life is everything I ever wanted and more than I ever dared to wish for. I think I loved you when we were seventeen, Mags, and I love you exponentially more now."

He kissed me again, and I leaned contentedly into the security of his arms. The odd girl out had finally found her happily ever after.

Note from the Author

Thanks for reading *Single Wish*! I hope you loved Luke and Magnolia.

Next up is *Single Desire*, Kemp and Anna's story.

If you missed the Henry Brothers series, you can dive into book one, *Unraveled*! Find out how a marriage of convenience can test even the best of friends!

Find *Unraveled* in ebook, audiobook, and paperback in my author store at amyknuppbooks.com!

Note from the Author

* * *

If you liked *Single Wish*, I hope you'll consider leaving a review for it. Reviews help other readers find books and can be as short (or long) as you feel comfortable with. Just a couple sentences is all it takes. I appreciate all honest reviews.

* * *

Single Wish is part of the Single Dads of Dragonfly Lake series, which includes:

- Singled Out
- Single All the Way
- Single Chance
- Single-Minded
- Single Wish
- Single Desire

Acknowledgments

Thank you to my alpha reader, Rachel, for reading multiple versions, for offering solid suggestions, and for always finding something positive to say about my chapters. Your encouragement is everything to me! I'm so lucky to have you on my team!

Thank you to my husband, Justin, who's been through so many books with me, which translates to so many meltdowns, losses of confidence, threats to quit, as well as the good stuff, like celebrating every finished draft, every release, every milestone. When I met you so many years ago, neither one of us had any idea what this journey had in store for us, certainly not the roller coaster that is being an author. I'd still choose you every time! I'm grateful for you every day. Thanks for being my sane half.

Also by Amy Knupp

North Brothers Box Sets:

North Brothers Books 1-3

North Brothers Books 4-5

North Brothers: The Complete Series

Or binge the North Brothers in audio:

North Brothers Audiobooks

Hale Street Series:

Sweet Spot

Sweet Dreams

Soft Spot

One and Only

Last First Kiss

Heartstrings

Hale Street Box Sets:

Meet Me at Clayborne's

Clayborne's After Hours

It Happened on Hale Street

Island Fire Series:

Playing with Fire

Heat of the Night

Fully Involved

Firestorm

Afterburn

Up in Flames

Flash Point

Fire Within

Impulse

Slow Burn

Island Fire Box Sets:

Sparked (books 1-3)

Ignited (books 4-6)

Enflamed (books 7-10)

OR

Island Fire: The Complete Series

<u>Themed Bundles</u>

<u>Single Dad</u>

Opposites Attract

Grumpy-Sunshine

Cinnamon Roll Heroes

Childhood Crush

Forbidden Love

Friends to Lovers

Coming Home

Musicians

Second Chance

Workplace Romance

Heroines Finding Their Path

About the Author

Amy Knupp is a *USA Today* Best-Selling author of contemporary romance. She loves words and grammar and meaty, engrossing stories with complex characters.

Amy lives in Wisconsin with her husband and has two adult children, two cats, and a box turtle. She graduated from the University of Kansas with degrees in French and journalism. In her spare time, she enjoys traveling, breaking up cat fights, watching college hoops, and annoying her family by correcting their grammar.

For more information:
https://www.amyknuppbooks.com

www.ingramcontent.com/pod-product-compliance
Lightning Source LLC
Chambersburg PA
CBHW061630190726
48289CB00006B/1551